"Try to get some more rest. You need it."

"Ravena," Tex called as she reached the door.

She blew out a sigh and turned to face him. "Yes?"

"Thank you for this. But you said one night, and I won't stay longer than that."

Gripping the edges of the tray until they dug into her palms, she willed the words she wanted to say to reach her lips. *Yes, Tex, you have to leave. I have enough concerns right now without worrying about you and the fragility of my heart.*

Whatever she said, there was no going back after this moment. She didn't understand why he'd come to the farm after all these years. But he was here—and she had the power to hold him to his word and make him leave, or extend his time.

She shut her eyes for a brief moment, praying for guidance. The smallest seed of peace germinated inside her. A whisper that everything would be all right.

Please help me trust You, God.

Opening her eyes, she peered straight at Tex. "I'm changing our agreement. You may stay until you're well."

Stacy Henrie has always had a love for history, fiction and chocolate. She earned her BA in public relations before turning her attentions to raising a family and writing inspirational historical romances. The wife of an entrepreneur husband and a mother of three, Stacy loves to live out history through her fictional characters. In addition to being an author, she is also a reader, a road-trip enthusiast and a novice interior decorator.

Books by Stacy Henrie

Love Inspired Historical

Lady Outlaw
The Express Rider's Lady
The Outlaw's Secret
The Renegade's Redemption

Visit the Author Profile page at Harlequin.com.

STACY HENRIE

The Renegade's Redemption

HARLEQUIN® LOVE INSPIRED® HISTORICAL

Recycling programs
for this product may
not exist in your area.

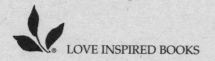

LOVE INSPIRED BOOKS

ISBN-13: 978-0-373-42532-7

The Renegade's Redemption

Copyright © 2017 by Stacy Henrie

And ye shall know the truth,
and the truth shall make you free.
—*John* 8:32

For T & G

A real man is honest, humble and responsible—
as Tex learns to be. And these same qualities are
exemplified in the young men you are both becoming.

Chapter One

Casper, Wyoming, April 1892

Tex Beckett twirled the gold coin back and forth between his fingers, its shiny surface catching the lamplight in the saloon. "Much obliged, Quincy," he said with a grin.

The barrel-chested cattle rustler visibly swallowed and inclined his head in somber acquiescence. His skin more closely matched the gray of his trimmed beard now that their poker game had come to an end.

Scooting the rest of his winnings toward himself, Tex picked up the weathered piece of parchment lying on top. "So this map shows the whereabouts of more gold coins like this one?"

One of Kip Quincy's partners piped up. "Not just gold but silver ones too." Tex blew out a whistle of appreciation at the potential wealth.

"Shut up, Lester," Quincy ground out, clearly sore over losing the treasure map after only having it in his possession a few weeks.

"When were you planning to head to Texas to search for the loot?" Tex asked.

Quincy's thunderous look flicked from Lester to Tex. "Planned to head south this week. What I hadn't planned on was losing tonight."

In all honesty, Tex hadn't really planned on winning; he'd never gambled before. And he wasn't entirely sure what had compelled him to accept Quincy's invitation this evening.

Maybe it was the loneliness that had been eating at his gut the last six months. Or maybe it was because he was closer to his home state of Idaho than he'd been in eight years. Or maybe it was staying this past week on the ranch of a family friendly to outlaws and rustlers that had him missing the company of would-be friends. Even the continued company of Quincy and his three henchmen, who'd also sought refuge at the ranch during Tex's time there, seemed a better substitute for friends than no friends at all. Spending the evening around the card table with them had seemed like a better prospect than spending it in his hotel room, alone.

Whatever the reason, Tex hadn't lost the game and he was grateful. Maybe he had his father's touch. Though more times than Tex could count, that "touch" had been as elusive to his father as rain in a drought. His jaw tightened just thinking of how he, his mother and his twin brother, Tate, had been forced to eek by for years, barely scraping together enough to live on, after his father had finally chosen the gambling life over a family life.

And that's why this would be his one and only game of poker.

"Thanks again for playing, boys," he said, scraping back his chair. The other four men did the same. Tex leaned forward to pocket his winnings, but Quincy reached out and clapped a hand onto a corner of the map.

"I'm thinking you don't need this old paper after all," the older man said, his expression no longer full of disbelief but anger.

Tex set his hand on the map as well, his other rising to the gun in his holster. "Now, Quincy," he crooned as if talking to a child. "You threw that map into the pile of your own volition and I won it fair and square." No one in the saloon would contest that.

Quincy's scowl deepened, but he lifted his hand and backed away from the table. "Should've known not to play poker with the *Texas Titan*." He hissed the words, though to Tex they sounded as loud as a train whistle. "How much did you tell us that Wanted poster said you were worth? Dead or alive."

Arranging his face so as not to show his alarm, Tex didn't answer. Instead he made a show of slowly pocketing the gold coin, the pile of cash in the center of the table and the map.

He'd known his acquaintance with Quincy came with the risk of having the man reveal Tex's outlaw identity. Prior to this, Tex had been enjoying going unrecognized, since folks this far north hadn't seemed to have heard of his heists. But they certainly would if Quincy started flapping his jaw about it. And it only took one person wanting to collect on the reward to send a telegram…or maybe Quincy was intending to double-cross him and turn Tex in himself.

That was the way with thieves, Tex supposed. They couldn't be trusted.

"As I said it's been a pleasure, *gentlemen*." He hardened his look as he gazed at Quincy. "Sounds a lot more polite and civil than calling you cattle rustlers, don't it?" Quincy's eyes narrowed, but Tex could tell the man understood the message. If Quincy ratted him out as an outlaw, he'd do the same, naming the man and his partners as cattle thieves.

Tipping his hat to the men, he exited the saloon. A brisk wind followed him up the twilight-lit street to the hotel where "Mr. Chancy" was greeted by the desk clerk on his way to his room. Once inside Tex locked his door and set his gun on the nearby table. He wouldn't put it past Quincy to try to get back the map. The man was that stubborn, but then again, so was Tex.

After slipping into bed, fully dressed, he linked his hands behind his head and stared at the ceiling. Where did he want to go next? He'd been working the last eight years in Texas and most recently in Utah Territory. Maybe he'd keep heading north to Buffalo or into Montana. But the thought of a new place, a new robbery didn't fill him with the usual rush of excitement.

Tex slid his hand into his vest pocket and pulled out the earrings he always kept there. They had been his mother's, the only memento he and Tate had been able to hold on to of hers after her death.

They weren't just a keepsake to Tex though. They were a symbol, a reminder, of why he'd left his brother and the farm behind, nearly a decade ago.

His plan had been to sell the earrings, but when it had come time to do so, Tex couldn't part with them. He kept seeing Tate's face, twisted with outrage and hurt, when he'd caught Tex preparing to leave. The realization that Tex intended to sell the earrings had led to a blazing row. How could he get rid of something their mother had so diligently cherished and hidden time and again from their gambler father?

In the end, the fight had turned violent. Tex had struck his brother, hard enough to knock him out, and then left him behind—sneaking away like the thief he hadn't yet been…but would soon become.

He and Tate hadn't spoken since. No visits. No letters. Nothing to remember his brother by except the earrings they'd fought over.

Each time he pulled them out, he was reminded of his mother, of his brother's cutting words that fateful night, and what Tex had been forced to do to survive these last eight years.

Feeling resolved once more, he secured the earrings back inside his pocket and turned over. Tomorrow he'd ride out of Casper, after he conducted a few matters of business, and then he'd move on to his next outlawing adventure.

Tex impatiently tapped his foot against the polished floor of the bank. The woman at the clerk's window had been there for seven minutes, according to his pocket watch. A gift from his mother, which she'd saved for months to buy, a watch for him and one for Tate. It wasn't the only thing the brothers had that was identical. Looking at Tate through the years had been like looking at Tex's own reflection.

Tamping down thoughts of his twin, Tex crossed his

arms and glared at the back of the woman's head. He needed to hurry and cash in his gold coin for money so he could send some more anonymous funds to Ravena Reid and her grandfather back in Idaho and slip out of town as soon as possible. For all he knew, Quincy was still around, and that meant it was time for Tex to leave. He didn't trust the cattle rustler. Especially not after seeing the desperate glint in Quincy's eyes last night when the man had realized he'd lost not only his coin and his cash but his precious map too. The older man had been boasting all week about how he'd won it himself from another outlaw in a card game in Colorado.

At last the woman thanked the clerk and walked away. Tex blew out a breath of relief. Stepping to the counter, he smiled at the clerk through the bars on the inner window. "Morning. Busy day at the bank, huh?"

He brought his hand to his pocket, intent on extracting the gold coin. But the sudden click of a gun from behind and the wide eyes of the clerk in front of him made Tex freeze.

"Caught you right in the act of robbing our bank," a firm voice intoned. "Didn't I, Mr. *Texas Titan*?"

Terror he hadn't felt since his first robbery coursed through Tex and robbed his mouth of moisture. He cautiously lifted his hands in surrender and turned to face the triumphant expression of the local sheriff. "There's been some mistake. I was simply conducting my banking affairs like everyone else."

The sheriff barked a humorless laugh. "I ain't a fool. The jig's up. Someone in town recognized you and I've been tracking you since you left the hotel ten minutes ago."

It had to be Quincy who had turned him in. Tex frowned, his stomach still lurching with panic. "Why don't we talk about this outside, Sheriff?"

"Not unless you're in handcuffs first."

Tex feigned a look of contrition as he fell back a small step, edging toward the wall that had a plateglass window. It stretched from waist high all the way up to the ceiling and looked out on an alley. "I can see how committed you are, Sheriff. And I applaud that."

His words seemed to confuse the man, just as Tex had hoped. "But I'm afraid..." He moved another tiny step backward. "That I'm going to have to pass on the suggestion."

With that he covered his face with his arm and dove for the window. The shatter of glass filled his ears and he felt it cut into the exposed skin along his jaw and hands. But better to deal with broken glass than a bullet.

He landed with a hard thud on the ground in the alley. Gulping for breath, he lumbered to his feet and started for the front of the building. The sheriff fired a shot through the window, but Tex ducked out of the way. Jerking his horse's reins free, he threw himself into the saddle. Out of the corner of his eye, he saw the sheriff barrel out of the bank, his face red with fury.

"You won't get away so easily," the man shouted.

Tex kicked his horse, his mind intent on fleeing. The horse leapt forward, and for one moment, Tex knew the familiar thrill of a clean escape. Then the sheriff shot at him again. This time the bullet found purchase. It struck Tex in his right side, and his body jerked hard to the left in reflexive response. He clung to the horse with trembling arms to keep from falling as searing fire registered through his shock.

Half blind with pain, he guided his horse down the alley and out the other side. As if from the end of a long train tunnel, he heard the sheriff hollering at him, but Tex couldn't make out the words over the roaring in his ears.

He urged his horse into a gallop, heedless of the outbursts from those leaping out of his way. Pressing a hand to his side, Tex fought off the blackness stealing onto the edges of his vision. If he lost consciousness and fell off his horse, he would lose his freedom too. He had to get away from Casper before he passed out. His few belongings, including his money and a dwindling supply of hardtack and jerky, were thankfully already ensconced inside his saddlebags.

As he reached the end of the street, he dizzily looked back over his shoulder. The sheriff was running hard after him and the man wasn't alone. Quincy and his friends were right behind him.

So it *had* been Quincy who'd revealed Tex's identity to the sheriff. Likely in an effort to get back the map.

Tex scowled as much from the pain of being shot as the realization he'd been framed. He wasn't giving up the map. Not when he'd won it fair and square. Quincy would have to pry it from Tex's dead hands…though his demise might be sooner than he anticipated with his side bleeding out all over.

He pushed his horse faster, though the increased speed jarred his injury even further. The stabbing in his side pierced his every thought and sense. He ground his teeth against it, refusing to falter. He'd need to stop soon and bandage the gunshot wound as best he could, but right now he had to focus his little remaining energy and awareness on escaping.

And Tex knew where he had to go.

There was only one place Quincy wouldn't think to look for him. One place he could convalesce in peace. One place where his outlaw past hadn't yet caught up to him.

The Texas Titan was headed home.

Idaho, five days later

"Mr. Grady, please." Ravena Reid tossed her dish towel on the porch rocker and trailed the middle-aged man into the yard. "You can't quit now. There are still two more fields to plow and the planting needs to be done."

He whirled on her, his face as red as his hair. "I ain't staying another day. Them rascally boys spooked the horses with their snake. And that's the second time they've made trouble for me in five days." Marching forward again, he tossed over his shoulder, "'Sides, I can earn far better wages somewhere else."

Desperation, in the form of a tight lump, lodged in Ravena's throat and slowed her steps. Not for the first time she wished her grandfather were still alive. The last three months of running the farm and caring for the orphan children by herself had taxed her to capacity. She felt twice as old as her twenty-seven years.

Without their two older orphans, who'd left the previous autumn to make their way into the world, she'd had to part with some of her precious savings to hire someone to help with the plowing and the planting. Mr. Grady was the second man she'd employed—and just like the first, he'd quit after less than a fortnight. In Mr. Grady's case it was less than a week. Clearly she wasn't as adept at keeping a hired hand or disciplining the children to leave them alone as her grandfather had been. The knowledge brought the hot press of tears that she barely managed to blink back.

They couldn't afford a delay in the planting. Not when she needed a good crop in order to provide for the children under her care and the other four orphans she and her grandfather had planned to bring to the farm this summer. There was also the matter of housing. She still needed to find a way to pay a carpenter to complete the lovely new house her grandfather had envisioned building. A house that would easily provide shelter for nine orphans and herself. And she owed it to Grandfather's memory to fulfill the plans he'd made. The thought of letting him down increased her heartache and fear.

"Will you at least finish plowing the field you were working on?" she urged.

Mr. Grady didn't answer. Instead he increased his agitated retreat to the barn. But Ravena wasn't giving up.

Before she reached the barn doors, the man came barreling out on his horse. Which meant he'd made up his mind and had the mount already saddled before he'd come into the kitchen to tell her that he'd quit and wanted his wages.

"I'll be takin' what I earned this week," he said, jerking his horse to a stop beside her.

Straightening her shoulders, Ravena leveled him with her firmest look. She might be a lone woman running the place now, but she wouldn't be cowed or swindled. "I'll pay you for five days of work, not six." She let the declaration hang in the air a moment before adding with a more entreating tone, "Unless you're willing to work the rest of the day. Then I'll pay you for six days."

He glared down at her. "I already done told you, I ain't staying."

She clenched her teeth, frustrated by his decision and his barnyard vernacular. "Very well." After fishing the required cash and coin from her apron pocket, she dropped them into his outstretched hand. "Good day, Mr. Grady."

He sniffed with disapproval as he pocketed the money, then dug his heels into his horse's flanks. Head held high, Ravena stepped back to avoid the kick of dirt from the animal's hooves. But her bravado ran out before the pair disappeared down the road.

Now that she'd lost another hired hand, the contents of the letter in her other pocket weighed heavier than a steer on her mind and heart. She moved to the porch and sat on the step. Pulling out the letter, she smoothed the wrinkles from it. If only she could smooth the troubled ripples in her life as easily.

Dear Miss Reid,
First let me offer my condolences at the loss of your grandfather. I never met a more gentle man and I'm grateful for my association with him these past few years.

Regarding the four brothers he planned to

bring to your farm this summer, I'm afraid I do not have the most comforting of news. After I received your letter sharing the sad tidings of your grandfather's passing and your limitation in providing any additional orphans with necessary housing, I felt it best to conduct a search for a permanent placement for the boys here in Boise but to no avail.

Here at the orphanage, we are quite at capacity at present. And unfortunately these boys, along with several of our older orphans, who have not found permanent homes either, will be joining the Orphan Train when it comes through on the first of July. As you are no doubt aware, the likelihood of the boys staying together once they leave here is quite low.

If you wish to follow through with your grandfather's wishes to provide a home for these four brothers, I would urge you to make the necessary plans posthaste. I will not be able to detain their departure. I eagerly await your response.

Sincerely,

Miss Gretchen Morley

Tears succeeded in blurring her vision this time as Ravena repocketed the letter. Those poor boys. Of course she wanted to honor her grandfather's wishes to bring them to the farm. As much for them as for herself. If she could fulfill Grandfather's wishes in these last plans he'd made before his death, then perhaps she could finally feel she had done enough to atone for nearly turning her back on him and the farm all those years ago.

Wiping the back of her hand at the useless moisture in her eyes, she shifted her gaze beyond the barn to the unfinished structure that sat there. Her grandfather, a skilled craftsman as well as farmer, had framed the outer walls of the ground floor. But his death had robbed the incomplete edifice of its talented creator, leaving the posts to look like leafless trees eyeing the distant sky.

How was she to provide a home for four more children without a bigger house? How could she feed and clothe the children she already had if a large portion of her money went to hiring workers? And that was *if* she could find someone to hire who'd be willing to stay until the plowing and planting were done. Otherwise, she wasn't sure what she'd do.

Even with the help of thirteen-year-old Jacob, the oldest of the orphans currently living at the farm, the two of them couldn't finish the plowing and planting on time. She needed an able-bodied man willing to work for little wages. One skilled in house building as well as farming would be even better. It was a rather tall order.

Movement by the barn drew her attention. Nine-year-old Mark and his seven-year-old brother, Luke, peered around the corner. No doubt they were the owners of the offending snake Mr. Grady had been complaining about. "Mark, Luke, come here, please."

The towheaded boys walked toward her, their chins dipped low to their chests. Sure enough, Mark carried a snake in his hand.

Though two years separated their ages, they looked as if they could be twins with their matching blond hair and brown eyes. They reminded her of a set of twins she'd known growing up—Tex and Tate Beckett. Even just the memory of the Beckett brothers caused a physical ache to lodge in her chest, especially any thought connected to Tex. He was the man she'd loved fully and agreed to elope with eight years earlier. Only Tex never came for her.

Which was good, she reminded herself. He'd saved her from making the two biggest mistakes of her life—leaving her grandfather behind and trusting Tex with her heart.

Pushing aside the painful recollections, she waited for the boys to shuffle to a stop in front of her. A shiver passed through her at seeing their reptile up close. She feared snakes every bit as much as the horses did. "Do you remember what I've told you, boys, about bringing snakes around the horses?"

Mark shot her a sad look. "We ain't supposed to do that."

"Aren't supposed to do that," she gently corrected. It was her duty to raise these children up right, and she would do it. A visit to their teacher might be in order to stress the importance of grammar and proper speech now that school was in session again.

"But it's a real beaut, Miss Ravena." Mark grinned, his sorrow forgotten, as he held the snake aloft.

Ravena scooted back against the porch column, eager to put distance between herself and the slithering creature. "Be that as it may, the rule still stands. As does the consequence. You, boys, will need to take over muck-ing the stalls for Jacob this week."

Mark and Luke exchanged pained glances.

"And," Ravena added, "if Mr. Grady were still here, you would need to apologize to him."

"Mr. Grady left?" Luke asked, his tone a mixture of regret and curiosity.

"Yes, he's left. Now please take that thing and re-lease it somewhere beyond the fields."

Mark frowned and eyed the snake dangling from his fingers. "Do we have to?"

Standing, Ravena fought an audible groan. "Yes," she intoned firmly.

They started to walk away, their heads low with dejection once more, then Mark turned around. Luke did the same. "If Mr. Grady's gone then how are we gonna..." Mark smiled sheepishly. "I mean *going* to do spring planting without any help? Can we still get those new brothers you told us about?"

Fresh apprehension washed through Ravena at hear-ing her own unanswered questions posed back to her. "We'll figure it out, Mark. All of it. About the planting and bringing those new brothers to the farm."

Satisfied, the boys scampered off. Thankfully they didn't see the droop to her shoulders or hear the heavy sigh that escaped her lips as she picked up her dish towel from off the rocker.

"Let my words be true, Lord," she prayed as she en-tered the house. "Please let them be true."

He might die. Right here on the front step of his childhood home. Gripping his side, Tex managed to haul himself off the new horse he'd bought from a livery in Boise that morning. How he'd survived his escape from Casper, the train journey west to Idaho, and the thirty-mile horse ride north from Boise to his hometown was beyond him. Some might say he'd had help from above, but Tex scoffed at the idea. He and God were as distant as he and his brother.

Or at least as distant as he and his brother *had been*. That was about to change when he came face-to-face with Tate again today.

Apprehension battled with the pain in Tex's gut as he stumbled toward the door. Would Tate take one look at him and throw him out? Tex couldn't say he'd blame Tate if he did. He'd probably do the same if their roles were reversed, given the way things had ended between them. His excessively serious brother, older by five minutes, might say Tex had gotten what he deserved. Tate might even call the law on him.

The thought sent a shudder of dread through Tex and had him tugging the brim of his hat lower. He nearly turned around…but he didn't know where else to go. If there was any chance of shelter to be found here, he had to try.

"Can I help you?" a man asked as he exited the nearby barn. He had a few years on Tex's twenty-nine.

"I'm looking for…" Tex swallowed. It was a struggle to say his brother's name for the first time in years. "Is Tate Beckett around?" Perhaps this man was a hired hand.

But the man shook his head. "Sorry. Beckett doesn't live here anymore. He sold me the place eight years ago. Said he was leaving the area for good."

Tate wasn't here? Tex sagged against the porch railing in disbelief. This was a possibility he'd never even considered. His brother had loved this land. While Tex had tolerated farm work, Tate had loved it, even when they were young. Why would he up and leave a place and an occupation he'd prized? And where had he gone?

"You all right?" The man peered hard at Tex. "You a relative of Beckett's?"

He didn't need anyone recognizing him—not as Tate's twin and certainly not as the Texas Titan. "Much obliged for the information, mister."

Mounting his horse left him sweating, despite the pleasant afternoon, and aggravated his wound even more. The makeshift bandage beneath his new set of clothes would likely be bloodied again. With great effort, he kept himself in the saddle and turned his horse.

Where should he go now? The question had barely entered his head when he found himself guiding the horse away from the road toward the shortcut between his old home and the next farm over.

He'd go to Ravena's; she'd likely still be there. If anyone loved this place more than his twin brother, it was Ravena Reid.

A feeling of dread and anticipation pushed through Tex's cloud of pain at the thought of seeing her again. It was quickly followed by a surge of memories, most prominent being the afternoon, eight years ago, when he'd last seen and spoken with her. They'd planned to run away together that night—had arranged for him to come and fetch her. But his brother had caught Tex as he was leaving. After that horrible fight, with Tate accusing him of ruining Ravena's life, Tex had run off alone, without a word to the girl he'd planned to marry.

He'd thought he'd never see her again, had believed she was better off without him. Now he had no choice but to turn to her. He needed to find somewhere safe where he could rest, or he'd run the risk of collapsing in the middle of the road…and no doubt find himself waking up in a jail cell.

Would she and her grandfather let him stay? Even a night or two in a real house, without being on the run, would surely help him heal faster.

Tex swiped at his brow with his sleeve. The temperature felt as if it kept soaring. Or maybe that was his fever. He'd contracted one at some point during the train ride to Idaho. In another hour or so, he'd probably be shivering with cold. And then there was the near-constant dizziness.

Trying to block out his intense discomfort, he turned his mind to Ravena once more. Would she be as beautiful as he remembered? It wasn't hard for him to conjure up the image of her dark, wavy hair, deep brown eyes and the smattering of freckles across the bridge of her nose. Tex had met plenty of women since leaving home, and yet, none of them affected him the way Ravena had. None of them had seen past his causal, lighthearted, adventure-seeking demeanor to the real man beneath, either.

The Reids' farm came into view, causing Tex's heart to flip painfully in his chest. He'd never allowed himself to believe he would ever come back. If he hadn't deserved Ravena years ago, he certainly didn't now. Fortunately, she and her grandfather, Ezra, weren't likely to know about his unlawful profession. And he wanted to keep it that way.

At the edge of one of the fields, which he absently noted was only a quarter of the way plowed, he climbed off his horse. If he thought facing Tate would be hard, facing Ravena was sure to be a thousand times more difficult.

Something akin to the fear he'd felt when the sheriff in Casper had recognized him twisted in Tex's stomach now. Could he face Ravena after all these years? What if she had learned he was an outlaw after all? His breath whooshed harder and faster through his lungs as the dizziness intensified. Tex tried to focus on leading his horse and staying upright. But after a few moments, the edges of his vision began to curdle like two-day-old milk and he found himself falling. The last thing to register in his mind was the feel of warm dirt against his face.

"Miss Ravena, Miss Ravena." Mark's frantic cry could be heard clear back to the kitchen.

What now? she wondered, wiping flour from her hands onto her apron. If their snake had gotten loose somewhere it wasn't supposed to... "I'll be right back, Ginny. Keep forming those biscuits, please."

The ten-year-old girl nodded, her red hair framing her pale face. She typically said little, even though she'd been with them for nearly a year now, but she was a quick learner and an efficient helper in the kitchen.

Ravena met Mark and his brother in the hallway. "What's going on?"

Hands on his knobby knees, Mark leaned over, trying to catch his breath. Luke copied his brother's stance. "There's somethin' you gotta see, Miss Ravena."

She forced a patient smile. "Ginny and I are making biscuits for supper. If it's another snake…"

"Not a snake," Mark said, panting. "It's a person."

"A person?"

Luke slipped his hand in hers and tugged her toward the front door. "He's dead, out in the field."

Ravena stopped short, horror coursing through her. "Dead? Are you sure?"

"Yes, ma'am." Mark gave a solemn nod as he rushed to push open the screen door. "He's lying in the dirt, not moving. Luke even poked him with a stick and he still ain't moved."

"Hasn't moved," she murmured. Were the boys serious? She almost wished it *were* a snake that had them overly excited.

"You gotta come see, Miss Ravena," Luke said, his eyes wide. "Besides, his horse is just standing there."

If what they were saying was true, she couldn't very well leave a…a dead person in her field. Though what exactly she'd do with him, she didn't know. *First Mr. Grady and now this.* But she refused to be beaten down by this day.

Taking the rifle from its pegs above the front door, she followed the boys outside and across the yard. She cast a glance at the barn where she knew Jacob was working and six-year-old Fanny would be playing with the new litter of kittens. Should she ask Jacob to tag along? But she dismissed the thought. She had the gun and it wasn't as if she'd never seen an expired person before.

Still, she gave a quick prayer for protection and a little added bravery as she trailed the boys to the fields. If she weren't on such a morbid errand, she might have paused to take in the view—one she never grew tired of. The farm sat on a hillside bench, overlooking the valley, the river and the mountains beyond. A stream ran along the edge of the property and boasted several nice-sized shade trees.

"There's his horse," Mark said, pointing.

Sure enough, a lone horse munched on the grass at the edge of one of the fields. The one Mr. Grady had left only partially plowed. Ravena shaded her eyes with her hand and was able to make out a figure lying face-down in the dirt.

Her heart sped up as she strode toward the body. The gentleman was tall and dressed like a cowboy or a farmhand, though even with the small amount of dust and dirt on his clothes, she could tell his were new. Ravena crouched beside him and set the gun within easy reach. There didn't seem to be any obvious reason for the man's demise. No limbs twisted at odd angles, no visible head injuries, no blood that she could see. And yet something had caused him to crumble in her field.

She watched the back of his coat for movement and felt immense relief when she saw it rise and fall with breath. A sick or injured man was a far cry better than a dead one.

"He's still alive," she announced in a half whisper, though she didn't know why she felt the need to speak quietly.

"How come he don't…*doesn't*…move then?" Mark asked from where he and Luke stood behind her.

"I believe he's unconscious." She glanced past the man, in the direction he appeared to have been riding before his collapse, and frowned. Why would a stranger take the shortcut between her place and the old Beckett farm instead of using the road?

Luke placed his hand on her shoulder in an oddly comforting gesture. "What are we going to do, Miss Ravena?"

She studied the man again. "We are going to gently roll him over and see if we can get him to come around. Hopefully long enough to tell us who he is."

Placing her hands along his arm and side, she nodded toward his legs. "Boys, you push from there."

They scrambled into position, their faces more alight with excitement than worry. *Boys will by boys*, she thought with a rueful shake of her head.

"Now we'll roll him over on the count of three." She took a deep breath, then began to count. When she reached *three*, she and the boys rolled him onto his back. The man cringed in pain, but his eyes remained shut.

A patch of red drew Ravena's attention to where his coat had fallen back from his shirt. She leaned closer to examine it. "I think he's been wounded." But how? A sliver of dread traveled up her spine. Had his injury been an unfortunate accident? Or had someone hurt him, and if so, was the offender still close by?

"He's wounded," Mark repeated with awe, sounding far too impressed.

"Go get Jacob from the barn, Mark," she directed. The injured man didn't need the boys gawking at him as she tried to clean the dirt from his face and revive him. "We'll need Jacob to help us assist this man to the house. Luke, get some water."

They took off at a dash, their childish voices full of wonder as they talked over each other. Ravena allowed herself a small smile at their antics. They might tire her out with their innocent mischief, especially since her grandfather's passing, but they were good boys.

Taking a corner of her apron in hand, she gently began wiping the dirt from the stranger's bearded face. He stirred, prompting her to console him. "We're here to help. You've passed out in our field, but we'll get you up to the house in a minute." She'd probably need to send one of the boys for the doctor. "Can you hear me, sir? We'll have you fixed up soon."

When he didn't respond, she resumed cleaning his face. She was concentrating on brushing the last of the dirt from his beard before she realized he'd gone completely still. Was he truly dead and gone this time? Jerking her gaze to his, Ravena found his eyes open. Brilliantly blue eyes—familiar eyes—which peered directly at her.

Her heart flew into her throat as she studied his face, now absent of dirt. There were age lines around his eyes that hadn't been there the last time she'd seen him, as well as tiny red cuts where his beard didn't cover his tanned skin. But the dark eyebrows, the arch of his jaw, the brown hair lying damp against his forehead were still as recognizable as they'd always been.

"Tex?" His name barely made it past her lips, but a faint smile creased his mouth at hearing it.

"Hello, Ravena," he murmured in a hoarse voice, which only confirmed the truth.

For better or worse, Tex Beckett had just stumbled back into her life.

Chapter Two

Despite his feverish haze, Tex caught a full glimpse of Ravena's face, furrowed in concern and shock. If possible, she looked even more beautiful than he remembered. The girl of nineteen he'd left behind was now a grown woman.

"Tex, what are you doing here?" Her compassionate tone of moments before had disappeared, replaced by one of firmness and cool indifference. He'd expected as much. Thankfully she hadn't yet walked away, leaving him to fend for himself.

He swallowed past his parched throat and shut his eyes against the glaring sun. "Could I…get some water?" he asked, dodging her question for the moment.

"Yes, Luke is on his way back with some right now."

Luke? Tex didn't remember anyone named Luke living here. Perhaps it was a hired hand or maybe one of the many orphans Ravena's grandfather had taken in through the years.

A young boy's excited voice pierced his thoughts. "We got the water and Jacob's coming."

"Thank you, Mark," Ravena replied.

At the mention of the needed water, Tex pried his eyes open to find Ravena leaning over him with a cup in her hand. Behind her, two boys, who must be Luke and Mark, stared wide-eyed at him. If he hadn't felt so near death, he might have chuckled at the horrified fascination on the orphans' young faces. He would've felt the same had a stranger collapsed in his family's field when he was a boy.

"I'll help you drink." Ravena lifted his head a few inches above the dirt and brought the cup to Tex's dry lips. Her cool fingers were a reprieve from the fever. After a few swallows, he turned his chin away to indicate he was finished.

His thirst abated, he realized his head and side felt awful. Still, there were questions that needed asking. "How many orphans do you have right now?" he questioned, trying to work up to what he really wanted to find out about her.

"Five."

"And your husband…" He wasn't under any illusion that Ravena hadn't married in his absence. It was only a matter of how much time had passed before she'd met someone else to claim her heart as Tex once had.

Her brow scrunched in confusion. "My husband?"

"Miss Ravena ain't married," the taller of the two boys volunteered. The news brought Tex unexplainable relief as did the shade from Ravena's shadow as she stood over him. It wasn't as if he'd come here to win her back. He'd slammed that door shut and locked it tight the moment he'd robbed his first bank. Still it pleased him to know no one else had captured her fancy.

Ravena appeared to draw in a steadying breath. "It's *isn't married*, Mark. Not *ain't married*." She glanced at Tex. "And Mark is correct. I'm not married."

"How's your grandfather?" Tex managed to ask next, though the pain and the heat were making it harder and harder to think clearly.

"He died three months ago." Her hair hid her expression as she bent to pick up a gun from off the grass, but her anguished tone told him what her face hadn't.

Sorrow flooded through Tex at the news. Not just for the loss of an honorable, generous man but for Ravena as well. She'd lost her parents to illness as a young child and now to have both grandparents gone too. Tex remembered a little about her grandmother, but her grandfather had been more of a father to him than his own father. He'd greatly admired Ezra Reid, even when they hadn't always seen eye to eye. Especially regarding Tex's ability to properly care for Ravena eight years ago.

"Ah, here's Jacob." She took a step away from Tex, allowing the harsh sun to beat down on him again. "He'll help us get you to the house."

Between the assistance of Ravena and the dark-haired youth named Jacob, Tex managed to get to his feet. Dizziness made the field seem like it was tipping one way, then the other, and he had to pause before he could start walking. He hated being at the mercy of others, but he had little choice. If he saw a doctor, he'd most likely be arrested, so he'd chosen to manage his gunshot wound himself. He'd done the best he could, and yet, he knew his current illness meant his efforts hadn't been as effective as he'd hoped. He needed rest and proper care if he wanted to heal.

"We'll get your horse, mister," Mark said, his eyes alight with childlike excitement.

"Thank you," he ground out between clenched teeth. Walking was proving more difficult than riding, even though Ravena and Jacob had him propped between them.

After a few minutes, the younger boys grew tired of Tex's laborious pace and moved ahead, leading his horse around them and toward the barn while Tex, Ravena and Jacob continued plodding along. Sweat slid down his temples and soaked the back of his shirt. It wasn't the most attractive way to greet one's former sweetheart. Ravena seemed to be repressing any further questions, which suited him just fine. If he didn't pass out before they reached the house, he would consider his first thirty minutes back in her presence a wild success.

"You have some older orphans or a hired hand helping out?" he asked, as much out of curiosity as to keep his mind off the pain radiating from his wound with each step forward. The Reid farm was on the smaller side, but with her grandfather gone, Ravena would still need help.

To his surprise, she shook her head. "Not anymore. The man I hired quit this morning."

He glanced over in time to catch the worry that flitted over her pretty features. No wonder the field he'd collapsed in hadn't been fully plowed. "What will you do now?"

He was pushing into her private life, a life he had no business learning more about. But he couldn't help it. He didn't like the thought of her in trouble. Or maybe he didn't like the way it pricked his conscience to know she was completely on her own now.

"I'll hire someone else." The determination in her voice might have fooled anyone else, but Tex still knew her well enough to recognize it masked deep fear.

"If there's anything I can do, Ravena…" He could stick around a little while, once he was well. Take more time to throw Quincy off his trail, since Tex felt certain the rustler wouldn't think to look for a notorious outlaw in this sleepy little hamlet.

She sucked her breath in sharply. "That won't be necessary."

"But, Miss Ravena," Jacob started to say.

"Mr. Beckett won't be staying." Ravena refused to look at Tex as she spoke. "And besides, he isn't in a position to help with much of anything right now."

Tex nearly laughed out loud at hearing her call him Mr. Beckett. That respectable-sounding name fit an entirely different person—one who'd stayed put on the farm, married Ravena and raised half a dozen kids along with the orphan children.

No, that name didn't fit him at all.

The three of them fell into a tense silence, injury and exhaustion robbing Tex of any further energy to speak. By the time they reached the house and he sat on the porch step, he felt more like a quivering mass of dizzying pain than an infamous, and temporarily retired, outlaw.

Ravena sent Jacob to the barn to see after the younger boys before she disappeared into the house, declaring she'd get Tex another drink of water. He leaned against the porch column, his gaze sweeping the familiar surroundings. He'd spent a good portion of each day at the Reids' farm until he'd left home. Beyond the worn red barn, he noticed a structure he'd never seen before. It appeared to be the outer walls of a house.

Ravena returned and handed him a full cup, then took a seat on the opposite side of the step. She seemed determined to keep her distance.

"Is that a house back there?" Tex asked, pointing in the direction with the cup. He wasn't sure what else it could be—but he also wasn't sure why she needed another house.

She followed his gaze. "It will be, when it's completed. Grandfather started it. It's twice as large as this one so we…" She lowered chin. "I mean, I…would be able to provide a home for more orphans."

Tex took a drink from the cup. He admired Ravena's dedication in continuing her grandfather's legacy. Any orphans she took in would find a good home at the farm. This place had certainly been his second home. Not only had he been welcomed day or night, but there'd always been someone to play with too.

"What are you doing here, Tex?" Her repeated question scattered his nostalgic thoughts.

"Thought it was time to see the ol' place again," he joked.

Her eyes narrowed in annoyance. "Be serious for once. You're hurt and you're sick. How did you get that wound in your side?"

He gulped down the rest of the water as he considered what to say. She'd made no mention of his being an outlaw, which he hoped confirmed his assumption that Ravena had no idea how he'd spent his time since he'd left here. "I was shot at," he said opting for some measure of honesty, "and who did it doesn't matter."

"But you're seriously injured." Her gaze darted to his and then away. "If you're hoping for a place to convalesce, it can't be here, Tex. It just can't. The farm and the children need all of my attention—I don't have time to play nursemaid. Besides, you need a doctor—"

"No, I don't. And you don't need to concern yourself with my injury. The bullet went clean through. It'll be fine." At least he hoped it would once he found some place to stop and rest for a time.

Her cheeks flushed with anger as she shot to her feet. "I can see you're just as stubborn as ever. You think you can just waltz in after nearly a decade of being gone and expect everything to be the same. Expect *me* to be the same." She turned her back to him and marched toward the screen door. "I should leave you to rot right there. Because if you had any idea of the pain…"

Her words faded out, but Tex didn't need her to finish to know what she'd meant to say.

Regret pulsed within him. He twisted around, ignoring the stab to his side. "Ravena, wait. It's asking too much. I know." He'd been a fool to think she'd take him in after all this time. And an even bigger fool to think that in coming here the past wouldn't creep into his mind and heart, making him consider things best left ignored.

But if he could have just one night's peace. One night without the fear of waking up to Quincy's enraged face, the same face that had been haunting his dreams since fleeing Casper. "What if I stay one night? I'll sleep in the barn. You won't have to know I'm here."

Would she agree? Her shoulders slumped forward and her chin dropped. "One night?" she echoed.

He had a sudden desire to stand and hold her in his arms, to bring her comfort. And yet, he'd forfeited that privilege a long time ago. "One night. That's all. I'll ride off tomorrow." How he'd be able to ride and where he'd go, he didn't know. But he wouldn't knowingly inflict more pain on her. Or himself. Coming back here hadn't been his most brilliant idea of late.

"Fine, you may stay one night." She lifted her head, steely resolve radiating from her stiff posture. "And since it's only one night and you're injured, you might as well sleep in the house. You can have my room. I'll go prepare it."

He considered arguing that he could sleep on the sofa instead, but he didn't want to raise her ire further. "Thank you."

She opened the screen and moved purposely inside, apparently ignoring him. But right before the door slammed shut, he heard her whisper, "You're welcome."

Ravena sat up, one hand pressed to her nightgown, over her pounding heart. A loud thud overhead had snatched her from sleep. Perhaps Ginny was having another nightmare. Which meant Ravena would need to hurry upstairs to the girls' room to console her before Fanny woke up too.

Throwing off her blankets, she rose from the sofa and lit a lamp to take with her. A peek into the girls' room showed her that both Ginny and Fanny were deep in slumber. Nothing appeared amiss in the boys' room either. Confused, Ravena paused outside her bedroom where Tex was sleeping. She'd bid him good-night after bringing him some of her grandfather's clothes, including a nightshirt. After her grandfather's funeral, she'd simply packed up his things and put them in the attic. Then she'd moved herself out of the girls' room into the master bedroom, much to the delight of Fanny and Ginny who each had a bed of their own now.

She couldn't hear any noise coming from Tex's room either. Perhaps the noise had come from outside? Flipping her long braid over her shoulder, she started back down the hall when an audible groan penetrated through her bedroom door. She moved back to it and called, "Tex? Are you all right?"

There was no reply. A flicker of concern prompted her to turn the knob and stick her head inside the room. "Tex?"

He wasn't in bed. Instead he lay sprawled on the floor, his bare feet sticking out of the borrowed trousers he wore beneath the long nightshirt. He was trembling from head to toe. Ravena inhaled a sharp gasp and rushed over.

"Tex?" She set the lamp aside and knelt next to him. "What happened?"

"Quincy," he murmured. "Can't find…"

Did he mean his horse? "Quincy's just fine," Ravena soothed. "We put him in the barn. He's safe."

Tex's eyes flew open, and he gazed wildly around until seeing her. He latched onto her wrist with surprising strength. "It's not safe, Ravena. He'll come for it. I know…" His words became incoherent mumbles, his eyes falling shut once more.

She lifted her hand and placed it against his forehead. He was burning with fever. Panic sliced through her. Tex was more ill than he'd let on earlier. And likely wouldn't be better by morning. Her concern ratcheted higher. "Tex, we need to get you back into bed."

He wouldn't be much help getting up in his fevered state, but she wasn't a weakling either. Gripping him under his arms, she wrested his upper body as gently as possible off the floor and onto the bed. She propped his legs up next, then repositioned the pillow beneath his head.

"I need to get a better look at your wound, all right?" She didn't really expect an answer, and yet, she felt compelled to explain why she needed to peek at his side, especially after his insistence that he'd be fine without her help. Tugging his nightshirt up, she wasn't surprised to find a bloodied bandage underneath.

She peeled back just enough of the soiled cloth to get a look at his injury and promptly gagged at his mottled flesh. Turning away, she clapped a hand over her mouth. She knew a little about sickness, farm injuries and medicine from her grandmother. Olive Reid had learned the skills of midwifery and nursing from her mother and had doctored most of the townsfolk during her lifetime, at least until an actual doctor had set up practice.

Tex's wound appeared to be more than a few days old, but it wasn't healing properly. No wonder he was feverish and delirious. He needed real medical care. And yet, he'd practically panicked when she'd suggested going for a doctor. It was something Ravena still didn't understand, but Tex wasn't in a position to explain.

She straightened, her arms folded tightly against her

middle. The lamp on the nearby table lit up Tex's features. How could they be so familiar and yet so foreign? Even now, creased with pain and fever, they still had the power to turn her insides to warm mush.

"What do I do, Lord?" How many times had she breathed this same prayer over the last three months? But having Tex here was nearly as daunting as having no hired hand for spring planting and not enough room to bring four more orphans to live on the farm.

Looking down at him, she felt as if she stood before a precipice. She didn't know if the right thing was to jump or turn and run the other way. Questions she'd stopped asking herself years ago rose painfully into her mind. Why hadn't Tex come back for her that night? Had his feelings for her changed so abruptly? Had she trusted where she shouldn't have? Had he loved her at all?

Even when his brother, Tate, had come over later that night and confessed that he and Tex had argued, she felt certain Tex would still return for her, once he'd had a chance to cool down. But the long hours became morning, and still there was no sign of him. Then a full day went by, then a week, then a month, and finally years. All without a single letter of explanation.

Now that Tex was here again, did she really want to know the answers to her questions? Could she bear to hear him say aloud that he'd changed his mind about her? The possibility made her heart thrum a ragged, aching beat beneath her nightgown. If he stayed, how would she keep the past from drawing away her focus? She had to remain strong in her dedication to provide a home for these orphans and those she would somehow bring to the farm as well.

She could send him away in the morning, ignoring the terrible state he was in. They had agreed on one night, and she didn't owe him anything.

Or she could do the Christian thing. She could allow him to stay however long he needed to fully recover.

Ravena eyed his bandage again, her mouth pursed in hesitation. Perhaps there was some way to speed up his recovery, then she wouldn't have to manage having him around for more than a few days. Grabbing the lamp, she padded out of the room and back downstairs to the parlor. She pulled one of her grandmother's journals, filled with Olive's medical notes and home remedies, from the shelf. She settled the book on her lap and began perusing the well-worn pages. There had to be something in here about dealing with bullet wounds and the illnesses they might produce.

The clock on the mantle struck two before Ravena found what she'd been looking for. She could mix up a special tea and a strong poultice from the herbs in the cellar, though her grandmother had noted that plenty of rest and little movement for the patient was also critical.

Shutting her mind to the latter advice, Ravena went to the kitchen, wrapped herself in a shawl and headed outside to the cellar, shivering in the cool predawn air. With the aid of the lamp, she located the needed herbs. In the kitchen, she stoked the fire and set the kettle on to boil. While she waited, she crushed the herbs in a bowl with her grandmother's old pestle.

The sharp scent of the crushed leaves awakened her further and reminded her of similar nights spent doing this very task as she'd assisted her grandmother. And now she was doing it alone—doing everything alone. A negligent tear rolled down her face, which she brushed away. Tears wouldn't solve her problems.

Once she had the tea and poultice ready, she placed everything on a tray, added a fresh roll of bandage, and carried the things up to her room. She was relieved to find Tex hadn't tumbled off the bed again. Her next task would be difficult, making her grateful Tex wasn't conscious. She had to remove his bandage, place the poultice against his wound, and tie a new cloth around his middle.

Uneasiness warred with her determination, and Ravena willed herself to take a steadying breath. She'd assisted her grandmother as Olive had attended to a number of men. This would be no different.

She managed to untie the old bandage without moving Tex too much, then she tossed the cloth on the floor to burn in the stove later. With that done, she placed the herb poultice against his side. Tex winced in his sleep, though Ravena wasn't sure if it was from the heat, the herbs or the pain of her jostling.

"Almost done," she murmured, as much to herself as to him.

She slid her arm and the bandage behind him before grabbing it with her other hand. Leaning forward, she made sure she had the cloth in the right position.

Holding him like this, in a half embrace, she felt beckoned to recall memories she'd buried long ago. Carefree days of strolling with Tex across the hills, walking hand in hand. Or kissing him as they stood beside the stream. Or speaking of their shared future. Those were the days when her world had been bright and happy, full of love and promise. She had Tex, her grandfather and the orphans.

Ravena suddenly felt Tex tense. Had she hurt him? She flicked her gaze to his and gave a soft yelp when she found his blue eyes watching her rather lucidly. Her cheeks burned with mortification as she scrambled away from him. "Y-you fell out of bed earlier. So I thought I'd just change your…um…your bandage."

The barest hint of amusement lit his face. "If you wanted to hug me," he said, his voice low and scratchy, "you could've just asked."

She leveled a glare at him, which only served to coax a faint smile from his lips. "I wished no such thing." Though she did feel some relief that he didn't seem angry at her for intervening when he'd told her not to.

"You can go ahead and finish." He closed his eyes, but now she had to complete the task with him awake.

Reminding herself she'd left her feelings for Tex in the past, as he'd clearly done with her, she set her chin and approached him again. She grabbed the ends of the bandage as hastily as she could, then she proceeded to tie them securely over the poultice.

"There," she announced, a bit breathlessly as she tugged his nightshirt back into place. Hopefully Tex didn't notice. "Since you're awake, you can have some of the tea I made."

"All right."

Her hands were trembling so that she rattled the teacup and saucer as she lifted them off the tray. Sitting on the very edge of the bed, she brought the cup to Tex's mouth. He took a swallow, but his face contorted in surprise and his eyes appeared to water.

"What's in that skunk brew?" he coughed out, pounding a hand to his chest.

Ravena shook her head with impatience. He was as bad as one of the younger boys. "It will help you heal. Now, drink up." She hoisted the cup again, half expecting him to clamp his lips shut like Mark did. But he didn't.

Even though he looked wary, he obediently drank several more swallows. "Enough," he wheezed after a minute.

"Try to get some more rest," she said as she stood. "You need it." After scooping up the soiled bandage, she gathered everything onto the tray. Exhaustion, and a healthy dose of apprehension and discomfort, pushed her toward the door. If she hurried, she could snatch a few more hours of sleep before it was time to start breakfast.

"Ravena," Tex called as she reached the door.

She blew out a sigh and turned to face him. "Yes?"

"Thank you for this." He motioned to his side. "But you said one night and I won't stay longer than that."

Gripping the edges of the tray until they dug into her palms, she willed the words she wanted to say to reach her lips. *Yes, Tex, you have to leave. I have enough concerns right now, without worrying about you and the fragileness of my heart.*

Whatever she said, there was no going back after this moment. She didn't understand why he'd come to the farm after all these years. But he was here—and she had the power to hold him to his word and make him leave or extend his time.

She shut her eyes for a brief moment, praying for

guidance. The smallest seed of peace, so delicate it might be uprooted in time, germinated inside her. A whisper that everything would be all right.

Please help me trust You, God.

Opening her eyes, she peered straight at Tex, her head and heart pounding in unison. "I'm changing our agreement. You may stay until you're well."

Chapter Three

Even after her conversation with Tex about staying as long as he needed, Ravena still harbored a secret hope that she would find him remarkably recovered when she looked in on him the next morning. But that hope was obliterated when she found him sweltering with fever again, his sleeping form shifting restlessly beneath his blankets. He didn't respond to her placing her hand on his forehead or calling his name.

"How come he still looks like he's half-dead?" Mark asked. He and Luke watched from the open doorway.

Ravena frowned as she checked Tex's wound. "Because he's very sick." It was time for a new poultice. "Hurry and eat, boys, so you can make it to church on time. I need to stay here and help care for Mr. Beckett, so Jacob will be in charge. Please mind him."

"Ah, Miss Ravena," Mark whined, "do we have to go?"

Fighting a small smile, she guided the boys down the hallway. She could understand why having a stranger on the farm, especially one who'd been shot, held more fascination for the two than singing hymns and hearing Bible stories. And if Tex was still here tomorrow, the boys weren't going to be thrilled about leaving him to attend school either.

Their help might come in handy if she kept them home. It would be difficult to tend to Tex, see to her regular tasks around the farm and try to finish the plowing too. At the thought of all of her responsibilities, Ravena felt a familiar weight settle onto her shoulders.

Then she recalled something her grandfather had often said. "Love, stability and education are the keys to success for any child." And she was doing all in her power to provide those, even by herself these past three months. She couldn't let this obstacle derail her.

She straightened her drooping back and willed away her worries. The children would go to church today and school tomorrow. Somehow a way would work out to care for everything and everyone. It had to, because she would not give up on fulfilling her grandfather's wishes for these orphans or for the other four he'd hoped to bring home as well.

After sending off all five of the children to church, she made a new herbal poultice for Tex's wound and some more tea. She found him still sleeping fitfully, so she chose to forego waking him. He could drink the tea later. She half expected him to wake as she redressed his side, but unlike the night before, he didn't open his eyes or make conversation with her.

Ravena also wet a cloth for his forehead. His agitation eased as she placed the cool fabric against his sweaty brow. "It's Quincy," he mumbled, when she stepped back. "He's still out there…"

The man certainly had an affinity for his horse. Too bad he hadn't displayed as much affection for those people he'd left behind.

She felt immediate guilt at the thought. In many ways, life had been more difficult for Tex and Tate than for her, what with their father always gambling, then up and leaving the family when the boys were only nine. They'd struggled for years to make it through, only to lose their mother in death when they were young adults. And then, there'd been the fight that had lost them to each other. Had they reconciled in the years since she'd seen them last? She hoped so…but she also doubted it. She knew firsthand just how stubborn those Beckett brothers could be.

"Your horse is just fine," she soothed, placing a tentative hand on the sleeve of his nightshirt. Jacob had fed the animal along with their two horses and the cow that morning. "You can see for yourself once you're well."

Leaving the tea behind should he wake, she started for the door when she noticed the pile of things in the corner, including Tex's bloodied shirt from the day before. It was a pity his new clothes might be permanently ruined. Perhaps if she washed them now they could still be salvaged.

She loaded the crook of her arm with his shirt, jacket and trousers. Underneath the clothes sat two saddlebags. Perhaps they held more clothing in need of washing. She threw back the flap of one of the bags. It contained a holster and gun and a few pieces of jerky. No clothes though. She opened the other bag and a startled cry spilled from her lips to find it half filled with neat bundles of cash. Surely there had to be several hundred dollars inside.

Closing up the bag, she stood and crept from the room, her mind churning as she set about boiling water for the washing. Why would Tex be carrying that much money inside his saddlebag? What line of work did he do to earn so much? Certainly not farming or ranching.

She still hadn't puzzled out any answers by the time the water was ready. Pushing the new questions to the back of her mind, along with the old ones regarding Tex, Ravena threw herself into the washing. Her hands were soon pink and wrinkled from the warm water.

Sunshine poured down on her bare head as she hung Tex's clothes on the line to dry. Her task complete, her thoughts went back to the money sitting upstairs. There was so much she could do if such a sum belonged to her. She could hire several farm hands and someone to finish the new house. There would be enough to feed, clothe and care for more orphans, including the four brothers in Boise.

Yet that money wasn't hers. It was Tex's and she wouldn't be beholden to him by asking for financial help or a personal loan. He'd turned his back on her, unlike Tate who she suspected of being the benefactor behind the mysterious envelopes that had come to the farm over the years. Each was addressed to her and contained a helpful sum of money.

The children returned from church a short time later, all talking at once about the experience. Except for Ginny. She silently jumped in to help Ravena finish preparing lunch, as usual. The simple act calmed

Ravena's troubled heart and thoughts, at least for the moment.

Once everyone had eaten, she sent the children outside to play. It was probably time to check on Tex again and see if he was awake and hungry. She prepared a fresh pot of tea and a bowl of broth, then carried the full tray upstairs. She secretly hoped to find Tex still sleeping, so she wouldn't have to make conversation. The less they had to speak the better.

Unfortunately his gaze followed her movement into the room. "Morning," he said, his voice rough.

Ravena added the untouched teacup from earlier to the tray and placed it on the bureau. "I think you mean *good afternoon*."

He eyed the window, where the curtains were still drawn. "What time is it?"

"After lunch. Are you hungry?" He'd declined eating anything the night before.

"A little." The lopsided grin he gave her, even with how ill and pale he looked, still made her pulse sputter as it had in the old days.

Steeling herself against the reaction, she helped him sit up and placed the tray across his lap. "Can you manage or do you need some help?"

He eyed the spoon and bowl. "I think I can handle it." She watched to make sure he got the spoon to his mouth, though her gaze lingered on his face, even after he'd swallowed and dipped into the bowl a second time. If he hadn't run off eight years ago, if he'd come back for her as he'd promised, he would be her husband and the sight of him and his tussled hair just after he woke every day would be wonderfully familiar.

Needing air, Ravena crossed to the window. She drew back the curtains and wrenched the sill upward. A nice breeze washed over her flushed cheeks. She could hear Mark, Luke and Fanny laughing below. "You don't need to worry about your horse," she said as a way to end the awkward silence.

"I'm not." Tex chuckled. "I imagine he's in good hands."

She crossed her arms and leaned her forehead against the glass. "Your sleeping self doesn't seem to believe it. You keep asking about him."

"What do you mean? Was I talking in my sleep?"

"Yes, you kept mentioning your horse Quincy," she said, turning around.

His entire upper body went very still, the spoon pausing halfway to his lips. "My horse Quincy?"

Ravena rolled her eyes. "Yes, Tex. Your horse named Quincy."

He seemed to snap out of whatever stupor he'd been in. "The man at the livery said the horse's name is Brutus. I kind of figured I'd keep that."

"Brutus?" she repeated, confused. "Then who is Quincy?"

Lowering his gaze to the tray, he sampled some more broth before answering. "He's a...an acquaintance of mine. You might say we had a disagreement over some property. Not sure how to reconcile it."

Something in his words and his neutral expression struck her as odd. "Must have been some disagreement if you keep mumbling about it in your sleep." She regarded him with a level look, but he only smiled. That slow, boyish smile she used to never tire of seeing.

"This is delicious, even for broth. But then you always were a good cook."

"Is that why you're back?" The words burst forth as irritation resurrected the heat on her face. He wasn't being honest with her; she could tell. He probably didn't think she could remember the signs, but she could. The casual demeanor, the deliberate smile, the shift in the conversation's topic. What was he keeping from her this time?

Tex set down his spoon. "You know that isn't why I'm back."

"No, I don't. You show up after all these years, without sending a single letter the entire time, and you're injured and you have all this money stashed away inside your saddlebag." She waved a hand toward the corner. "Did you rob a bank or something, Tex? Why are you here?"

The little bit of color he'd regained bled away, making his blue eyes stand out starkly. Eyes that were wide with shock. "Wh-what did you say?"

Was he really that surprised that she'd lose her temper? Surely he knew he had it coming. She threw her arms in the air. "I said why are you here, *now*, after all this time."

His Adam's apple bobbed up and down as he swallowed, though he hadn't sampled another spoonful of broth. "I went to the old farm, to see if…if Tate…was there."

So the two had never reconciled after all. Even in her frustration, Ravena felt a measure of sadness for both of them. "Tate stayed another few months after you left, then he sold the place. Didn't you write him?"

Tex shook his head.

Her sadness deepened at knowing there was still a rift between the brothers. The sorrow was followed by sharp disappointment she didn't understand. Why should it hurt her that Tex hadn't come here out of any desire to see her? She should be grateful for that, but she wasn't.

"I understand why you're here," she said, taking a step toward the door. She wanted an end to this conversation. "You're injured and you thought Tate would be here to help you."

"Ravena." Tex's voice sounded as tortured as her heart in that moment. "I didn't want to impose on you. Not after…everything."

"But you did." He was still making choices that affected her, that hurt her. Even after all these years. She had trouble enough without Tex dredging up the past and confusing her emotions.

"I needed a place to rest."

Rest, yes, that was his real motive for being here. And she would do well to remember that. "As I told you last night, you're welcome to rest here as long as you need to." Though she prayed once more that his departure would be soon. Very soon. "Now if you'll excuse me, I have a farm to run."

The creak of the door interrupted Tex's nap two days later. He jerked awake, wondering how long he'd been asleep this time. He was trying to stay awake whenever he heard Ravena or the children moving about below stairs. That way he wouldn't unknowingly spill any more information about Quincy, or worse, talk about his career as an outlaw.

From the bed, he caught sight of Mark slipping into the room, followed closely by Luke. "Mr. Beckett?" the older of the brothers whispered. "Are you awake?"

Tex fought a smile. "No. I'm fast asleep. So that must mean you're in my dream."

That made the boys pause in their stealthy advance toward the bed. "He's still sleeping," Mark hissed.

"Then how come he's talking?" Luke questioned with a note of skepticism.

"Maybe he talks when he's dreaming."

Tex peeked above the blankets at his chin to see them creeping forward again. Promptly shutting his eyes, he held back a chuckle as he waited for them to reach him.

"Whatdaya think he's dreaming about that has us in it?" Tex recognized Luke's voice.

"Don't know."

"We could ask him."

He opened his eyes to find the boys standing right beside him. "Except Miss Ravena might not like that. Or the fact that you're in here." Tex had heard her telling the children more than once to leave him be.

"You ain't asleep," Mark protested with a glare.

Luke grinned. "I knew it."

"Did not."

"Did too."

"What can I do for you, boys?" he asked, hoping to end their argument.

"We wanna know how you got shot." Mark leaned close as he lowered his voice. "Did it hurt?"

Tex shifted carefully up onto his pillow. The slight

movement still had him sucking in a hard breath. What could he say that wouldn't reveal too much? "A very angry man shot me over a misunderstanding. And as far as if it hurt or not. I'd say it hurts like—"

Luke's hand shot out and covered Tex's mouth. "Shh. If you say a curse, Miss Ravena will make you muck the stalls *by yourself*—for a whole week."

Tex burst out laughing at the boy's warning, then regretted it at once. It felt like his side was splitting in two. Luke lowered his hand, his brow pinched in confusion. "Thanks for the advice. I'll remember that," Tex said. "What I was going to say is that getting shot hurts like when you slam your finger in a door, but then doing it about a million times over."

Both boys' eyes widened. "Whoa," Mark whispered. "But you ain't dead?"

"I ain't dead."

Luke solemnly shook his head. "You can't say that either, Mr. Beckett."

Tex feigned a look of contrition. "My apologies, young man. I am not dead." And he was glad for it. It had been nice to see Ravena one more time before he had to leave.

And leave he must. Especially after Ravena's innocent, but all too accurate remark about him robbing a bank in order to have that much money in his saddlebag. Tex had been so terrified she suspected the truth that he hadn't been able to get back to sleep for hours that night. If he stayed any longer than he had to, she was sure to discover who he'd become and Tex couldn't stomach the idea of her revulsion. At least if he rode away now, he could tell himself that she wouldn't completely hate him once she learned the truth.

"What do you do, 'sides getting shot?" Mark rested his elbows on the edge of the bed.

The question so closely matched his thoughts just now that Tex gulped, searching for a suitable answer. "I ride from one place to another, picking up jobs along on the way."

Luke placed his head in his palm as he regarded Tex. "Do you have a home?"

Tex shook his head. "Nope."

"Is that because you're an orphan?" Mark asked.

He thought about that a moment, then nodded. "I guess I am."

"Well, Miss Ravena will give you a home here with us," Mark said emphatically.

The boy's assurance pierced straight through Tex's tired, pain-filled mind. If only those words could be true for him.

Movement at the door drew his attention. "Boys," Ravena said as she hurried inside. "You need to leave Mr. Beckett alone."

"They're all right," he said.

But she ignored him. "Let's go." She placed a hand on each of their shoulders and steered them toward the door. "Please let me know if they bother you again, Tex."

"They weren't a…" The door shut before he could finish.

A feeling of desolation washed over him as the quiet in the room pressed in. Pushing out a sigh, he slid back beneath the covers. He was grateful for Ravena's help, truly grateful, but he couldn't linger here.

After spending a total of five and a half days in bed, Tex felt more than ready to be up and about. And to leave. Under Ravena's capable hands, his wound had almost completely healed, though there were still moments when he wished he could sleep for a month. Mark and Luke hadn't come to see him again, so he guessed Ravena had stopped any further attempts at visits. He had been amused by the occasional appearance of a smiling little girl with dark brown braids and blue eyes who held up her kitten for him to see.

Without anyone to talk to, other than short conversations with Ravena when she carried in his food or rebandaged his side, he kept busy resting or reading. He read more while convalescing than he had in years. Books mostly, ones Ravena brought him from downstairs, but also a newspaper, which he'd perused front and back, relieved when he didn't find mention of himself.

But now it was time to move on. Tex finished putting on his boots and stood. Hefting his saddlebags and throwing his jacket over his arm, he observed the room. It looked as if he hadn't been here at all. The thought brought a flicker of emotion. Was it disappointment? Had he really left no trace of himself behind when he'd left eight years ago? Maybe, maybe not. But either way, everyone else's lives had continued on.

He ignored the introspective thoughts and questions as he made his way downstairs. Outside he caught sight of Mark and Luke dashing through the afternoon shadows near the corner of the barn. Ginny, the older girl with red hair whom he'd met during his first day here, sat on the porch step. She was peeling potatoes, her green gaze darting toward him before skittering away.

"You don't want to sit in the rocker?" he asked, motioning to it.

She shook her head. "The seat is broken."

It was something he could fix, if he were staying. Which he wasn't.

"Well, I'm off," he announced into the ensuing silence. Where was Ravena?

"She's plowing one of the fields," Ginny said with canny perceptiveness.

Tex nodded. "Thank you." He'd see to his horse, then find Ravena to say goodbye. The imminent farewell made his gut twist with apprehension, though he wasn't sure why. He couldn't stay. Now that he could walk around with relative ease, it was time to go.

He ducked into the barn, blinking in the dim light. Jacob had already saddled Brutus as Tex had asked him to earlier. "Thanks for seeing to my horse." The boy gave a wordless nod. Placing the saddlebags in their proper place, Tex slipped into his jacket and gathered the reins in his hand.

"Goodbye, Mr. Beckett," a small voice called from above. Tex squinted at the hayloft to see the dark-haired little girl sitting there with her kitten in tow, her legs dangling over the ladder.

"Goodbye…" He realized he didn't know her name.

Jacob answered his unspoken question. "Her name's Fanny. She's my sister."

"Ah. Goodbye then, Fanny." He doffed his hat to her. "Thank you for sharing your kitten with me."

She grinned as if she'd shared something more precious than gold with him, a stranger. "Whiskers likes you and so do I."

Tex wasn't sure how to respond, so he simply lifted his hand in a goodbye wave and led his horse outside. Jacob followed him. "Can you hold Brutus while I go say goodbye to Miss Ravena?"

Taking the reins from him, Jacob tossed a challenging look at Tex. "You're gonna up and leave her without help?"

"Pardon me?"

The lad might only be thirteen, but he stood as tall and determined as any man in that moment. "Miss Ravena. She told us that you two were once friends. So why are you up and leaving?"

Tex rubbed a hand over his jaw—this afternoon he'd finally shaved the beard that had taken up residence on his face. "We were friends, but I was just here to rest, Jacob. Nothing more. I've got to, you know..." He gestured toward the road. "I had a life before coming here."

The intensity left Jacob's gaze and he lowered his chin. "I know," he murmured. "It's just that...well, she needs help. We won't finish the plowing and get the planting in on time if everyone she hires up and quits."

A gnawing guilt began to creep over him. Tex folded his arms against it. "Did they give a reason?"

"They say they don't like havin' the younger kids underfoot, but I think it's more the wages." Jacob pushed at the dirt with the toe of his boot. "Miss Ravena doesn't have much money to pay them. She still needs to finish the bigger house too, so we can take care of the four boys Mr. Ezra wanted to bring to the farm."

Tex cut a look over his shoulder in the direction of the fields. "That is a difficult predicament all around." He might have turned his back on farming years ago, but he'd grown up in this life and remembered well the importance of planting on time in order to reap at harvest.

"I told her I can help with the planting." Jacob's boyish shoulders lifted in a shrug. "Other boys my age miss school to help out that way. I can too."

"That's not a bad idea, kid." Tex turned and started walking away. "I'll talk to her."

The late-afternoon sunlight warmed him through his jacket as he tromped toward the fields. Up ahead he spied Ravena guiding the plow and the team of horses. He stopped to watch her a moment. Her head was down, so she hadn't seen him yet, her concentration fully on her task. A worn straw hat shaded her from the sun. Her hair, which she typically wore long and flowing, had been braided and lay down her back.

Even from a distance, her natural beauty struck him hard in the chest. She'd been his world and he hers for so long. And they'd both believed that would never change.

She deserves better than a thief. Tate's angry words from that night eight years ago were even more true now than they'd been at the time. Tex wasn't just a thief but an outlaw, with a price on his head, and an angry enemy on his trail. Ravena deserved better than him as a sweetheart or a friend. Regret built beneath his collar and he plucked at it in order to breathe.

Ravena paused in her task to brush her sleeve across

her forehead. Her expression changed from one of focus to complete exhaustion as she dropped her chin. She was likely praying, Tex guessed, or crying—or maybe both. Her visible despondency seemed to reach across the field and twist at his heart. She couldn't spend all of her money on hired help when she had a houseful of children to care for and a desire to bring others to the farm. But she couldn't afford a delay in getting her crops planted either.

As Tex watched, Ravena lifted her head, pulling strength from somewhere, and clucked to the horses to keep moving. It would take her weeks to complete the planting, even with Jacob's help. And what about everything else that needed doing around the farm in the meantime? While he'd heard the children going about their chores morning and evening, none of them were old enough to take the place of an able-bodied man.

But if he stayed…

Tex blew out his breath, certain the heat must be getting to him after so many days inside. That would explain the crazy notion attempting to take shape inside his head. Staying was a foolish idea. If he wanted to help, he could give her money, as he had in the past, though he suspected she didn't know those anonymous envelopes of cash were from him.

Ravena wasn't likely to accept his offer of money though. She would likely see it as him buying her off, attempting to monetarily make up for the pain of the past. And she'd be right, wouldn't she?

He paced the grass, his side and head beginning to ache. Did she have to be so stubborn? *Do you?* a gentle thought from deep inside him countered.

Yanking off his hat, he slapped it against his leg. He had to leave. What if she learned he was the Texas Titan? He spun around, determined to bid her goodbye after insisting she take some of his money. But Ravena was no longer plowing. Instead she stood still, her eyes meeting his across the field.

There was more than freshly-turned earth between them—there was a chasm of regrets and heartache. And yet, he hadn't stopped caring about her and likely never would. She'd been his greatest friend and his first and only love. How could he turn his back on her a second time?

The answer came swift and firm: he couldn't.

Plopping his hat back on, he marched toward the house. Jacob guided his horse forward as Tex drew closer. "What did she say about me missing school to help?"

"Nothing. I didn't ask her, but you can put the horse away."

The boy's brow scrunched in bewilderment. "Put him away? Why?"

After removing his jacket, Tex tossed it to Jacob who caught it one-handed. "Because," he said, rolling up his sleeves, "I'm staying to help, kid."

Chapter Four

With heavy heart, Ravena watched Tex walk away. He'd appeared to be feeling well enough today that she'd considered inviting him to eat supper in the kitchen with them tonight, but that would no longer be an option. He was already leaving, without saying goodbye. Just as he'd done once before. She told herself she ought to be glad, relieved even, that he was finally going. One of her many problems had solved itself. Tex would no longer be a constant and painful reminder of the past.

But she didn't feel happy. She felt like slipping to the dirt and giving in to the desolation threatening to consume her.

Checking her emotions, she gave the horses a gentle slap with the reins and called, "Walk on." The plowing wouldn't get done if she didn't do it herself, whether she felt up to the task or not.

Everything would work out, she firmly told herself, with the Lord's help. It was something her grandparents had taught her over and over again. Something she'd clung to when Tex hadn't returned. And she would hold to that hope now. Somehow, some way, she would finish plowing her fields, get the crops planted and build the house. She had to. For herself, for the five children under her care and for those four boys she hoped to bring home soon. They were counting on her and so was her grandfather, whether he was here or not.

As she turned the horses at the edge of the field and lined them up for the next furrow, a flash of movement caught her eye. Ravena twisted to see what it was and felt the breath leave her lungs when she saw Tex stalking back toward her.

"Whoa." She stopped the horses, her heartbeat thrashing with confusion. What was he doing? Had he decided to say goodbye after all?

Stepping away from the team, she crossed her arms tightly against her worn dress as she waited for Tex to approach. Not for the first time she wondered what sort of young women he'd met or fallen in love with during his time away. If his new clothes and the money in his saddlebags were any indication, he'd likely been associated with wealthy, sophisticated girls. Not farm women with patched clothes and five children to care for.

"I figured you'd be gone by now, Tex," she said in an icy tone when he was still a few feet away. Anger was her ally, her protection, against having her heart broken again. "Did you forget something?" Maybe it was his jacket. He was no longer wearing it and his sleeves had been rolled back.

"Nope," he answered. He strode right past her and grabbed the reins.

Ravena stared at him in bewilderment. "What are

you doing?" she repeated. Why wasn't he saying good-bye? Why wouldn't he just let her be?

"This field needs plowing," he said before clucking to the horses.

"Of course it needs plowing." She hurried to keep in step with him and the team. "Which is why *I've* been plowing it, all day."

Tex didn't slow. "Now you don't have to do it. According to Jacob, you've got a real need for help this year." He cast a glance at her. "He seems like a good kid. And stronger than you might think. I'd let him do more."

Ravena's mouth fell open and she stopped walking. Was he trying to tell her how to run the farm? Indignation rose inside her as hot as the sun on her back and arms.

"You have no right, Tex Beckett," she said, her voice shaking with fury. "No right to plow my field before you disappear again or offer your completely unsolicited advice. You left, Tex. By your own volition last time, but this time, I'm demanding that you go."

Her words had the desired effect. Tex jerked back on the reins and turned to face her. "I'm not leaving, Ravena. Not yet."

"Yes, you are." She clenched her hands into fists at her sides, anger and fear dueling inside her. "I will not allow you to manipulate me or think that plowing my field somehow makes up for…for…" She swallowed the fast-forming lump in her throat. "That it somehow makes up for everything else. I want you to leave. And if you don't, I'm sending Jacob for the sheriff."

She spun on her heel, intent on making good on her

threat, but Tex moved quicker and stopped her with a hand to her elbow. At his touch, her pulse galloped for an entirely different reason than resentment or panic. "Ravena, wait. You're right."

Searching his blue gaze, she couldn't detect any deceit there. But how well did she really know him now? "Right about what?"

"Plowing your field doesn't make up for the past. And it isn't supposed to." He lowered his hand and a traitorous prick of disappointment shot through her. "I want to help with the rest of the plowing and the planting too."

She folded her arms, suspicious. "Why?" What made him want to stick around this time when he hadn't all those years ago?

Tex ran his hand over his clean-shaven jaw in a gesture of pure agitation. "I'd like to help because you need it."

When she opened her mouth to protest, he forged on, "I know you'll say you don't. But Jacob says otherwise, and I can see with my own eyes how much work there is right now. You've helped me more than your fair share this last week. So let me help you."

She sensed only sincerity behind his admission, but she still wanted to tell him no. She needed him gone, away, and no longer wreaking havoc in her life and with her feelings. But would she be able to find someone else as willing to help as he seemed to be?

"I can only pay you the same wage I did the other hired hands," she said, her chin held firm and aloft. She wouldn't let him see yet that she was beginning to waver in her resolve to turn him out.

"I don't want your money, Ravena. I'm offering to help without pay." He pushed his hat up, then tugged it back down as if embarrassed. "It's the least I can do after all you've done to help me get well."

He'd work for free? Her adamancy that he leave was weakening by the second. "How long will you stay?"

A slow smile lifted his mouth and brightened his blue eyes. The kind of smile that had once lit her world. "Does that mean you accept my offer?"

"Answer the question first, Tex." She bristled. "How long?"

He glanced at the field. "Until the spring planting's completed."

It was a tempting offer. Ravena fiddled with the end of her braid as she considered it. She would only need to manage having him around for another few weeks.

Could he be an answer to her prayers? If so, she might need to be more specific with the Lord in the future about whom she could and could not put up with for help. Still, with Tex's assistance, they would likely get the planting done on time. And since she wouldn't be paying him a wage, she could use that money to hopefully hire someone willing to work for cheap to finish building the larger house.

She threw him a glance to find him watching her, and suddenly, she needed to know why he'd disappeared that night. If she was going to agree to let him stay on or not, she needed an answer to the question that had haunted her for so long. "Why didn't you come back, Tex?"

A puzzled expression settled onto his handsome face. "I did. That's why I'm standing here."

"No." She shook her head, her heart thrashing faster. Did she want to know the answer? There'd be no un-hearing Tex's response. "I mean," she plunged on, "why didn't you come for me like we'd planned?"

Understanding washed the color from his jaw and he shifted his weight. Would he tell her the truth? Ravena clasped her hands tightly together, hoping she looked more brave and unaffected than she felt.

"I planned to. But then…" He wiped his hand over his chin. Ravena held her breath. "I realized you deserved far better than me."

She released the pressure in her lungs in a soft whoosh, feeling just as deflated. He'd decided she deserved better, but he hadn't bothered to ask if she felt that way too. "I see."

But she didn't, not completely. Something had happened that night, between the time they'd finalized their plans to elope and Tate showing up at the farm to say Tex had disappeared.

She considered pressing Tex for more of an explanation, and yet, she couldn't stomach reopening the old wounds any more than they'd already been. His answer wasn't as satisfying as she'd hoped…but it didn't hurt as much as she'd feared either. And really, what did it matter in the end?

Tex hadn't come back for her, which meant she hadn't made the mistake of leaving her grandfather alone. Those were the realities of the past. But she hated that she'd pinned everything on Tex's word and had come so close to turning her back on the home she'd loved for the man she'd trusted. A man who'd gone back on his promise to be there for her always and come for her that night. A man who stood before her now, offering to help when she needed it most.

Can I do it, Lord? If Tex stuck around, the past was likely to keep eating at her. But surely she could endure some discomfort over the next few weeks if it made her better able to care for the children—and bring the other four boys to the farm.

"All right." Ravena stuck out her hand for him to shake. "I accept your offer."

His hand closed over hers. "You won't regret it, Ravena," he said, his gaze unusually serious. "I promise."

She'd heard those words before. Breaking his hold, she strode toward the house to see how Ginny was coming at starting supper. Everything inside her hoped that Tex would fulfill his promise. Because she wasn't the only one counting on him this time.

Tex hobbled toward the porch, the sun's dying rays a fitting backdrop to how he felt. His body, and particularly his healing wound, protested each step. And he'd only been plowing that field for a couple hours. Outlawing wasn't exactly a life free of activity, but he hadn't done hard labor like this in years and every one of his muscles was determined to remind him of that fact.

Opening the screen and then the front door, he entered to the murmur of conversation coming from the back of the house. Mark and Luke had found him in the barn a few minutes earlier, seeing to the horses, and had announced it was time for supper. "And Miss Ravena ain't partial to latecomers," Mark warned.

Tex managed to work up a small smile at the memory of the boy's words as he moved slowly down the hall.

Ravena might run the farm with a steady hand, but she was compassionate too. It wasn't hard to see how much the children loved and respected her. That was something he could easily relate to—she'd always engendered his love and respect as well.

Until you abandoned her.

A tremor of shame and guilt rocked him at the errant thought and stole what little strength he had left. Tex splayed his hand against the wall to hold himself upright. He'd thought he'd suppressed his regret over not coming back for Ravena that night. But being here again and having her ask him earlier about the past was making it harder and harder to ignore.

Laughter floated toward him, beckoning him forward, and away from the painful past. He hadn't yet eaten in the kitchen with Ravena and the children. Tex gritted his teeth against his despondency, fighting it back with reminders that he was here to help her now. Surely that was something. Pushing away from the wall, he forced himself to walk instead of limp into the kitchen.

All of the children were seated, except for Ginny who assisted Ravena in carrying the dishes to the table. The laughter faded as he stepped through the doorway.

"Smells good," Tex said, a little louder than necessary. But he was desperate for an escape from the physical and emotional pain battling inside himself. "Then again, it usually does."

He noticed Ravena's cheeks flush pink, though she didn't change her passive expression. "You're welcome to take a seat after you wash up." She and Ginny sat at the table.

Crossing to the sink, he lifted the pump and began to wash his hands in the stream of water. "What's for supper?"

His only response came in the form of a girlish giggle. Tex turned to see Fanny covering her mouth with her hands. The rest of the children were staring down at their empty plates, but they were all fighting smiles.

"All right," he half growled, trying to sound stern. He'd never cared for being the butt of a joke, but the children's smiles were irresistible. He dried his hands on the nearby towel and turned to face them. "What's got Fanny in stitches?"

Another giggle leaked between the girl's small fingers and nearly prompted a grin from Tex. But he hid it as he folded his arms and regarded each of the children in turn with a shrewd look. When his gaze fell on Ravena, he was surprised to find a half smile on her face. The sight of it was like sampling a cool drink of water after trekking through the hot desert.

"We were having a rather amusing conversation, which Mark started," Ravena offered by way of explanation as she began dishing up the food.

Tex took a seat beside Ginny. "And what did you say?" he asked, turning to Mark. But the boy took one look at his little brother and they both burst out laughing.

"I'll tell it." Jacob placed a roll on his plate and passed the bowl with the rest of the bread to Ginny. "He and Luke were telling us how they found you asleep just now, standing in the barn and holding the pitchfork." The boys were right—Tex had been so tired that he'd nodded off for a moment. "Then Fanny wanted to

know if that meant you were half horse since they sometimes sleep standing up. And Ginny said she's read that
elephants often nap the same way. So then Luke wondered, if like an elephant, you'd eat all the food and then
you came in and said 'Smells good...'"

"Ah, makes sense now." Accepting the bowl of bread
from Ginny, he made sure to catch Luke's eye. Then
he proceeded to set one roll after another onto his plate
until there were none left. "Now that I think about it, I
am rather famished."

Luke's mouth formed a silent O, which succeeded in
eliciting more laughter from everyone around the table,
including Ravena. The sound of her laughter wound
its way straight into Tex's chest, both comforting and
sad. It had been far too many years since he'd heard
her laugh. When her eyes met his, her open and happy
countenance disappeared and her smile faded. He'd seen
them, though, and he knew he'd inspired them. It was
a small victory but a victory nonetheless.

Piling all but one roll back into the bowl, he passed
it to Fanny at his left. Luke appeared visibly relieved.
Soon Tex had his plate heaped high with warm food.
He was starving. Lifting his fork, he scooped up a full
bite. Before he could bring it to his mouth though, Mark
declared, "You ain't supposed to eat before the prayer,
Mr. Beckett."

"Aren't supposed to eat." Ravena threw Tex a quick
look. "And Mark is right. We say the blessing on our
meal first."

Tex squirmed a little in his chair as all eyes rested
on him again. Removing his hat, he bowed his head as
much in compliance as to hide from the children's scru-

tiny. Could they see that he was as far from religious as a man could likely get?

"It's your turn, Fanny," Ravena said kindly.

As the little girl began praying, Tex obediently shut his eyes. "Our Father in Heaven, bless our supper. And bless me, and Jacob, and Ginny, and Mark, and Luke, and Miss Ravena. And bless Mr. Beckett…"

Tex's eyelids flew open. He stared in shock at Fanny's bent head and clasped hands, missing the rest of her words. When was the last time someone had prayed for him? Probably not since before his mother had passed away. But he amended that thought with the recollection that at one time his brother Tate used to pray for him. Did Tate still do that? Or was his twin still as angry as he'd been the last time Tex had seen him?

Fanny ended her prayer, a chorus of amens following hers. It was a signal to Tex to set aside thoughts of the past—once again. Why did they keep plaguing him today? he wondered as he put his hat back on. Perhaps it was because he was nearly recovered from his injury and not concentrating anymore on healing or revealing too much in his feverish state. But he hadn't counted on coming face-to-face with his history when he'd made his decision to stick around and help Ravena with the planting.

The itch inside him, the one that had always indicated he'd stayed too long in one spot, began nibbling at him as it had earlier. He lifted his fork again and glanced up to find Ravena watching him. Could she see him wrestling with himself?

Frowning, Ravena looked away. But Tex felt certain she'd seen something on his face. *She thinks I'm still going to up and leave, even after my offer to help.* The realization shouldn't have shocked him, but it did. At one time his word had meant something to her. And yet...

The children's conversation bounced back and forth across the table, but Tex felt detached from it. He managed to eat most of the delicious meal, but his sour thoughts soon soured his stomach. Pushing back from the table, he gathered up his dishes and moved toward the sink.

"Should I wash my things now?" He avoided looking directly at Ravena.

"No, it's all right," she answered. "Mark and Jacob have dishes tonight."

The younger boy's audible groans coaxed a bit of a smile from Tex before he headed outside. Gulping in the night air, he winced at the pain in his side. He had to believe at some point it would cease bothering him, though he doubted he'd done himself any favors with the labor he'd undertaken that afternoon. Riding a horse full out, to escape both the sheriff and Quincy, felt like easy work after plowing that field. He probably ought to get to sleep, but he didn't feel like being cooped up in the house right now.

He moved slowly to the corral and rested his boot on the lowest rung of the fence. Nearly every corner of this place held memories for him—ones with him and Ravena, and ones with both of them and Tate. Tex pushed out a long breath, desperate to clear his head.

Ravena might expect him to leave, but he wasn't going anywhere. Not until he'd fulfilled his promise to help her with the planting. Hopefully by then Quincy would have given up searching for Tex and he'd be free to return to the life he'd chosen.

"Not hungry? Or did the food taste badly?"

Tex waited for Ravena to walk closer before he responded, slightly surprised she'd sought him out. "The meal was excellent, as always. So I guess it's the former."

Resting her arms on the fence rail, she glanced up at the twilight sky. "How's your side feeling tonight?"

"Right as rain after your doctoring." He forced a smile.

Instead of prompting one in return with his compliment, Ravena frowned. "I know that isn't true, Tex. You can't be injured like that and not have it aggravate you when you start to move about and work."

"Fine." Something in him hardened at her keen perceptiveness and the fact that maybe he was losing his ability to sweet-talk a woman. "Truth is I feel like death walking. Is that better?"

Ravena gave a light laugh, catching him off guard once more. "That's refreshingly better. I'm tired of men coming around and overpromising what they can do, how much they can handle, just to back out in the end."

Tex had a sinking feeling in the pit of his stomach that she wasn't just talking about farm hands. "Is that what you think I'm doing, overpromising?"

"Aren't you?" She twisted to face him, her expression a mixture of determined pride and frightened vulnerability. He'd seen that same look, nearly a decade ago, when he'd asked her to elope with him. Then and now, it made him want to pull her into his arms. His only defense was to harden himself against getting too close.

He feigned a nonchalant posture. "Still looking for rain when there isn't a cloud in the sky, huh?"

Her shoulders stiffened and she reared back slightly. A prick of pain flicked through him—he'd hurt her with his deliberate teasing. But he had to keep his distance. For her protection…and for his. The more she questioned him about the past, the closer she'd likely come to unearthing the truth about what he'd done since leaving the first time.

"Perhaps in that I haven't changed," Ravena said, her voice as tight as her folded arms. "But as you'll recall, the last time you were here, Tex, the sky was sparkling blue and then you dropped a hurricane on me. Without ever bothering to look back and see the damage and debris."

The guilt he'd been dodging all day wound around his lungs and squeezed. But he wasn't ready to voice it, let alone feel it. "Look. I said I'd stay for the planting. And I aim to. I will."

"I guess we'll see." She started to walk away before calling back, "A warm poultice on your side might help with the soreness. Let me know if you want one." Then she moved at a steady pace back toward the house.

Tex faced the corral again, but not before kicking at one of the posts with his boot. He was trying, couldn't she see that? He wasn't any more thrilled with doing farm work than Ravena clearly was with him staying. Still, beneath all that probably needed saying between them, he knew he had a debt to pay. Ravena had been right when she'd said he hadn't looked back to see how his choices had affected her and her life. And though everything inside him was urging him to saddle up

Brutus and ride away a second time, he couldn't do it. Maybe it was only to prove to Ravena that he wasn't all bad.

Or maybe it was to prove that to himself.

Either way, he wasn't leaving. He'd come here seeking help and now he'd give it in return. Only then would he be able to leave with a clear conscience.

Ravena knelt on the rug beside the sofa for her nightly prayers—she'd insisted Tex continue to use her room until he was fully recovered. Exhaustion haunted her, and it stemmed from far more than plowing the field earlier that day before Tex had taken over. This fatigue was born from trying to navigate things with him. He'd spoken the truth when he had teased her about looking for rain when there was no sign of it. But she still believed his being here might prove as much a burden as a blessing.

"Lord," she whispered as she shut her eyes. "I'm afraid of him staying longer, even though I need his help."

A memory she hadn't recalled since her grandfather's funeral entered her thoughts and pushed at her fears. It was something Grandfather had said years earlier, after another long cry over Tex's silence. "Remember that the Lord has got this in His hands, Ravena. He's got you."

Isn't that what the Lord was trying to show her now, by bringing Tex here and having him offer to help with the planting? She might not understand all of the reasons for his sudden appearance in her life, but she had enough faith to understand that trusting God didn't always make sense.

Feeling a bit more at peace, she began to pray for each of the children by name and for the strength to keep going. She started to climb to her feet when she remembered Fanny's sweet prayer at supper and how the little girl had prayed for Tex. Fanny wasn't the first one to have prayed for him since his arrival. In contrast, it had been years since Ravena had prayed for him.

She lowered herself to her knees once more and folded her arms, her heart knocking faster against her ribs. *The Lord has got this in His hands, Ravena*, she reminded herself. *He's got you.*

"You know how hard this is for me, Lord. Having Tex here after all this time." Her voice wobbled with emotion, but she forged ahead. "I do still care for him, though. And so I ask You…" She swallowed hard. "Please bless him too."

Tex slipped upstairs, grateful his stocking feet made no noise. He hadn't meant to eavesdrop. Feeling thirsty, he'd decided to head to the kitchen for a drink of water. He'd heard Ravena's voice as he started down the stairs and had assumed she was talking to one of the children in the parlor. But he'd paused on the second step when he'd discovered she was praying. For him.

Rubbing his hand over his face, he crept back to his room and sat on the bed, his thoughts as stirred up as the dust in a windstorm. Why had two people prayed for him tonight? First Fanny, then Ravena. Of course Ravena had also expressed how difficult his being here was for her—a realization that physically pained him to hear her say out loud. And yet she'd still asked God to bless him. Why? More important, why did both their prayers give him a hopeful feeling deep down in his gut? It was a feeling he both welcomed and feared.

It was likely just the pull of being connected to someone or something, like what he'd felt at first being around Quincy and his cronies. But this…emotion…, wasn't the same, he realized. Deep down he'd felt desperate and lonely, even after befriending Quincy.

As an outlaw, he'd always worked alone—unable to find any comrades who would hold to his rules of never harming women or children. With Quincy, he hadn't been looking for someone he could trust or rely on—just someone to keep the loneliness at bay for a few hours.

Tonight he felt something akin to familiarity and comfort. It reminded him of the time his mother would pull out the winter quilts each year and he and Tate would burrow into the familiar cozy warmth.

That was it, he felt cozy.

Tex climbed back into bed, no longer thirsty. "I'm not coming back," he whispered fiercely in the direction of the ceiling. "They can pray for me all they like. But I'm not coming back to You or them. I picked my course and it's the one I'm happy with. So don't go blessing me and expecting I'll return."

Releasing a huff of irritation, he turned on his good side. But he couldn't help wondering as he shut his eyes why he'd bothered talking to Someone he'd told himself a long time ago he no longer cared about.

Chapter Five

Pushing up his hat, Tex swiped at his sweaty brow with his sleeve. His side didn't ache as much today, in spite of driving the plow and team for the last few hours, thanks to Ravena's poultice last night. But he could still tell he wasn't completely back to full health. There'd been a time when half a day of regular farm work hadn't worked up this much sweat and exhaustion in him.

He lifted the reins of the horses to start them moving again when he caught sight of Ravena walking toward him. The sight of a covered dish and a canteen in her hands prompted a tired smile. It must be time for lunch. The horses could use another rest too. Ducking into the shade of a nearby tree, Tex removed his hat and waited for her approach.

"You're almost done," Ravena commented as she came to a stop beside him. "Only one more field to plow."

"Then it's on to spring planting."

She nodded. "Here's your lunch and some water."

"Thanks." Tex accepted the canteen from her before

downing a throatful of the cool liquid. Brushing the lingering moisture from his mouth, he took a seat on the ground and settled the covered dish on his knee. "Did you eat already?"

"Yes." He expected her to leave, to retreat to the house, but instead she lingered.

"Care to sit for a spell?" he asked, patting the dirt next to him.

Her upper lip pressed in on the bottom one, but after a moment, she took a seat next to him on the ground. "It's rather warm today." She lifted her long dark hair off her neck and shut her eyes.

Tex uncovered his lunch, but he couldn't help glancing at her once, then twice. Light and shadow chased each other across her face and the slight breeze ruffled the hair along her cheekbones. He'd always thought her pretty—inside and out. Even when they'd been younger. And yet there was a graceful, sophisticated quality to her beauty now that hadn't been there eight years ago.

Looking away, he bit into one of the hard boiled eggs she'd made him. "So how long have these kids been with you?" he asked after swallowing.

Ravena leaned against the tree trunk. "Let's see. Mark and Luke came to the farm two years ago. Jacob and Fanny have only been here six months, and Ginny has lived here a year."

"She doesn't say much, does she?"

A slight frown pulled at her mouth as she shook her head. "No, she doesn't. She used to have awful nightmares, though they aren't as frequent now. I don't know what happened to her and she's not saying, but I hate the thought of anyone mistreating her. She's such a good girl, very smart and respectful. She's a real help to me in the kitchen. And I will say, the quiet makes it down-right peaceful when we're cooking together while the others do their chores."

Tex took another bite and swallowed. "Now Fanny on the other hand…"

"Can talk a streak when she wants to, I know." Ravena gave a light laugh. "And then Mark and Luke are double the trouble sometimes."

"Reminds me of two other boys who used to live around here."

She shot him guarded look, but it soon relaxed into a smile. "I've thought the same. Although, unlike Tate, Mark is more the instigator of the fun."

"That would not be Tate." Tex smirked. "He was usu-ally wound tighter than a spool of thread and as humor-ous as a porcupine." It was the wrong thing to say. He saw it at once in the way Ravena's shoulders stiffened.

She scooted a few inches away from him, putting more distance between them. "Please don't speak ill of him, Tex. I know things were strained between the two of you at the end. But he's done far more to help me than you may know."

His gut twisted with apprehension—and jealousy, if he was honest with himself. "What do you mean by that?" he asked, far more casually than he felt. Had his brother come back to see Ravena?

Plucking up one tiny flower and then another, she began plaiting them together. Tex remembered how she'd done that as a girl. Then insisted he or Tate or both of them wear her homemade "crowns." Tex and his brother would protest at first, but eventually they'd give in to Ravena's big, pleading eyes. "Before he left for good, he came to apologize. For what he felt was his part in…in that night."

So Tate had apologized to Ravena? Well, Tex was glad to hear it. Although his brother hadn't seen fit to apologize to him too. *And did you?* his conscience prodded. Tex frowned. What about this place was nudging his inner moral compass to start yapping at him again?

"He's also sent me money through the years," Ravena added, her tone full of gratitude.

Tex choked on his next bite and hurried to wash it down with water from the canteen. Why did Ravena think Tate had been the one to send her money? Unless perhaps his twin had been mailing her cash too.

"That's awfully generous," he remarked. "Did he send it in a letter or something?"

"No," she said, shaking her head. "There's never been a return address, though most of the postal marks have been from Texas. Just a plain envelope with a little money inside. It helped us pull through more than once."

At her words, Tex felt like he could breathe again. She was describing the envelopes he'd mailed her, which meant the little bit of money coming to the farm was from him. Not Tate. Why then did Ravena suspect his twin of the generosity and not him?

"You sweet on him again like you were when you were fifteen?" he asked before downing more water. He wasn't sure he wanted to hear the answer, and yet, he needed to know.

There'd been a time before Tex had won Ravena's heart completely when she'd been sure she was smitten with Tate. As for Tate, he'd been awfully interested in her himself—though he hadn't been very good at showing it. Mixed signals and hurt feelings had ended Ravena's fascination back then, and Tex had been careful to make sure he was there to step in. But when he was gone, perhaps those old feelings had sprung up once more.

Storm clouds flashed in her dark brown eyes, making him wince inwardly. "That is no longer any of your business, Tex."

Remorse coursed through him. It was another emotion he hadn't felt in a long time. "I only meant—"

"I know what you meant," she snapped. "And no, I'm not sweet on him like I was then. Although…" She dropped her flower chain to the ground and lifted her dress-clad knees. "You ought to know that I did ask him before he left if he thought we could try again." She leveled Tex with a stern look as if daring him to challenge such a decision. He kept his mouth shut. "But Tate said no."

Tex shifted uneasily on the ground, wishing he'd never brought up his brother. This conversation was pushing him down a rocky path he wasn't comfortable traversing, now or maybe ever.

Still he felt compelled to ask, "Did Tate give you a reason?"

It was Ravena's turn to appear ill at ease. "He said he didn't think he and I could have what you and I once did." The truth behind his brother's admission clouded the air between them with thick silence.

Tex tried to think of some way to lighten it, but he came up empty. Anything he said would likely anger her further or prompt her to dig even deeper into the past—and Tex couldn't abide either.

Thankfully Ravena spoke first. "I'm grateful for your help with the plowing. We'll be spring planting much sooner than I'd thought after that last hired hand quit."

"You're welcome." Tex wrapped up the rest of his lunch to save for later. He wasn't sure how much more he could stomach, of the food or this conversation. "I guess you can take the boy from the farm but not the farm out of the boy, huh?"

A light laugh accompanied his weak joke. "Is that what you did all of these years? Farming?" Why did she sound less curious and more suspicious?

Despite the temperate day and his earlier exertion, a sudden shiver rocked through him. "Uh, no," he said, putting his hat back on and standing. He hoped his vague answer would head off the dangerous turn to their conversation.

Ravena stood as well, but she didn't make a move to leave or stop talking. "I suppose I'm not entirely surprised. You never did love farming in the same way Tate did."

He shot her a thin smile of agreement.

"So if you weren't farming, what were you doing these last eight years?"

Ice-cold panic gripped his throat, cutting off any words. Ravena couldn't learn of his outlawing career. At least not until he was far away from here. Even then, he didn't like to think of her hating him once she found out.

Tex coughed to clear his throat of the fear. "I drifted here and there." Which was true. "Didn't ever really settle in one place for long."

She studied him a moment, which only increased his uneasiness. "That sounds rather lonely, even for a bachelor."

Feigning an indifferent shrug, he stepped toward the horses. "It was a nice way to see places I never would've seen otherwise." Another truth. "Thanks again for the lunch, Ravena. Better get back to plowing the field. It isn't going to do it on its own." His laugh sounded wholly forced, even to himself.

Her brow pinched together, but he walked away to escape seeing any more of her reaction. *Avoid conversations about the past*, he told himself, as he gathered the reins once more and urged the horses to walk on. It was the only way to stick around and not reveal the truth.

She'd made it through another awkward conversation with Tex. Ravena wanted to shout the victory to the world. Instead she decided to celebrate by walking down the road to meet the children coming home from school. It was a luxury she hadn't been able to afford while she'd played nursemaid, run the farm, and tried to finish the plowing all on her own. But now with Tex's help…

That help still comes with a price. She'd do well to remember that.

Things were far from simple with Tex around. She hadn't intended to bring up Tate or question Tex about the past either, but the words had slipped largely unbidden from her lips.

There were still things she didn't understand about Tex—why he'd felt he hadn't deserved her or what exactly he'd been doing as he'd wandered from one place to another. She didn't think a drifter would have as much money as she'd seen inside his saddlebag. And yet, the more she poked at the past, the more she was liable to get hurt again.

She folded her arms against a sudden shiver, though the sun warmed the dirt road in front and behind her. Maybe holding back any more questions about the past was the smarter course of action.

Shading her eyes, she smiled as she saw the children come tromping up the road. She'd given up her girlhood dreams of marrying and having a family of her own, and yet, she loved these orphans every bit as much as she imagined she would have any children she might have birthed herself.

As usual Mark was in the lead followed closely by Luke. Ginny took up the middle, while Jacob hung back with his sister to accommodate Fanny's shorter steps.

"Miss Ravena," Mark hollered with a vigorous wave when he saw her. She waved back.

"How was school?" she asked as the group drew closer.

As usual all of them began talking at once, with the exception of Ginny. Ravena shook her head with a laugh, realizing her own foolishness in asking a question they would all wish to answer. "Let's start with Fanny, since she's the youngest, and everyone can have a turn."

Fanny grinned and began chattering about recess and eating lunch outside. Then each of the other children took their turns, regaling Ravena with experiences from the day. Even Ginny proudly announced she'd been the only one in her grade to get all of the spelling words correct.

After everyone had a chance to share, Mark, Ginny, Fanny and Jacob hurried toward the house, eager for a slice of the bread she told them was waiting. Luke hung back though, to Ravena's surprise. He was rarely far from Mark's side.

"What is it, Luke?"

He slipped his hand into hers in a spontanteous show of affection, and Ravena's heart swelled. "I have to bring something to school on Monday to show the class."

"Ah. And what do you want to bring?"

Kicking at a rock with the toe of his shoe, he shrugged. "I don't know. I want to bring something really neat though, Miss Ravena. 'Cause Ollie in my grade, he keeps saying I don't have anything neat 'cause I'm an orphan."

Ravena squeezed his hand and bit back an unkind remark about Ollie. "Are you sad about what he said?"

Luke's thin shoulders lifted in a shrug. "Naw. Just mad."

"I think I'd feel mad too," she pretended to confide in a loud whisper, coaxing a small smile from Luke. "Do you think Ollie's right? That you don't have anything neat?"

The boy's face scrunched in thought. "No. 'Cause I got you and Mark and Ginny and Fanny and Jacob. And Mr. Beckett now too."

Ravena nodded in agreement. "That's a good list."

Suddenly Luke tugged her to a stop. "Do you think Mr. Beckett would be my thing to share with the class?"

She pressed her lips over a laugh when she realized he was in earnest. "That would be very neat, Luke. But I don't think Mr. Beckett will be able to stop plowing to come to school."

"Yeah, I guess you're right. But that's too bad. 'Cause he's nice and he's funny."

They started walking again, but his words kept circling through Ravena's mind. Luke's admiration for Tex wasn't unique. She'd seen how all of the children had warmed to him, more so than to either of the hired hands she'd employed. Of course the other two had kept mostly to themselves, insisting on sleeping in the extra room off the barn and eating alone. Tex was the first to ingratiate himself into their makeshift family.

Which, she thought, looking at Luke again, *could be good*. With her grandfather gone, it might be nice for the boys especially to have a grown man about the place to look up to. Even if it would only be for a few weeks.

"I'm sure you'll think of something neat to bring," she said as they neared the porch. "And Luke..." She waited for him to stop and look at her. Crouching down, she released his hand to put hers on his shoulder. "I agree with you. Ollie isn't right. You have people in your life who love you very much. And you know what?"

He shook his head, his large brown eyes somber. "What?"

"I became an orphan when I was about your age." She swallowed back the lump in her throat when she thought of all the people she'd lost—her parents, her grandmother, Tate, her grandfather and Tex, the man she'd loved with all of her heart back then. She knew what it meant to feel different, even if she'd had grand-parents who'd stepped in to raise her. "I'm familiar with the Ollies of this world and what they say. But we know the truth about us and what we have, don't we?"

Luke's expression brightened. "We sure do, Miss Ravena. Now I'm going to get some bread." He darted onto the porch as she rose to her feet, then he spun back. "You don't have to be mad or sad about being an orphan either. 'Cause you got neat people too. Me and Mark and Jacob and Ginny and Fanny and Mr. Beckett."

Ravena offered him an encouraging smile, though she didn't feel quite so confident about including the last person on her list. "Thank you, Luke."

She did have much to be grateful for, including Tex's help. Beyond that, she would simply have to hold out hope that all of Luke's words would prove true—that having Tex back in her life would be a good thing.

"Mr. Beckett! Mr. Beckett!"

Tex glanced over his shoulder to see Mark and Luke racing toward him. School must have concluded for the day. He grinned at the thought of someone to talk to. Plowing the field had left him with little else to do but think. And that was something he didn't want to do, especially after his conversation with Ravena at lunch.

He faced forward again as the boys ran into view. "How was schoo—" The question hadn't fully exited his mouth when the horses suddenly reared in fright. Tex was jerked forward by their abrupt movement, but he managed to keep the reins in his grip.

"What in the world..." he muttered as the team danced nervously.

"Look what we caught just now," Mark hollered as he hoisted a snake in the air.

The boy's loud cry and the dangling reptile spooked the horses again. They charged forward, dragging Tex along at a jog.

"Get that snake away from here," he shouted, hoping the boys would be quick to comply.

He let the horses have their heads for half the field, then he pulled back on the reins. After a minute or so, the team came to a stuttering halt. Tex released the reins and flexed his burning fingers within his gloves. Circling in front of the horses, he rubbed their heads and spoke in soothing tones until they'd both calmed.

Deciding to call it a day after their ordeal, he unhitched the pair from the plow and led them to the barn. Mark and Luke were nowhere in sight. Tex brushed and fed the two horses, taking extra time and care with each.

As he finished up, he saw two flashes of blond hair outside the barn doors. "Mark?" he called. "Luke? Can you come here?"

The boys didn't appear immediately, but after a long moment, they slunk inside. "Are you gonna leave now?" Mark asked without looking up.

Tex stared at them in confusion. "What are you talking about?"

"Mr. Grady up and left after we spooked the horses last time."

Understanding flooded his thoughts. "This isn't the first time you've brought a snake around the horses, is it?"

Both boys shook their heads, their chins tipped low.

After locating an empty milk bucket, Tex turned it over and sat down. "We need to talk."

The brothers inched forward in tandem as if headed to the executioner's block. Tex suppressed a chuckle. He wasn't going to rant at them, but they needed to understand the seriousness of their actions. "Boys, do you understand how dangerous it is to bring a snake around a team of horses?"

Mark nodded solemnly and Luke copied the gesture, but Tex guessed they didn't fully grasp what he was asking. Otherwise they would've stopped the last time.

"Mark," he said, trying a different tactic, "is there anything you're scared of?"

"No sir, Mr. Beckett," the boy blurted out, then he ducked his head again. "Well, maybe one thing."

"And what's that?"

Mark toed the dirt. "I never did like that old goose we had when me and Luke still lived with our parents before they died."

A measure of sadness filled him at the boy's words. While Tex and Tate had been adults when their mother died, they hadn't been much older than Mark was now when their father had up and abandoned the family. Tex swallowed back the bite of grief and anger such memories provoked. "Did the goose ever chase you?"

"All the time," Luke piped up.

"Is that what you're scared of too, Luke?"

Mark shook his head. "Nah. He don't like spiders."

"I've been known to get the shivers around attacking geese and large spiders myself," Tex said gravely. "So tell me this. What would you do if say Jacob came and found you and wanted to show you a big fat goose or a spider?"

Luke's eyes widened, but it was Mark who protested aloud. "I'd run away so it wouldn't get me."

"I agree." He turned to look at the younger brother. "Is that what you'd do, Luke?" ·

"Uh-huh."

Tex placed a firm but gentle hand on each of their shoulders. "Want to know something?" He dropped his voice to a conspiratorial whisper. "Did you know horses are as afraid of snakes as you are of geese or spiders?"

Mark frowned. "But they're way bigger than a little ol' snake."

"And you and me are way bigger than a little ol' spider or even a grown goose." He let his words hang there a moment before he continued. "Just like you wouldn't stand there gawking at something you're afraid of, the horses don't want to stick around either. And when they bolt they can hurt themselves or someone else."

"Like you, Mr. Beckett?" Luke asked.

Tex dipped his head again. "Me or you or even someone small like Fanny. A frightened horse team is a dangerous thing." Releasing his grip, he rested his elbows on his knees and leveled each boy with a stern look. "Which is why I'm going to ask you to promise me and Miss Ravena that you won't bring any more snakes around the horses. Will you promise us that?"

"Yes," the brothers said together, their gazes on the ground.

Standing, he nudged them both toward the barn doors. "Let's go share your promise with Miss Ravena then."

"So you aren't leaving?" Luke's expression appeared full of hope and trepidation. It cut straight through Tex's heart.

He cleared his throat of emotion. "No, I'm not leaving yet."

Tex guided them toward the house, passing Jacob in the yard as the older boy headed to the barn to milk the cow. Inside the kitchen, Ravena and the girls were preparing supper. "You're done for the day?" she asked, glancing up.

"Yes. And the boys have something to say."

She paused, searching the brothers' faces. "Mark? Luke?"

Mark glanced up at Tex and he nodded for the boy to speak. "It was for Luke, see. For him to show the class on his sharing day."

"Yep," Luke said glumly.

"What was for Luke?" Ravena asked, sounding resigned, as if she knew she wouldn't like the answer.

"We found another snake and wanted to show Mr. Beckett…" Mark explained.

Shutting her eyes, Ravena visibly blew out a breath. "Did they spook the horses again?" she asked Tex as she opened her eyes. "Boys, we've talked about this."

"We won't do it again, Miss Ravena. Honest." Mark pointed his thumb at Tex. "We promised Mr. Beckett that we wouldn't."

"I told them they needed to make that same promise to you," Tex added. Something flickered through her gaze, but he couldn't identify the emotion. Was she thinking of other promises made and broken?

Luke took up the thread of conversation. "We won't bring any more snakes around the horses. 'Cause even if they're big they don't like 'em any more than me and Mark don't like that old goose or a big, ugly spider."

Ravena threw Tex a perplexed look and he couldn't help chuckling. "Let's just say I attempted to put things into perspective for them."

"Thank you," she said with evident sincerity before turning her focus back to the boys. "Remember what the consequence is for bringing another snake around the horses?"

"Yes, Miss Ravena," they intoned in gloomy unison.

"In addition to mucking the stalls for a week…" She motioned to the table where Tex noticed a lovely, golden pie. "There will also be no pie for either of you after supper tonight."

The boys groaned loudly with regret, but they made no further complaint. Tex hoped his little talk in the barn, a week of mucking stalls and the forgoing of Ravena's delicious pie would be enough to convince them to change their behavior.

"What'll I bring to show the class on Monday, Mr. Beckett?" Luke regarded him sadly. "'Cause it's real important I have something neat to bring."

The way the boy was looking up at him as if he had all the answers did something funny to Tex's lungs. It wasn't an unpleasant sensation either and one he felt certain he'd experienced in the past.

Maybe it was a feeling of being needed. No one had needed him in years and he had to admit it felt real nice not to solely be looking out for himself at present. "I've got an idea, Luke. Wait here. I'll be right back."

With that he headed for the stairs, feeling lighter and more agile than he had in days.

Chapter Six

Ravena stared in bewilderment at the spot where Tex had been standing. She wasn't sure which she found more perplexing—whatever he'd said to the boys to help them understand snakes and horses don't mix or the fact that he'd taken the time to teach them at all.

She still struggled to believe that Tex wasn't going to up and quit on her as the other two hired hands had. If anyone had more inclination for riding away and not looking back, it would be Tex. He'd already done it once.

Blowing out her breath, Ravena allowed her posture to relax slightly. Tex could still choose to leave at any time, whether the planting was done or not, but it seemed that his going wouldn't be because of the boys' mischief. There was some comfort in that. "Do you, boys, understand the importance of never doing this again?"

"We sure do, Miss Ravena," Luke answered.

Mark agreed. "We ain't never going to bring a snake around the horses again."

She let his *ain't* slide this time, certain they'd had more than enough correction today. "I'm glad to hear it."

Footsteps sounded on the stairs and she glanced up to find Tex returning to the kitchen. Seeing him looking hale and handsome and eager to help her boys brought sudden warmth to her heart that was both unwanted and welcome. Here was the Tex Beckett she'd fallen in love with all those years ago.

"Whatcha got there, Mr. Beckett?" Luke asked as he and Mark rushed over to him. Tex crouched in front of the boys and held his fist out. There was something concealed inside. Ginny and Fanny sidled forward to get a peek and Ravena couldn't help doing the same.

Tex aimed a grave look at Luke. "I have something pretty special here, Luke. Can you take good care of it? And make sure I get it back after school on Monday?"

"I sure will, Mr. Beckett. Honest."

A boyish grin tugged at Tex's mouth and stirred flurries inside Ravena's stomach. Even after all this time, she still found him charming when he smiled. "All right then. Let me show you what I've got."

After turning his hand palm up, he uncurled his fingers. There against his tanned skin lay a gold coin. Ravena released a gasp. Tex not only had several hundreds of dollars inside his saddlebag, but he also had a gold coin in his possession. Her earlier doubts about his story of drifting rose anew within her. Drifters lived hand to mouth—they didn't have small fortunes tucked away.

"Is that real gold?" Mark's voice dripped with awe.

Luke reached out and ran a finger over the coin. "Where'd you get it?"

If she hadn't already been watching Tex, Ravena would've missed the flicker of what appeared to be regret that crossed his face. But it disappeared as quickly as it came. "I won it, though it's not important how or from whom."

Disappointment cut sharply through her. She could easily guess what the boys wouldn't from Tex's explanation. He had won the coin by gambling, a vice his father had given in to over and over again throughout Tex's childhood, to the detriment and heartbreak of the Beckett family. How often had she listened to Tex rant about how his father had gambled away the family's money? That Tex would choose to gamble after what he'd experienced felt like a deep betrayal.

"I'm sure we can find something else," she announced in a firm voice, her gaze locked on Tex's. "You do not need to take a gold coin won in a poker game to school."

Luke's eyes rounded. "You won it in a poker game, Mr. Beckett?"

His fingers closed over the coin as Tex frowned and rose to his feet. "It was one game, Ravena. One game. And I didn't lose."

"No, someone else did."

"Aw, Miss Ravena," Luke whined. "Can't I still take it to school? Ollie's eyes will bug out when he sees it."

She shook her head, adamant about not backing down. "We'll find something else, Luke. I promise." Tex continued to level her with a glare, but she ignored him. The girls went back to their supper tasks as Ravena searched her memory for anything out of the ordinary her grandfather had owned. "I have an idea. What about an old tricorn hat?"

Mark grimaced. "How's that better than a gold coin?"

Biting back a retort, she knelt beside Luke, hoping to persuade his interest. "It isn't any old hat, Luke. My ancestor Jedediah Reid wore it during the Revolutionary War when he was just fifteen years old." As she'd hoped, those few details drew expressions of curiosity from both boys. "The story goes that he came face-to-face with a group of redcoats. After praying for help, he used his musket and his impressive height to fool them into thinking he was older and not alone. To his surprise, they surrendered. Just as he was taking their guns, his father and several other men showed up to aid him in capturing their enemies."

"And you have his hat?" Luke whispered, prompting a smile from Ravena.

She stood and reached for his hand. "Yes, I do. Jedediah passed it down to his son who passed it to his son and so on until my grandfather came to have it. The hat is in the attic. We can go get it right now."

Mark gave a whoop of excitement. "I'm comin' too. I wanna see Jedediah's tricorn hat."

Heading to the attic from the kitchen meant passing by Tex to reach the stairs. He still regarded her grimly. Ravena felt a twinge of guilt herself—he'd attempted to help, even if she didn't agree with his way of doing it.

"Boys, go ahead. I'll be there in a minute." With her permission, the brothers raced down the hallway.

"I was trying to help," he said, confirming her thoughts. His low voice was full of frustration as he ran his hand over the bristles on his jaw. "It's just a coin, Ravena. Nothing more, nothing less."

But it wasn't just a coin and she wished he could see that. "I appreciate your help with the boys. I truly do. But I'm trying to raise these children up right and that means I can't, in good conscience, allow them to take winnings from a poker game to school."

The exasperation didn't completely leave his demeanor, though he did nod. "I never gambled before that game and I don't plan on doing it again." He glanced down at his hand and rubbed the shiny coin between his fingers. "I want you to know that."

When he lifted his chin, she had a clear view of his blue eyes and once again she caught a glimpse of the old Tex within their depths. The man who had been at the center of her heart and her dreams for so long.

At that moment she realized how close she stood to him, his gaze locked with hers. Her heartbeat thundered as hard and as fast as the boys' footsteps on the stairs.

She was relieved to know Tex didn't plan to gamble again. Maybe it was more evidence, like his helping the boys tonight, that he wasn't the irresponsible, unfeeling scoundrel she'd believed him to be after he'd failed to come back for her.

The memory of that night poked painfully at her as it had over and over since Tex had shown up in her field. It resurrected some of the grief she'd felt then and for so long afterward. Only the intense sadness she'd experienced at her grandfather's passing could compare.

"Thank you for sharing that with me." Her voice came out far more calm than she felt. Ravena took a deliberate step past him. "I'd better see to the boys before they unpack everything in their search for that hat."

She didn't wait for him to respond. Instead she moved purposely down the hall toward the stairs. Away from Tex. The plowing and planting couldn't be finished soon enough in her opinion—for the crops and for her own sanity. Once they were finished, Tex could leave.

Then she could return her focus to bringing the four brothers from Boise to the farm, and in turn, feeling that she'd finally made up for the ways she'd let her grandfather down in the past. Only then would she have peace.

Tex's second full week at the farm had passed more quickly than his first. He was grateful, especially to be moving about with greater ease. He'd insisted on switching Ravena for the sofa in the parlor now that he was nearly all healed. It felt good to be one step closer to his old physical stamina and to fulfilling his promise to help Ravena.

Once Tex had finished the plowing, he, Ravena and Jacob had started on the planting. The older boy had told her that missing some school to help wouldn't prove fatal to his education and that the work would go faster with three. Ravena had finally relented. They were making good progress, but Tex still felt bushed each night. After assisting with the evening chores, he ate supper with the family and then went straight to bed. While being an outlaw came with its own mental and physical tasks, he hadn't experienced this level of exhaustion in years.

In spite of seeing each other every day, Ravena said

very little to him, and when she did, the conversation re-
volved around the planting, the children or the weather.
Tex wasn't surprised. Ever since he'd shown her and the
children the coin he'd won from Quincy, Ravena had
been polite but cool toward him.

He told himself it was a good lesson to learn. If Ravena couldn't stomach him gambling, even once, she'd
never be able to swallow his outlawing career. Tex had
taken to keeping the coin in his pocket, alongside his
mother's earrings, as another reminder. He couldn't get
too comfortable here—he was an outlaw, not a farmer.
And once he'd satisfied his obligation to Ravena, he
would move on before she learned of his other choices,
choices he felt certain she would condemn.

"Seeing to the animals is sure a lot faster with two,"
Jacob said, bringing Tex back to the present.

He chuckled as he added Jacob's pitchfork to his own
and put them away. "That it is. My brother and I used
to complain about the chores, to my mother's constant
frustration, but it never seemed so bad when you knew
you had someone else working next to you."

His words brought several happy memories flitting
through his mind, times when he and Tate would com-
pete to see who could finish their chores first and end
up chucking hay at each other. Tate was usually the
one in the lead and Tex would be the one to start bal-
ing hay on his brother. They were like night and day in
how they viewed the world, and yet, they'd once been
the best of friends.

Remorse followed on the heels of his thoughts. Tex
had made the choice not to contact Tate after riding
away from the farm eight years ago, but now... A sud-

den longing filled him to know where his brother was and how he fared.

Jacob followed Tex to the barn doors. "You have a brother?"

"A twin, actually."

"Do you look alike?"

Tex shot the older boy a grin. "The mirror image of each other. Used to give our schoolteacher fits whenever we pretended to be the other. Our ma, on the other hand, she could always tell who was who."

Jacob laughed, though a wistful expression settled onto his face. "I think I'd like having a twin or an older brother."

"Is it just you and Fanny?" Tex asked as he secured the doors behind them.

"It is now." Tex waited for Jacob to elaborate, and after a long moment of staring at the ground, he continued. "Ma died pretty soon after Fanny was born, so our older sister took care of us while our pa was away working. But last year we got word that Pa was killed. Felicity didn't want us to go to an orphanage so she didn't tell anyone what happened to our pa—she insisted we tell Fanny and our neighbors that he was still away working."

Jacob pocketed his hands and kicked at a clod of dirt, his chin low. "Then Felicity got real sick. I went for the doctor, but it took a long time to get him, because it was snowing. She died the next day."

Stepping up to the boy, Tex laid a comforting hand on Jacob's shoulder. He could feel it trembling beneath his fingers. "So you took over caring for Fanny."

The boy nodded, then swiped a hand beneath his

nose. "I knew Felicity hadn't wanted us to go to an orphanage, so I didn't want to go there either. We ended up here in the valley and someone told me about Miss Ravena. Me and Fanny have been here ever since."

Shared grief and compassion welled up inside Tex. Even if he'd been older when his mother had died, he knew the pain of losing a loved one. "Sounds like you did the best you could to keep you and Fanny together. And to help your sister Felicity too."

"You really think so?" The earnest look in Jacob's eyes as he lifted his head pierced Tex's heart. The boy was looking to him for help. "I tried, Mr. Beckett..." His voice wobbled. "But maybe...maybe it wasn't enough for either of my sisters."

Tex gave Jacob's shoulder a firm squeeze, then lowered his hand. "You did all that you could, kid. And I imagine Felicity and your parents are real proud of you."

Jacob visibly relaxed. "I hope so."

Was Tex's mother proud of him? He tensed at the thought, certain he knew the answer.

"So do you think that maybe..." Jacob shrugged, not quite looking at Tex. "Well, that maybe you could be like an older brother, to me?" He cleared his throat. "I mean to all of us kids here at Miss Ravena's."

The inquiry took Tex by surprise. He hadn't been a part of a family in ages. The idea was more tempting than he'd expected. But even as he wanted to answer in the affirmative, he couldn't. He wasn't staying. "I don't know that I'll be here that long, kid."

Jacob's hopeful countenance fell, stirring guilt in Tex's gut. "Right. I meant just until the planting's done."

What was it about being here that kept pricking at his

conscience? He swallowed hard, wondering how much more prodding he could take before he'd have to flee. "Tell you what. Until the work is finished here, you're welcome to think of me as an older brother."

"Really? That'd be great, Mr. Beckett." Jacob's eyes widened with eagerness, making him appear younger. Tex couldn't help thinking of the childhood the boy had lost. Jacob had been forced to grow up quick, just as Tex and Tate did after their father had up and left the family.

Up and left. The words sprouted inside Tex's mind and wouldn't let him go. His father had up and left them just as Tex had later up and left Ravena and Tate. The similarities between him and his father rocked Tex to his core, as they had in the past. Was he destined to leave broken hearts and homes behind him wherever he went, same as his father? *But I'm back now and trying to make some amends.* He clung to that thought with all of his remaining strength. Because that was something his father hadn't done after walking out on them that last time.

Tex shook himself and strolled toward the house, Jacob right beside him. What had they been talking about? "If I'm going to be an older brother, I guess you'd better stop calling me Mr. Beckett. Call me Tex instead."

"Tex," Jacob repeated. "Is that short for something?"

He shook his head. "Nope. My mother's family is originally from Texas."

"You ever been there?"

Opening the screen door for them, Tex paused to consider his answer. He didn't want to give any information, even to Jacob, that might tie him to the Texas Titan. "I have been through there, yes."

"When I'm older," Jacob said in a determined tone as he ambled inside, "I want to travel. See more of this country than what's right here."

That had been Tex's boyhood wish too. And he'd certainly done his fair share of travelling, even if it was mostly throughout Texas. But as he trailed Jacob inside, his gaze moving to the kitchen where he could see Ravena wiping the table, he didn't feel the same satisfaction that living a vagrant life usually brought.

"Nothing wrong with wishing, kid," he said, clapping Jacob on the back. "Just remember there is something special about having a home to eventually come home to." Even if Tex couldn't stay, even if a real home was no longer a possibility for him, he sincerely hoped it would be for Jacob and each of these orphans.

They joined Ravena in the kitchen. "Chores are all done, Miss Ravena," Jacob announced.

She ran her rag over the corner of the table and straightened. "That was even faster than last night. Thank you. Both of you," she added with a glance at Tex. He nodded in acknowledgment. "I have your slices of pie."

"Oh good. I'm starved." Jacob plunked into a chair.

Tex laughed. "You just ate supper," he said, taking a seat as well.

"There's always room for pie, especially Miss Ravena's."

"I can't argue with you there, kid." Tex shot her a smile, which succeeded in pinking her cheeks, as she set a plate of pie in front of Jacob. The boy began wolfing it down.

She brought Tex his plate next, but unlike Jacob's, his held two slices. He'd seen the pie earlier and knew there were enough slices to go around with one extra.

"You don't want the extra slice?" he asked.

Ravena shook her head. "No, you can have it. I know it's your favorite."

The kind gesture resurrected the cozy feeling he'd experienced the other night. "Thank you."

"I'll have it," Jacob said around a full bite.

"No, it's for Mr. Beckett."

The boy shrugged and returned his attention to his own slice.

Tex forked some of the pie and slid it into his mouth. Ravena had always been an excellent cook. Even the fare he'd sampled in fancy restaurants couldn't compare to her food. "This is amazing, Ravena."

Her blush increased, though this time it was accompanied by a small smile. It was the first one he'd seen aimed at him in several days.

"You…uh…have some pie…right there." She touched a spot near her own lips to indicate where he needed to wipe his face. Tex swiped his hand across his mouth, but he knew he wasn't successful, when Ravena chuckled. "I can get it, if you'd like…"

Tex nodded for her to go ahead. Reaching out, she brushed her thumb against the corner of his mouth. The familiarity of her soft touch set his heart clanging inside his chest. He felt as weak as he had that first afternoon of plowing, and at the same time, he felt as if he could run to the top of the nearest hill and back without getting winded. The last time he'd felt this way was right before he'd asked Ravena to elope with him.

"There, I got it," she said, lowering her hand.

The poignancy of the moment ended when Jacob declared he was finished. Tex had forgotten the boy was there at all.

But as Tex nodded his thanks to Ravena and resumed eating, he couldn't help thinking that perhaps there was another way to look at his remaining time here besides as a thing to be endured. Maybe he could let himself enjoy the time, just a little, too.

Ravena was grateful for the excuse to leave the table and wash Jacob's plate. Her pulse still pattered rapidly after touching Tex's face. She'd been pleased at his compliments about her pie and his evident surprise in her offering him the extra slice. She'd hoped to let him know, in a personal way, how grateful she was for his help. The planting was coming along and she had Tex—and the Lord—to thank for that.

But what had compelled her to touch him? Her cheeks heated again, even as the water from the pump cooled her hands.

From behind, she half listened to Jacob and Tex talking. The teenage boy was asking questions about what Tex had seen in his travels across Texas. She hadn't known he had been there. How odd that he and Tate would wind up in the same state and not know it, though she knew Texas was quite large. Had Tex gone to see his mother's family? Although, if Ravena remembered right, his relatives had already passed on by the time his mother had died.

She turned to ask him, but she didn't get the words out before a loud squeak filled the air. It was followed by a low groan.

"What was that?" Jacob asked.

Ravena lifted her shoulders in confusion. "I guess I'd better find out." The other children were supposed to be readying themselves for bed.

"Sounds like a goose in the throes of death," Tex remarked as he stood and carried his plate to the sink. The apt description drew a full smile to Ravena's lips.

The awful sound started again, but this time Fanny's unmistakable giggle accompanied it. Ravena followed the girl's laughter down the hall to the stairs, where she found Fanny, Ginny and the boys seated on the steps in their nightgowns. "You are all supposed to be in bed," she said half with exasperation and half with affection as she regarded them. Jacob and Tex came to a stop behind her.

Mark held up a harmonica. "We found this in the parlor." The awful racket of moments ago was no longer a mystery.

Taking the instrument in hand, Ravena ran her fingers over the worn metal. She could almost hear an echo of the melodies her grandfather used to play. The harmonica reminded her of summer nights, sitting on the porch and listening to her grandfather play while she and her grandmother sang along. He hadn't played much in the years before his death, and Ravena suddenly realized how much she'd missed his music.

"I brought it down from the attic last week," she explained, "when we went to find Jedediah's hat. It was Mr. Ezra's harmonica."

"Can you play it?" Mark asked, his expression hopeful.

"No," Ravena said with a laugh. "Anything I played sounded far less like music and more like a chorus of bullfrogs."

"Sort of like Mark's music just now?" Jacob teased.

"Hey." The younger boy scowled. "It ain't as easy to play as it looks."

"Isn't as easy," Ravena corrected. "And you are absolutely right, Mark. Playing the harmonica requires practice and skill. Like any instrument, one isn't simply able to play it just because one wants to."

Shooting a smug look in Jacob's direction, Mark stood. "Guess there's nothin' to do but go to bed then. Come on, Luke." His little brother hopped up.

"I can play," Tex volunteered. Ravena had forgotten her grandfather had taught him. "At least I used to."

Fanny clasped her hands together and gazed adoringly at Tex. "Will you play somethin' for us, Mr. Beckett? Please?"

A smile nudged the corners of his mouth. "If it's all right with Miss Ravena."

The rest of the children took up Fanny's plea, but Ravena hesitated, knowing a musical performance would likely mean a later bedtime. It might be Sunday tomorrow, which meant no school, but they would still be attending church.

A longing to hear the old instrument played again finally overrode her remaining reluctance. "All right." She passed the harmonica to Tex. "But just a few songs."

Cheers erupted from the children. The four on the stairs clamored into the parlor and settled onto the rug. Jacob sat on the sofa, while Ravena chose one of the chairs. Putting the harmonica to his lips, Tex played a series of running notes.

"Doesn't sound much better than me," Mark said, crossing his arms. The rest of them laughed.

A few moments later, Tex drew a jaunty tune from the instrument. Mark instantly brightened. Fanny and Luke began clapping their hands in time with the music and Ravena tapped her foot against the floor. It had been too long since they'd last had music in the house.

When he concluded that number, Tex played two more lively songs, both of which Ravena recognized as ones her grandfather had known. A keen sense of missing him filled her head to toe, winding in and through the pleasure of the music.

"This next one is a dancin' number," Tex announced. "So choose your partners."

If there hadn't been music in a while, there hadn't been dancing in ages. Ravena stood and claimed a reticent Mark as her dancing companion. Jacob took Fanny's hands in his, and even Ginny linked arms with Luke. Each couple began do-si-doing around the room. The children's laughter accompanied Tex's song, and Ravena found herself smiling at the merriment. She swung Mark one direction, then the other, her eyes catching and holding Tex's. His blue gaze sparked with enjoyment and reminded her of other days when anything and everything had felt possible for them.

When the song ended, all five children collapsed onto the floor or the sofa. Their happy chatter attested to their delight—and the fact that they were no longer settled for bed.

"Why don't we have Mr. Beckett play a slow one this time?" she suggested.

"Aw, Miss Ravena," the brothers chorused, while Fanny emphatically shook her head.

Ravena sat back in her chair. "A slow one please, Tex."

With a nod he began to play a soft, sweet melody. Fanny climbed onto Ravena's lap and she placed her arms around the little girl, feeling a swell of gratitude and contentment. Jacob and the younger boys spread out on the rug, while Ginny rested her cheek beside Ravena's knee.

"Any requests?" Tex asked when he finished the languid song.

Mark hollered out a few suggestions, all of which would surely rouse the children again.

Ravena thought a moment. "How about 'Amazing Grace'?" It had been her grandfather's favorite.

Tex nodded slowly. "If you'll sing along."

"You sing here at home, Miss Ravena? Not just at church?" The soft questions came from Ginny.

Ravena glanced down at the girl, feeling the others' eyes on her. "Sometimes, yes." Though she couldn't recall the last time she'd sung at home.

"Miss Ravena has the voice of a songbird," Tex said, his tone animated but genuine, "but she's twice as nice and four times as pretty."

Fanny giggled behind her hand, and Ravena blushed again. Her cheeks were likely to stay pink forever after all the compliments she'd received from Tex tonight. She couldn't deny that she liked them. It had been so long since she'd received any sort of tribute from a handsome man.

"Come on, Miss Ravena." Mark scrambled to his knees. "Sing it for us."

She blew out her breath in self-consciousness. "Do the rest of you know the words?" The children collectively shook their heads. Which meant she was singing a solo. "Very well. Though after tonight I intend to teach it to all of you."

Throwing her a satisfied glance, Tex played an introduction to the song, then tipped his head to her when it was time to sing. Ravena sang the words, though she kept her voice quiet. As the message and the melody grew within her, though, she forgot her embarrassment and let herself sing with more volume and feeling.

When she'd sung the final words and Tex had played the last note, he lowered the harmonica from his mouth. "As breathtaking a voice as I remember."

"Thank you," she said, ducking her chin and feigning interest in smoothing Fanny's hair from her face. "And now, children, it's time for bed."

The younger boys emitted grumbles of protest as they rose to their feet, but Ravena could see their objections were half-hearted. The gentle music had worked to settle all of them. The children headed to the stairs, and Ravena rose to her feet as Tex approached her.

"Thank you for playing, Tex. They thoroughly enjoyed it."

His mouth kicked up into a smile. "I think they enjoyed the dancing and your singing just as much."

A laugh spilled from her. "Perhaps." Glancing at the children as they made their way upstairs, she sobered her tone. "I don't know that any of them have had that sort of fun in a long time."

"Neither have I," Tex replied, his voice quiet.

Questions rose once more inside her mind, about what he'd seen and experienced during his time away. He'd always possessed a zest for life, but Ravena could see he'd lost some of that since the last time he'd been here. What had stolen that joy from him?

Then he grinned at her and the openness and honesty dropped from his face, bringing her a sliver of disappointment. She admired his charm, but she longed for authenticity in him too.

"Your instrument, my lady." He held out the harmonica to her.

Ravena considered putting it back in the attic or here in the parlor, but instead, she gently pushed the instrument back into his hand. "Keep it, please. Grandfather would have wanted you to have it."

Surprise furrowed his expression. "What about when I leave?" His eyes were no longer lit with amusement. They regarded her solemnly.

A physical ache pressed hard against her chest. In spite of everything, there were things she liked about having Tex around that went beyond his help with the planting. He had a way with the children and his lighthearted demeanor brought a needed breath of fresh air to the farm. Ravena never would have imagined he'd show up in her life after all these years, but she couldn't say she wasn't a little grateful.

Tilting her chin upward, she matched his level gaze with one of her own. "Even when you leave. And maybe you could play for us again?" It wouldn't hurt to allow a little more fun into their lives.

"I think that can be arranged," he said with half a smile.

She gave a poised nod of acceptance. But as she moved up the stairs, Tex's smile just now had her knees and heartbeat feeling far less steady than she was pretending to be.

Chapter Seven

The dream felt so real that Tex could smell Quincy's drunken breath, could hear the cock of the outlaw's gun, could feel the cold press of the barrel in his side. "You're gonna give me my map, Tex," the man snarled. "If I have to take it from your cold, lifeless hand, so be it. Wherever you run, I'm gonna find you. You can't hide forever…"

Tex startled awake and swung at the air in defense, certain Quincy was standing over him. When he realized he was alone in the parlor, he lowered his arms and stared at the ceiling. His nightshirt was soaked with sweat and his heart still pounded like a runaway horse inside his chest.

While he still felt certain Quincy didn't know where he was hiding out, the man wasn't one to let go of a grudge. Tex had figured that out after only a few minutes in Quincy's presence. Hence the continued nightmares.

Throwing off his blanket, Tex sat, his bare feet on the floor, and willed his heart rate to slow. He'd stowed his saddlebags behind the sofa for safekeeping but also for quick access—day or night. It would be so easy to pull them out now, saddle up Brutus and disappear again. And yet he couldn't do it. Not when he hadn't fully completed his commitment to Ravena. And not after last night.

Ravena might not fully welcome his presence here, but she'd offered him an olive branch in the form of the extra piece of pie, the brief but sweet touch to his face and her offer to Tex of her grandfather's harmonica. And he had to admit, he'd play the instrument for her and the children over and over again if it meant another chance to hear her sing.

The moment she'd started, something inside him had broken loose. He didn't want to keep up this formal, distant relationship between them anymore; he wanted to be friends again. And after last night, he believed Ravena might want that too.

The thought filled him with both fear and tentative happiness. Tex hadn't met anyone in years who he could call a true friend. Instead he'd operated under the knowledge that at any moment a comrade could become an enemy if there was money, the law or a woman involved. But he liked being around Ravena and he liked being around the children. And the idea of forming deeper bonds with someone felt good.

Even if it couldn't be permanent.

Certain he wouldn't fall back asleep now, Tex rose and dressed for the day. He'd get an earlier start on the morning chores and surprise Jacob. He smiled to himself at the thought of the boy coming downstairs in a few hours to discover everything was already done.

Tex lit a lamp and made his way onto the porch and into the shadowed yard. The warmth and smell of the barn felt almost welcoming as he slipped through the doors and set the lamp down. He threw himself into his tasks, eager to drive away any lingering thoughts about Quincy. But the thoughts wouldn't depart.

Even if Quincy had followed him after he'd fled Casper, Tex had made sure to keep his trail as untraceable as possible. He'd bought new clothes at the first available store and had purchased multiple train tickets for places he didn't intend to see, all in an attempt to throw off Quincy's pursuit. Hopefully the rustler would assume Tex had died as a result of the sheriff's bullet or that he'd fled farther north to Montana or Canada. But Tex couldn't know that for certain, and the unknown gnawed at him like a tick on a horse.

Tex had the chores finished and was exiting the barn as the first rays of sunrise were peeking over the hills. His surprise was complete. He whistled to himself as he headed around the back of the house to the kitchen.

A light shone inside, which meant Ravena was likely up and starting breakfast. He would've liked to surprise her too, after her kindness last night. Tex wiped his boots and pushed the door open wide enough to see her standing at the stove. The sight of her stole the tune from his lips.

Her dark hair gleamed in the lamplight and her cheeks had been turned a pretty pink from the stove's heat. But it was more than her physical beauty that stopped him cold. In this moment he could plainly see the way she radiated innocence, compassion and honesty. Qualities his mother had demonstrated to him and

Tate, and yet, Tex had chosen a path that encompassed none of those things.

For the first time since coming to the farm, Tex felt as if the dirt and manure that had coated his boots only moments ago covered him inside. He wasn't just trespassing on Ravena's hospitality; he was also trespassing on her goodness. His earlier desire to flee rose with greater urgency inside him. He cast a look at the horizon and fell back a step.

"Tex?" Ravena's voice pierced the choke hold of his panic. "I didn't know you were up already."

He swallowed hard and forced himself to step inside the kitchen. The horizon wasn't going anywhere and neither was he. If nothing else, he hoped keeping his word to her this time would blot out some of the inner stain he'd collected.

"Morning," he said with forced ease and cheerfulness. "I couldn't sleep and thought I'd get an early start to the chores."

"Should I wake Jacob?" She stepped toward the inner doorway.

Tex shook his head. "Let him sleep in for once. Everything's finished."

Her bright smile only prompted greater guilt within him. "That was very kind of you." She returned to the stove, saying over her shoulder, "Next time you can't sleep, I'd be happy to make some tea for you. It's guaranteed to put a body to sleep within minutes."

He offered the laugh she likely expected from him, but he felt no real merriment. "I'll remember that. For now, I'll take some strong coffee."

"Coming up." When he stood there, unsure what to do next, she waved toward the table. "Have a seat."

Pulling out a chair, he dropped into it. *I'm here to help her*, he told himself. *And that's got to amount to something, for both of us.*

"Care to talk about why you couldn't sleep?" He could easily picture her asking the same question of one of the children. But the parallel didn't offend him. Instead it reminded him of how well Ravena had stepped into the role of nurturing parent, even if it was in a less conventional way.

He shrugged as he put on a nonchalant expression. "Just a bad dream."

"Like the ones you had when you were sick?"

Since he couldn't recall any of those dreams, he wasn't sure, but it was likely he'd been plagued by nightmares of Quincy then too. "I think so."

"The sofa's not too uncomfortable, is it?" she asked next.

He'd slept on far worse, especially during his flight from Casper. "No, it's just fine."

"Because if you want to switch for the bed again…"

"Ravena," he said, waiting for her to turn around. Her compassion aggravated his already guilty conscience. "The arrangement we have is more than suitable."

Her brow furrowed and Tex wondered if she could sense he was talking about far more than the sleeping arrangements. He meant his being here and helping. It was more than suitable, wasn't it? He could've left much sooner as he'd planned, but he hadn't.

After a few minutes of tense silence, Ravena plunked

a cup onto the table in front of him. "Here's your coffee." She was irritated with him.

Tex frowned as he took a sip of the drink.

"Thank you for the coffee," he said in a genuine tone as he twisted in his chair to face her. "And thank you for the use of the sofa." She could have insisted he stay out in the barn as the other hired hands had done.

Ravena glanced at him, and like the night before, some of the guardedness dropped from her beautiful, dark eyes. "You're welcome."

How many times had he gazed into those eyes and thought he was the most fortunate man in the world to have won her heart? The reality that she no longer looked back at him with that same tenderness and adoration hit him hard. Mustering up a feigned smile, he turned back to his coffee.

Jacob rushed into the kitchen at that moment, hastily trying to tuck his shirt into his trousers and pull up his suspenders at the same time. His sudden appearance gave Tex something else to focus on besides the past and he gratefully clung to it.

"You're late," he said to the boy. He shot Ravena a look, hoping she'd play along.

"Chores are already done, Jacob. Mr. Beckett did all of them." She kept a deadpan expression, which prompted Tex to hide a grin behind the lip of his coffee cup.

Jacob ground to a stop as he ran his hand through his mussed hair. "I'm sorry, Miss Ravena. I don't know what happened. I don't usually sleep—"

"It's all right, kid." Tex let his smile break free and pulled out the chair next to him. "I was up early and thought I'd get everything done and out of the way so you could sleep a little longer."

Jacob's face changed in an instant from downtrodden and confused to relieved and happy. "Wow, thanks, Tex," he said, plopping into the chair.

"Mr. Beckett," Ravena corrected. Tex cringed, realizing that he probably should have talked to her before giving Jacob permission to call him by his first name.

Jacob spun in his chair, looking uncertain. "He told me I could call him that. Didn't you, Tex?"

He dipped his head in a nod, even as he kept his gaze on Ravena. He couldn't quite read the emotions flashing in her eyes. Did she wish for him to keep his interactions with the children stiff and formal? He hoped not. While he knew they shouldn't get too attached, he liked the idea of being a big brother to them while he was here.

"If *Tex* said to call him that, then I suppose that's fine."

Jacob wasn't the only one to release a breath; Tex did the same. The rest of the children trooped into the kitchen after that, looking sleepy, except for Mark. The boy moved about with the energy of a jackrabbit. Tex almost envied him.

After Ginny blessed the food, Ravena joined them at the table to eat breakfast. Tex had only managed to down a few bites when Fanny, seated at his left, glanced at him, her young face lit with earnestness.

"Mr. Beckett," she asked in her sweet voice, "are you comin' to church with us today?"

Tex coughed with embarrassment as the rest of the children turned expectant gazes in his direction. Lifting his cup, he downed more of his coffee—not just to clear his throat but to stall for an answer. How could he tell her that he had no desire to set foot inside a church?

"I was planning on staying here at the farm today, Fanny," he hedged.

Her small mouth pursed into a frown. "But you didn't come last week neither. And Miss Ravena says church is as important as school."

Glancing at Ravena, Tex silently pleaded for her to help him explain. But instead of jumping in to rescue him, she simply smiled at him over the brim of her cup and said, "That is true, Fanny. Church is as important as school."

Tex cleared his throat, feeling irritation and shame lodging there. He'd committed to helping with the planting, not attending church. He might have gone regularly with his family when his mother was alive, but he'd gone less and less after her death as the distance increased between him and God—and him and Tate, who had continued to go every Sunday. Besides, he couldn't afford being recognized in town.

"I'm afraid that isn't going to work today," he said, scooting his chair back and standing. "But I'll get the wagon and the horses ready for you."

The little girl's expression remained sad, but he wouldn't give her false promises. He'd had enough of those from his father growing up.

After clearing his dishes to the sink, Tex slipped back outside. He hated the disappointment he'd seen on all the children's faces just now. But he was here to do a job, not join them at church as if they were a family.

He busied himself with shaving in the extra room

off the barn and then with hitching the horses to the wagon. After that he took a walk to look over the fields they'd already planted. He didn't have any desire to hear a repeat of Fanny's request before she and the rest of them left. When he returned to the house, the wagon was gone.

What to do now? He could get a little more of the planting done on his own, but Ravena had told him that he could have the day off on Sundays. Which suited him fine, except he had no place to go and nothing to do. He wandered over to the porch and went to sit in the rocker before remembering it was broken.

One look revealed one of the runners was missing. Perhaps it had been placed inside the barn on the table with Ravena's grandfather's woodworking tools. He could recall watching Ezra make the rocker when the older man had taught Tex all about carpentry years ago. The rocker shouldn't be too difficult to fix and would be something he could surprise Ravena with. It would be a way to thank her, with more than words, for all of her help while he'd been ill.

Hoisting the rocker, he carried it to the barn. He opened the doors to allow in some of the bright morning sunshine, then set the piece of furniture next to Ezra's woodworking table. Sure enough he found the broken runner lying among the man's tools. Tex picked up one of the chisels, his mind filling with memories.

As a boy, he'd trailed Ezra Reid around the farm, eager for a man to talk to besides his always-absent father. And Ezra hadn't let him down. The man had taught Tex how to farm, how to play the harmonica, how to build more out of wood than a fence, how to be a gentleman. Tex had loved hearing Ezra's stories about heading West as a boy, about meeting his sweetheart Olive, about buying this spread of land. He'd given Tex a glimpse of life beyond this little valley and whetted his appetite to see it for himself one day.

"Guess I did, Ezra," he murmured as he set down the chisel to pick up a mallet.

How had Ravena's grandfather felt about him when Tex ran off, leaving Ravena behind? The thought wasn't a new one, but the possibility of Ezra thinking poorly of him still had the power to bring a sharp ache to Tex's chest. He'd tried so hard, even before asking Ravena to elope, to prove to her grandfather and to himself that he was worthy of such a woman. But the truth was he hadn't been. Not then or now.

Worse than that, he'd convinced Ravena to come away with him without telling her grandfather because Tex had been sure Ezra wouldn't condone their actions. Would her grandfather have eventually given his consent to their marriage if Tex had stuck around? He closed his mind to the prospect. It didn't matter anymore. He'd done what he'd done and he couldn't undo it. But he could still try to make things up to Ravena— and in the process, maybe he could feel he'd made peace with Ezra too.

Determined, he located two sawhorses and propped the runner between them. He used a small saw to remove the broken parts of the runner, then went to work carving new dowels from some lumber he found behind the barn.

The smell of wood and shavings filled his nose as Tex worked, bringing a smile to his mouth. It had been far too long since he'd made or repaired something with his own two hands. Regret crept in, stealing some of his contentment.

He'd once envisioned living a life similar to Ezra Reid's—a loving wife, a family, a home full of people and laughter. That had been his plan when he and Ravena talked of eloping. But first he wanted to see the world outside their valley home. So he'd taken his mother's earrings, in the hopes of selling them to support him and Ravena as they travelled about the country. Eventually they'd settle down somewhere and he'd become a farmer or a carpenter. It didn't matter what he did so long as it was in some distant place with Ravena.

No wonder Tate had accused him that night of being a thief. It wasn't just in regards to taking their mother's earrings. Tex had planned to steal Ravena away as well, from her grandfather and from her life here, and disappear like a thief in the night.

Tex had felt the truth of Tate's words and it had burned him inside. He'd been tired of working so hard on a farm he couldn't call his own, not completely. He'd been tired of living in Tate's shadow too, of feeling like the rebellious, irresponsible twin just because he wasn't as serious or because he only liked farming instead of loving it the way his brother did. And when Tate had threatened to ride over to the Reids' and reveal Tex's plan to Ezra, Tex had panicked. He'd knocked his twin out cold, jumped on his horse and rode as fast and as far as he could.

When Tex had finally stopped, it was full dark. He felt cold and tired, though no longer as angry. He turned the horse around, with every intention of going back, but fear suddenly gripped him. What would Ravena and Ezra think if they learned he'd taken his mother's earrings from his own brother and knocked him unconscious? And if Tate had followed through on his threat, would Ezra forgive Tex for wanting to take away the man's only living family member?

He'd asked himself that night why he wanted to slip away in the first place, without telling anyone. And he didn't like the answer—that he'd been looking for the easy way out, like his father had always done. Ravena did deserve better. She deserved someone like Tate who was honest and responsible, who didn't favor their father in temperament like Tex did. Maybe his leaving was more proof that he, like his father, wouldn't ever change.

With those thoughts as his companions, Tex had pointed his horse south once more and kept riding, without looking back. If Tate thought him a thief, then the life of a thief was what he'd embrace. But he wouldn't drag Ravena down with him.

Tex gulped in a breath of barn air and wood, desperate to end the parade of recollections through his mind. He'd made his choice, and it wasn't honorable; still, he'd been successful, happy even. At least to some degree.

As he fitted the runner with the new dowels and put it back on the rocker, he couldn't help comparing his life to the broken piece of furniture. It had looked purposeful, efficient and even nice until he'd taken the time to examine it up close.

Coming back here to Ravena's was making him look at his life more closely than he had in years. And while he enjoyed the freedom and adventure of the outlaw life, it looked a bit lopsided, a bit broken, when compared to what she and the orphans had here.

"Enough," he growled at himself, his voice echoing off the rafters and disturbing a pair of birds. He had half a mind to go to church with them next week, just so he wouldn't have to face the solitude of his own thoughts.

He set the rocker on its runners and gave the seat a gentle push. The thing began rocking at once. Tex grinned—he'd fixed it. If nothing else, Ezra would surely be proud of him for that.

Carrying the rocker out of the barn, across the yard and to the porch, he set it down in its original spot. He considered pointing it out to Ravena the moment she and the children returned. But then he changed his mind. He'd hoped to surprise her earlier with the chores and hadn't. So this would be his surprise instead.

His smile deepened when he imagined the look on her pretty face when she discovered the rocker had been mysteriously fixed. It would've been the type of thing he would have done had they married. The thought caused his smile to slip, but he forced it back into place.

Things were going well—the planting was coming along, Quincy hadn't tracked him down yet, and he and Ravena were tentative friends again. He wouldn't wish for anything more. It would only make things harder when it came time to leave.

"Children," Ravena called up the stairs. "It's time to read the Bible." Her grandfather had started the Sunday evening tradition when she was a girl and she had kept it up after his passing.

"I suppose it's time for me to move then," Tex said

from the parlor as he folded the newspaper he'd been reading and set it aside. He rose to his feet. "I think I'll head outside for some air."

She chastised herself for the pang of disappointment his words inspired. Why should he stay and listen? He hadn't last Sunday and today he'd practically expired over Fanny's invitation to attend church with them.

The rest of the day had been rather nice, though. Tex had gone out into the yard before supper to play a game of blindman's bluff with the children, and even Ginny had participated. Ravena had caught him smiling secretively to himself more than once too. Not in an alarming way but in a way that reminded her of times past when Tex used to bring her little gifts or plan some adventure for them.

Maybe that's it, she thought, her discontent changing to sorrow. *Maybe he's just planning his next adventure for after he leaves here.*

Well, he had a right to do that. It wasn't as if he had a real reason to stay or any permanent ties to the farm.

She put on a smile as the children came downstairs and arranged themselves on the parlor furniture. Picking up the Bible from off the side table, she took a seat on the sofa. "Now, does anyone remember—"

"Mr. Beckett?" Fanny called as Tex opened the screen door. "Aren't you comin' to Bible reading?"

He cut a look at Ravena and she found herself holding her breath, even as she knew she was being silly. It wasn't as if his staying to listen to the Bible meant anything. But she couldn't squelch the hope that Tex would accept Fanny's invitation this time, though Ravena had no illusions that his faith was stronger than when he'd last been here. Quite the contrary.

"You know, I was just waitin' for a pretty little girl to ask me," Tex said, letting the screen fall shut as he walked back into the room. Ravena let her breath out in a puff of surprise. Fanny beamed as if she'd known all along that her solicitation would be accepted this time.

Tex settled onto the opposite end of the sofa and Fanny scrambled up beside him. Though four feet and one happy little girl separated them, Ravena felt suddenly aware of Tex's presence. Like the way the lamplight revealed the bristles on his face that had grown back since his morning shave, or the way his warm blue eyes held hers just now and made her heart trip.

Clearing her throat, Ravena dipped her chin and opened the Bible to her bookmark. "Now, as I was saying, does anyone remember what story we read last week?"

"Ohhhh." Mark waved his arm about in the air, then blurted out an answer before Ravena could call on him. "It was about a lost sheep and a lost coin. Ain't that right, Miss Ravena?"

She nodded, ignoring his grammar in light of his enthusiasm. "Yes, that's right, Mark. Thank you. And tonight, we'll be reading about the prodigal son."

After reading a few verses, and seeing the younger boys' eyes begin to glaze over, Ravena opted to tell the rest of the story in her own words. When she'd finished her retelling, she read the final verse of the parable from the Bible. "'It was meet that we should make merry, and be glad: for this thy brother was dead, and is alive again; and was lost, and is found.'"

"Why did he have to eat with the pigs?" Luke asked when she shut the Bible.

Ravena bit back a laugh at the boy's repulsed expression. "He didn't have to—he chose to. And his earlier choices meant he had nothing to eat. We get to choose what we do with our lives, but like the younger son in the story, we don't get to choose our consequences."

"How come the older brother got mad?" Mark cocked his head, his brow furrowed in deep thought. "Didn't he want to come to the party?"

"Well, he was upset because he'd stayed and done all that was asked of him by his father." A tremor of regret rocked through Ravena as she listened to her own words. Like the older brother in the story, she'd stayed, but she might have made a very different choice if Tex had shown up that night. She reined her thoughts in to finish explaining. "He couldn't understand why the younger brother would get a reward when he'd made foolish choices while the older brother had made wise choices and never got a party as a reward for them."

Jacob lifted his arms and leaned his head back on his hands. "It does seem a little unfair that the younger one got a party."

"Perhaps," Ravena consented, "but we have to remember he didn't have a home or a life free of guilt and remorse like his older brother did. He might have had his fun for a time, but he realized, in the end, that what he really wanted wasn't what he had. It was everything he'd left behind." From the corner of her eye, she saw Tex visibly wince. Was he comparing the story to his own life? She suddenly wondered how many parallels there were between he and Tate and these two brothers.

"Anyway, the father recognized the humble change in his son and wanted him to know he was still welcomed back, no matter what his choices had been."

"I guess that makes sense," Jacob said. "He lost out on a lot of things that the older brother didn't."

Ravena smiled at the boy. "Yes, Jacob, that's right. What about you, Fanny? What did you like about the story?"

The little girl leaned forward. "That there was music and dancing."

Everyone but Tex laughed at that. "Ginny, anything you liked or had questions about?" Ravena asked. "Or maybe you can tell us why you think Jesus told the story."

Ginny glanced down at her lap. "I think He wanted the people to know that no one is ever lost to Him, no matter what."

Ravena sat back, both pleased and surprised at the depth to Ginny's comment. "That is a beautiful way to put it." The girl blushed, but the briefest of smiles tugged at her mouth. "And now, it's bedtime."

Mark led Luke in a squirming groan that ended with both of them wrestling on the floor. With a sigh, Ravena stood and gently pulled Luke to his feet. "Go on, now. Both of you."

"I'll beat you," Mark called, scrambling up and dashing past his brother.

Luke rushed after him. "No, I'll beat you."

Jacob and Ginny rolled their eyes and followed at a plodding pace. Only Fanny remained.

"Come on, Fanny," Ravena reminded. "You too."

The little girl bobbed her head, then climbing to her

knees, she pressed a kiss to Tex's cheek. He looked startled, but Ravena wasn't sure if it was from Fanny's show of affection or from something he'd been mulling over. He recovered quickly though.

"Why thank you, little lady." He pretended as if he were doffing his hat to her, which made Fanny giggle. "Now scoot along."

She hopped down from the sofa and took Ravena's hand. "'Night, Mr. Beckett. Thanks for coming to Bible reading."

"'Night, Fanny." The gentleness in his voice made Ravena wish, for a moment, that he was talking to her.

What would they do when he left? she wondered as she and Fanny climbed the stairs. The children were all enamored with him, and Jacob was already calling Tex by his first name. As for herself… She was beginning to see that Tex's leaving wouldn't be so different than the last time. He would leave a hole in all of their hearts that only he, and he alone, could ever fill.

Chapter Eight

Tex couldn't escape the house fast enough once Ravena and Fanny headed upstairs. Did Ravena suspect the sort of life he'd led—and was still leading? Is that why she'd selected that Bible story? Or was it merely a coincidence?

Stepping out onto the porch, he sunk down on the step, much as he had that first day two weeks ago when he'd come here, wounded and sick. He ran a hand over his jaw and blew out a long breath. Try as he might, he couldn't flee his own thoughts as easily as he could the claustrophobic feeling inside the house. His mind kept plowing down the same furrow.

It was unsettling how closely his and Tate's lives matched that of the brothers in the story. Of course their father hadn't stuck around and eventually neither had Tate, but there were enough similarities to leave Tex feeling uncomfortable. Thankfully the children had seemed too interested in the story and in Ravena's answers to their questions to notice.

He was sure he'd heard the story of the prodigal

son before, but he couldn't recall what he'd thought of it back then. It likely hadn't struck him with as much force as it had tonight. The life of the younger brother, according to Ravena's retelling, sounded eerily familiar to him—the leaving of home in search of adventure, the finding of said adventure and the realization of how empty it could be. His only defense was that he hadn't squandered any of his family's money in the process, or really much of what he'd stolen as an outlaw. The bulk of what he'd taken during his bank and train heists was hidden in several locations, known only to himself.

But those facts still didn't stop the story from eating at his conscience. Why had the wayward son been welcomed back by his father, after all the young man had done? Tex shifted on the hard planks of the porch, leaning his elbows on his knees. From behind, he heard the screen door squeak open. He glanced over his shoulder to find Ravena there.

"I was getting the younger boys a drink and saw that you were out here."

He grunted in response, not sure whether he preferred her company or the companionship of his own thoughts.

Stepping to the opposite porch column, Ravena rested her shoulder against it and loosely folded her arms. "It's a beautiful night," she said, staring up at the starry sky.

Tex found himself staring at her rather than at the majesty of the sky above. Had he stuck around and they'd married, he could have climbed to his feet right now and wrapped his arms around her from behind. She would've rested her head on his shoulder and he would've thought how grateful he felt to be here, with her.

But he hadn't stuck around. And instead of holding Ravena as his wife, he was alone and troubled as he compared his life to that of the Bible story he'd just heard.

"You haven't said much tonight." She twisted to look at him.

He shrugged, for once not caring that he didn't appear easygoing or carefree. "Not much to say."

"Fanny appreciated you joining us." He heard her exhale a long breath before adding, "I thought it was nice to have you there too."

Her admission surprised him, but Tex forced himself to harden his heart against her compassion. He wasn't worthy of her. "Is that why you picked that story?" His accusing tone made him wince.

Ravena straightened away from the column. "Is that what you think?"

"Just answer the question, Ravena."

Instead of firing back a harsh retort as he'd expected—wanted even, so he could justify his anger—she shook her head sadly. "I told that story because that's the one we're on. If you didn't like it, you could've walked out."

She was right and they both knew it.

"Which part did you find most troubling?" she asked, her voice surprisingly gentle.

Tex dug a groove into the dirt with his heel, stalling. He kept forgetting how well she knew him, even after all these years. "Why would I be troubled over a story?"

"Never mind." She took a step toward the door. Tex didn't dare peek at her expression. He didn't want to see the disappointment there. "I won't force you to talk, Tex. But I also don't have to sit here and take your sullen mood. Good night."

"Why'd he forgive him?" he blurted out, desperate to know and yet fearing the answer.

"What do you mean?"

Now that he'd asked it, there was no going back. He gripped his hands together and forced the words from his arid throat. "Why did the father forgive the younger son? He could've slammed the door in his face or made him be his servant like the kid thought he would. But he didn't. Why?"

Lowering herself onto the opposite side of the porch step, Ravena faced his profile. "He forgave him because he loved his son. Because he saw that the young man had turned his back on his old life. That he chose humility and repentance and change instead. That's why he forgave him."

Tex considered her response. "And what about what Ginny said? Is that really the lesson in that story?"

Her answering smile was as much a balm as her words. "Yes. We are never lost to the Lord. He loves and forgives us, like the father in the story, each and every time we err as long as we then choose to come back to Him."

He wanted to believe it. But he couldn't ask for forgiveness if he planned to make the same choices. And he did. He was in too deep to turn back now. The only life open to him was the one he'd already chosen. "Does it work that way with people too?"

Ravena's expression fell. "You mean do they forgive us as easily as the Lord does?"

Tex nodded.

"Sometimes," she said, though this time her tone held less conviction. "If we earnestly seek the Lord's forgiveness, we'll receive it, but that isn't a guarantee others will forgive us too. They still have a choice."

Her explanation made sense. He still had one more question to ask though. "Do you think the older brother forgave the younger one?"

Ravena appeared to ponder that. "I don't know for certain, since the story doesn't say. But I could see him eventually forgiving his younger brother, especially after seeing the example their father set. It might not have happened as quickly between the brothers, but I think it could have."

Nodding, he unclasped his fingers and relaxed them. The earlier choke hold of uneasiness had loosened a bit while they'd talked.

"Were you thinking about you and Tate during the story?"

Among other things, he thought ruefully. "Yeah I suppose I was."

"Do you think you two will ever forgive each other?"

Tex stiffened, his relief fleeing like a coyote for the hills. Why should he seek Tate's forgiveness? He wasn't the only one who'd hurled angry insults that night, though he knew he'd been wrong to knock Tate out and leave him there unconscious. All he'd wanted was for Tate to have his back, to support his decision to elope with Ravena. Instead his only living family member had accused him of being a thief.

A memory pushed through his anger. He'd accused Tate that night of being sweet on Ravena, of not being able to accept that she'd chosen Tex over him. The recollection made him cringe. He'd also taken their mother's earrings without telling Tate, largely because Tex knew his brother wouldn't approve.

So apparently there were things he needed to seek Tate's forgiveness for. He shot a sideways glance at Ravena and felt another wave of guilt threatening him. There were things he needed to apologize for with her too. But could he do it, without revealing who and what he was now?

"I should've written," he admitted in a voice not much louder than a whisper. "To let you know it wasn't you, Ravena. You weren't the reason I didn't come back."

He watched her swallow hard and her expression change from interest to pain. "What was the reason then?"

Staring down at his hands, Tex tried to think how to explain. "It was partly Tate," he said after a long moment. "You see, I took something of his. Well, it was both of ours, really. And I was going to sell it…" He glanced up to see she was still listening. "That way you and I could travel around for a time before settling somewhere and getting our own place. But Tate discovered what I'd taken."

Ravena crossed her arms, probably an unconscious gesture to protect herself. And Tex hated that she felt she needed to around him. "What did Tate do?"

"He told me you deserved better than a thief."

"Oh, I see." She stared down at the toes of her shoes peeking out from her dress hem. "Is that what you meant the other day, when you said I deserved better? Did you decide not to come back for me because you'd taken and sold that thing that belonged to you and Tate?"

Tex dipped his head in a nod. "I didn't sell the keepsake, though, Ravena." He needed her to know that, even if Tate still didn't.

"Then you aren't a thief."

Her innocent remark speared straight through his chest, igniting a flame of remorse, until he could sit no longer. He climbed to his feet and paced a few steps away from the porch. What would Ravena think or say if she knew about all he'd stolen since?

"Is there something else?" she asked.

He whirled around, panic sluicing through him. "What do you mean?"

"You said it was partly because of Tate that you didn't come back. What was the other part?"

The conversation was moving dangerously close to the truth about his current life. He needed to steer it back on course, while still giving her an honest answer. "I was stubborn, and for that I'm truly sorry, Ravena."

Would she realize how much he meant it? He'd hurt her back then—now that he was here again, he could see that—and he wished he hadn't been the cause of pain for her.

"Thank you, for telling me and for apologizing." She stood, her arms still a shield against him. "I… I've forgiven you, Tex. For not coming back. I did so several years ago."

She didn't say anything more, but Tex understood the things she'd left unspoken. That forgiving him and trusting him were two very different things. They might even be friends now, but that was all.

"Good night, Tex."

"'Night, Ravena."

He watched her slip back inside as the earlier heaviness descended on him again. The only way he knew to escape it was to leave—to leave behind this place, the past and his mistakes.

As soon as he'd fulfilled his promise, he'd be gone.

Ravena bent to stretch the sore muscles of her back, her gaze jumping to where Tex and Jacob were working ahead of her. The planting was going well. In contrast, progress on the larger house hadn't changed. She'd hoped to find someone to start working on it by now, but when she'd asked around at church on Sunday, there hadn't been anyone interested in taking time away from their own farms to take on a building job for such low wages.

Someone would turn up, at least that's what she kept telling herself. And in the meantime, her crops would all be planted soon. The realization brought a bittersweet feeling. Once the planting was finished, Tex would be leaving.

Her thoughts returned to their conversation on the porch two nights ago. Some of her long unanswered questions surrounding Tex had been resolved, and yet, she still felt restless. There were things she didn't understand. Though she took comfort in knowing that she'd meant her words about forgiving him for not coming back. And she'd been more than a little shocked and grateful when he'd acknowledged the pain he'd caused with an apology.

Feeling thirsty, she walked to the edge of the field where she'd placed her canteen in the grass. She took a long swallow of water and recapped the canteen. As she went to set it back down, a familiar rattling noise made her freeze. There, coiled, in the grass lay a rattlesnake.

Terror sent icy shards racing through her body and made her heart thrash against her ribs. She couldn't move, couldn't call for help, out of fear of being bitten. It was exactly like the time she'd been a girl and came across a rattler in a field. Thankfully she hadn't been alone then; her grandfather had been with her. But no one was beside her now.

Help, Lord. It was the only prayer she could manage. She kept her gaze fixed on the snake's head, the *rattle, rattle* of its tail as loud as the roaring in her ears.

"Ravena?" she heard Tex call from across the field. She couldn't answer. Her chest felt tight from her shallow breaths, but she didn't dare drag in a gulp of air, worried the snake would hear and feel threatened.

Tex called to her again, but she ignored him. If she died from a snakebite, what would happen to the children? Who would care for them? Who would carry on her grandfather's legacy?

Please, Lord, help me.

The rattler kept a steady beat, out of rhythm with the pounding of Ravena's heart. Her fingers began to ache where they gripped the canteen.

The canteen. She could use it as a weapon. But she would have to be accurate with her aim.

"Ravena? What's going on?" Tex sounded closer.

She'd have to hurry and act to keep him from startling the snake further.

She eyed the reptile's head, then sucking in her breath, she dropped the canteen on the snake. Then she ran. She was scrambling so quickly to get away she didn't realize her shoes had become entangled in her skirt until she was pitching forward. With a cry, she landed in a heap, her left foot caught beneath her.

Tex and Jacob were standing over her a moment later. "What happened?" Tex asked.

"Are you all right, Miss Ravena?"

She felt far from all right. "There was…a…a…" Her teeth began to chatter as the adrenaline ebbed and the pain in her ankle registered in her mind. Tears filled her eyes and Ravena was powerless to stop them.

After lifting her to a sitting position, Tex crouched in front of her. Jacob's concerned expression mirrored his.

"It was a…" She couldn't push the word from her mouth.

Tex's blue eyes lit with sudden understanding. "Was it a snake?" His remembering one of her biggest fears brought her the tiniest comfort.

Ravena managed a nod in response, even as she shuddered. Things might have gone so differently had she not had the thought to drop the canteen.

"A rattler?" Tex kept his gaze locked with hers. "Did it bite you, Ravena?"

She shook her head and whispered, "No." His relief was palpable. "I…I dropped my canteen on it." She brushed at her cheeks, but the tears wouldn't stop their course down her face. "Then I fell and my ankle…"

"Let's get you back to the house." He scooped her up

in his arms. "Jacob," he directed, "keep planting where we were working. I'll be right back."

With that he began carrying her away from the field. Over his shoulder, Ravena watched Jacob move to the other side of the field, away from the rattlesnake.

"I can get back on my own," she said, feeling the need to protest his help. Or was it how nice she felt being in Tex's arms that she was protesting? Either way, she was secretly grateful when he ignored her half-hearted objection. She didn't think she could stand, let alone make her way slowly and painfully to the house.

Tex tossed her a look. "That was a real smart thing to do with the canteen."

"Was it?" The words were half sob, half laugh. Her head felt too heavy to hold up, so she reluctantly leaned it onto Tex's shoulder.

His jaw came to rest against her forehead in a tender gesture that both unnerved and comforted her. "That was fast-thinking, especially when I imagine you were terrified."

"I was." Another shiver ran through her. "But I think the idea to drop the canteen was an answer to prayer."

She expected him to balk at that, but he simply nodded. When he reached the porch, Tex didn't slow. Instead he carried her inside and into the parlor. There he set her gently on the sofa. Ravena was grateful the children were still at school. She felt in no condition to answer their questions.

"We probably ought to get a look at that ankle," Tex said as he knelt before her.

Ravena agreed. But bending forward to unlace her

boot proved harder in her present state than she'd anticipated.

Tex's hand closed over hers. "Let me."

Untying the laces, he worked them loose, then slid
her foot from her shoe. Ravena pulled in a gasp between
her teeth, as much at the throbbing in her foot as from
the gentleness of his touch. An ache for what they'd
once had filled her with longing and regret.

Pushing the past aside and steeling herself against
the emotional and physical pain, she felt her ankle for
any fractures. "I think it's just sprained," she declared
with relief. But it was short-lived. She would need to
be careful so her foot healed properly, and that meant
doing less around the farm at a time when she couldn't
afford to hold back.

Fresh tears leaked from her eyes and she covered
her face with her hands. Desperation like she hadn't
felt since her grandfather's passing clogged her throat.

"Hey now," Tex soothed. Cupping her head, he drew
her forward onto his shoulder. Ravena willingly went.
She was so tired of doing things on her own, of being
the only adult. "It's going to be okay. You were smart
about the snake and it didn't hurt you."

She squeezed her eyes shut. "But it could have."

"Yes, though you aren't that helpless, little girl you
were the last time you encountered a rattler." His hand
ran the length of her hair, bringing reassurance. "Your
grandfather was there to help you last time, but this
time you helped yourself." He cleared his throat as if
embarrassed, then added, "Well, I suppose you'd say
God aided you too."

Ravena released a sigh and sat back. "It isn't just the

snake, Tex." She glanced down at her hands. "How do I assist with the planting and do everything else when I need to rest my foot?"

Lifting his hand, he brought it to rest alongside her cheek. Her heart picked up its swift rhythm as it had earlier in the field. "Jacob and I will keep planting. You just try to stay off that foot." He winked, prompting a quick smile from her, which was likely what he'd hoped for.

But her worries wouldn't be silenced. "With just you and Jacob working, the planting is going to take longer. Likely longer than you'd planned to stay."

"I said I'd stay until it was done." He rose slowly to his feet, his blue eyes unusually serious. "And that's what I'm going to do—whether it takes five more days or five weeks."

She wanted to stand and throw her arms around him, but the resignation rolling off him tethered her to the sofa. He was committed to seeing the planting through, yes, and she was grateful for that, but she could see that he didn't want to stay.

Had that been his other reason for not coming back for her? Tex had cited Tate's false accusation and his own stubbornness, but maybe another reason was he hadn't wanted to stay tethered to the farm anymore. She'd seen the glint of wanderlust in his eyes more than once since his arrival, just as she had the night he'd asked her to elope. Only then, she hadn't recognized it for what it was.

"Thank you," she voiced into the silence, "for carrying me to the house."

Tex nodded. "You're welcome. I'd better go help Jacob. Will you be all right here?"

"Go ahead." She could limp to wherever she needed to inside the house. And what she *needed* right now was a little space. Because, as she watched Tex disappear out the door, she couldn't help wishing once again that her hopes didn't lie with a man who had no wish or reason to stay.

Tex strode away from the house, back toward the fields. A few extra days or a week to complete the planting, while Ravena rested her foot, wouldn't make too much of a difference with his plans. At least that's what he told himself. But he felt the familiar itch for freedom creep up his collar and he loosened his bandanna in a vain effort to squelch it.

Had Ravena pretended to sprain her ankle so that he'd stick around longer? Tex shook his head, feeling badly for even thinking such a thing. Ravena was no liar, and the fear and pain he'd seen in her big dark eyes just now hadn't been imagined.

He'd felt confused in the field, watching her stand there frozen, then he'd felt alarmed. Especially when she'd bolted in his direction and had fallen. The pure terror of her expression when he reached her had told him what she hadn't been able to put into words—she'd had an encounter with a snake.

Pushing up his hat, he brushed his sleeve over his forehead. The afternoon felt overly warm. Or maybe it was just his churning emotions.

Tex had initially felt relieved to learn the snake hadn't bitten Ravena. That relief soon gave way to compassion when she'd confessed her concerns over having a sprained ankle and what effect that would have on the planting and running the farm. In that moment, seeing a crack in her usual strength and determination, he'd felt determined himself to see the planting through, no matter how much longer it took. He couldn't turn his back on her. If he did, this time would be worse than the last. Because unlike eight years ago, Ravena no longer had any other adult around to rely on. In that they were the same.

At the thought of Ravena being alone, just as he was, an unexplainable longing rose inside Tex—an image of what it could be if they were a family. She and he and all of these orphans. It wasn't difficult to contemplate. All he had to do was think about how right and wonderful it had felt to hold her in his arms just now. To run his hand over her long, silky hair. To touch her tearstained cheek to comfort her, as if he had a right to.

Tex allowed himself a full minute to entertain the thought of being part of a real family with Ravena. Then he dug it up and tossed it out before it could take root inside him. She'd never marry an outlaw, and he couldn't change what he was. He'd set himself on a road that he couldn't simply walk away from. He had Quincy out there, looking for him, and he was a wanted man throughout most of the West. It wasn't like he could just settle down and hope no one ever recognized him. Not when there was reward on his head.

"Besides," he grumbled to himself, "I don't want to be tied to one place forever." Wasn't that partly why he'd left in the first place?

But as he neared the field where he could see Jacob

still hard at work, Tex felt suddenly tired. Tired of wrestling with the past. Tired of wrestling with himself and his conscience. And most of all, tired of wrestling with his growing attraction to Ravena and her life here.

Half walking, half hobbling, Ravena made her way to the field where she knew Tex and Jacob were working. Four days had passed since she'd sprained her ankle, but she couldn't stay confined to the house any longer. She wanted to see for herself how the planting was going—and convince Tex that she was well enough to help. That's why she'd prepared some of his favorite foods, including pie, for lunch.

She paused near the field to catch her breath and to ease the aching in her foot. All right, so maybe it wasn't completely healed. It wasn't as if she hadn't rested it. She had. But she was anxious to see the planting completed in a timely manner. Tex had committed to seeing it through, and yet, Ravena couldn't help wondering if he would really do it or if he'd grow tired of the endless work. He wasn't getting paid after all.

Catching sight of her, Jacob waved. Ravena pushed aside the pain in her foot and shifted her load to wave back. Tex slowly straightened, his gaze capturing hers from across the field. Her pulse picked up tempo, though she wasn't sure if it was out of concern that he'd see through her plan or out of awareness of him.

"I've brought lunch," she called as she shuffled forward.

They both approached, wiping at their foreheads with their bandannas. "We could have come to the house for it, like we've been doing," Tex said, throwing a level look her way.

Ravena shrugged. "I decided I could use a little air." Which was also the truth. She took a seat on the ground and they followed suit. "Eat up. There's plenty."

"Looks delicious, Miss Ravena," Jacob said, pulling things from the lunch pails.

Arching an eyebrow, Tex made slow work of spreading out his lunch. "It does look good. Smells good too. And all my favorite foods."

She felt a blush steal over her cheeks. "Well, you're both working hard. How's the planting going?" She glanced past Tex to the field, eager for something else to focus on.

"It's going well, same as I told you last night." He'd been giving her an update each evening at supper.

Ignoring his pointed remark, she steered the discussion to other things. Jacob tossed in a comment or two, but he mostly just ate. Tex took his time eating, though he did keep up his end of the conversation, sprinkling it with liberal compliments about her food.

Ravena smiled. Her plan was working.

Once they had both finished eating, they gathered up what little remained of the food as well as the napkins. "Thanks again for lunch, Ravena." Tex climbed to his feet, then helped her stand as well. Hoisting the lunch pails, he extended them toward her.

"I…um…" She gestured toward the field. "I thought since I'm out here and don't need to start supper for a while longer that I might help."

Tex set the pails back down. "No."

She shot Jacob a firm glance when he snickered. "What do you mean, *no*?"

"Is your foot fully healed?" He fell back a step, motioning for Jacob to join him.

"It's much better. I only have to rest it a few times a day now."

Shaking his head, Tex turned and led Jacob back toward the field. "Then the answer is still no," he said over his shoulder.

Ravena balled her hands into fists at the realization that he'd known exactly what she was doing, plying him with his favorite foods to soften him up. "Tex Beckett, this is not your farm. I can work in my field if I want to, with or without your permission."

"Is that so?" He spun back, a surprisingly gentle expression on his face. "And what will you do if your foot doesn't heal properly? How will you manage things then?"

His words stole the bluster from her anger. He was right. But she wouldn't let him see that. "I'll be fine for one afternoon." She limped forward.

Tex blocked her way. "So help me, Ravena, if you step into this field on that injured foot, I'm going to throw you over my shoulder and carry you back to the house."

"You wouldn't dare…"

But the amusing look in his blue eyes and his smug grin told a different story, even before he leaned close to say, "I would."

Ravena narrowed her eyes at him. "Fine." Scooping up the lunch pails, she hobbled away with all the dignity she could muster. She was more than frustrated at him and her ankle was throbbing.

Deep down, though, she felt a splinter of disappointment that he hadn't thrown her over his shoulder and carried her to the house after all. The idea sounded far from unpleasant. It actually sounded fun. And that realization scared her as much as his words about running the farm alone with an improperly healed foot. Because whatever happened, she could not—would not—fall for Tex a second time.

Chapter Nine

Two weeks after her sly attempt to help with the planting, Ravena woke in the night to the sound of crying. After wrapping a shawl over her nightgown, she hurried to light a lamp, then padded down the hall to the girls' bedroom. She found Ginny sitting up in bed, her thin arms hugging her knees, her cheeks tearstained.

"Oh, Ginny." Ravena set the lamp on the bureau and sat beside the weeping girl. "Was it another bad dream?"

Ginny gave a wordless nod.

Gathering the girl into her arms, she rocked her back and forth, just as her grandmother had done whenever Ravena had a nightmare. Movement at the open door drew her attention. She was surprised to see Tex standing there. Ginny's crying must have woken him too.

"I heard a noise," he said, keeping his voice low in consideration for Fanny, who still slept soundly in the other bed. "Is Ginny all right?"

Ravena eased back to smooth the girl's red hair from her face. "She had a bad dream."

Stepping into the room, Tex crouched beside the bed. "Do you want to talk about it?" he asked Ginny.

She looked to Ravena who nodded encouragement. But would the girl actually share her dream with Tex? Both Ravena and her grandfather had tried to explain that talking about her fears might help, but Ginny refused. It had been several months since the girl had last had a bad dream, and Ravena had hoped that meant they were gone altogether. Apparently that wasn't the truth though.

"I was havin' a bad dream too." Tex leaned forward as if confiding a great secret. "I dreamed Mark and Luke made me supper, which they said I could only eat on the roof with the cow for company."

A tiny smile appeared on Ginny's lips.

Tex shook his head with mock severity and Ravena had to tamp down a chuckle at his performance. "The cow didn't like the biscuits they made, so it kicked them off the roof. And I was so hungry, I jumped down to grab them. Then I woke up."

Ginny's smile widened a little more.

"Now that you've heard my dream, what do you say about sharing yours?"

Ravena held her breath as the girl fiddled with the bed quilt. After a moment, Ginny glanced at Tex and whispered, "Okay." Then she shot Ravena a hesitant look. "Can I just tell it to Mr. Beckett first?"

Her desire to hear and comfort Ginny quickly gave way to gratitude that at least the girl was willing to open up to Tex. Ravena wanted to hug him. Instead she exchanged a smile with him and stood. "That would be just fine, Ginny. Let's all go downstairs. I'll make some tea, to help you get back to sleep. And you two can talk in the parlor."

She took Ginny's hand in her own, then picked up the lamp. They walked out of the room, Tex coming behind them. When they reached the parlor, Ravena motioned for Ginny to take a seat.

"Thank you for telling her that story," she said softly to Tex.

His gaze appeared bright with amusement in the lamplight. "What do you mean 'story'? That was a bona fide dream I had." He bent toward her and lowered his voice, causing her pulse to trip. "Only I dreamt it last night instead of tonight."

Her answering chuckle sounded more nervous than merry in her ears. Ravena passed him the lamp and took a deliberate step toward the kitchen. "I'll make that tea, while you talk to her."

If Tex noticed her flustered manner, he didn't comment. To her great relief. Instead he walked into the parlor, set down the lamp and pulled one of the armchairs in front of the sofa where Ginny now sat.

"How does the dream start?" he asked in a kind tone.

Ravena made herself walk away, though she wanted to stick around. Not only to hear what Ginny would say but to watch Tex. She was finding it harder and harder to steel herself against her growing affection for him. It had been blossoming ever since he'd agreed to help with the planting. And seeing him, once again, respond to the children and to her in that gentle, teasing, caring manner of his only increased her attraction for him.

Which will only lead to trouble, she reminded herself as she lit another lamp in the kitchen and set about making the tea. If only she would listen to that rational part of her. But tonight, working together like this to help one of the children, she found she wanted these moments to continue for a very long time

"It always starts with me in the cabin," Ginny said, her voice soft and tinged with pain.

Tex rested his arms on his knees, to show he was listening. He'd felt as surprised as Ravena had looked when the girl agreed to talk about her dream with him, but he was determined not to let either Ginny or Ravena down.

"Who's there with you?"

Ginny drew her legs up underneath her long nightgown. "It's me and my ma and pa at first. But then Mama waves goodbye and disappears out the door."

Sadness began to well up inside Tex. The words were more than he'd ever heard Ginny speak at one time, and yet, they were so full of grief. "Where does your mother go?"

The girl's eyes glittered with more tears. "She got sick and died."

Tex cleared his throat. "I'm real sorry, Ginny. You must miss her." He still missed his mother. And he knew how helpless it felt to watch a loved one slowly lose a fight with illness. "What happens next in the dream?"

"Pa kneels by my bed and says he has to go too." A shudder ran through her and she folded her arms tightly. "I beg him to stay, Mr. Beckett," she said, her voice wobbling with emotion. "But he keeps saying no. Now that Mama's gone, he can't stay."

Tex lowered his gaze to his hands and squeezed them

together. Ginny's story inspired painful memories of his own. And he realized this wasn't just a dream for her; this was something Ginny had actually experienced. "So does he go?"

"Yes." When he lifted his chin, he saw the tears rushing down her cheeks. "He tells me our neighbor will come take care of me. But I didn't like Mrs. Goff. She was mean and would always say my pa was a no-account and that Mama and me were better off without him."

"Then what happens?"

Ginny hung her head so he had to bend forward to hear what she said next. "I beg and cry and tell Pa not to leave. And he says, 'Stop crying.' So I do, but he still walks out the door." Tex reached forward and clasped her hand in his, sensing the next part wouldn't be any less difficult to share. "Then I'm all alone and crying and Mrs. Goff comes and she has a wagon. She tells me, 'Climb in,' but I can't, Mr. Beckett. I can't."

"Is there someone already in the wagon?"

Ginny nodded vigorously and lifted her eyes to his. Her tortured look reminded him of what he'd felt after his own father failed to return after that last disappearance. "My pa is there, in the wagon, but he's dead too."

Giving her hand a squeeze, Tex coughed again to dislodge the solid lump in his throat. "What happened to him in real life?"

Her shoulders rose and fell. "I don't know. When the sheriff found him near the gulch the day after he left, he was already dead." Tex guessed the man had likely drunk himself to death after losing his wife.

"That's awful, Ginny." He wished there was more

he could say. "I don't blame you for not wanting to go with Mrs. Goff or get in the wagon."

"But why did Pa leave, Mr. Beckett?" Her plaintive tone tore at his heart. "Is it because I didn't stop crying fast enough?"

The question prompted further memories, ones he'd suppressed years ago. Tex could recall how he and Tate had asked their mother nearly the same thing Ginny was asking him now. *What had they done to make their father leave?*

"Will you listen real hard to what I'm going to tell you?" Tex waited for her to nod before continuing. "All right. I'm going to share a secret with you."

Her green eyes lit with mild interest.

"Your pa was every bit as ill as your mama."

She cocked her head. "He was?"

"Yes, but it wasn't an illness you could see with your eyes or hear with your ears." He pointed to his chest with his finger. "It happens in your heart, and it's pretty hard to make it get better. And it isn't something a little girl can help with all by herself."

Ginny's brow furrowed in thought. "So he left because he was sick too? And not because of me?"

"His leaving had nothing to do with you," Tex stated firmly, his gaze locked on hers. "And nothing you could have done to help him would have made him well again, Ginny. He had to choose to get better himself."

The girl bolted forward and wrapped her arms around Tex's neck. "He didn't leave because of me," she repeated, this time in a whisper, but her voice rang with conviction.

Tex couldn't have spoken if he'd wanted to. Tears

brimmed his own eyes as he hugged her back. Could the same be true for him? he wondered. He knew without a doubt that Ginny wasn't responsible for her father's leaving. But wasn't that also the truth for him and Tate and their father? They weren't responsible for his leaving either.

Some of the hardness that had collected around his heart over the last two decades, since his own father's leaving, chipped off.

"Feel any better?" he asked when Ginny eased back.

A rare full smile brightened her entire face. "Yes."

"Come get some tea," Ravena announced from the hallway. "It's ready."

Tex pushed back his chair and stood, offering Ginny the crook of his arm. "Shall we take our tea now, my lady?"

She giggled—another rarity for Ginny—and slipped her arm in his. As he guided her down the hall to the kitchen, the tinkle of her laughter followed them.

In spite of drinking some of Ravena's tea himself, Tex didn't feel sleepy. Not with Ginny's story—and its similarities to his and Tate's experiences—still running through his mind. After Ginny and Ravena had gone back upstairs, he'd wandered outside and took his customary seat on the step, his back against one of the porch columns. This was becoming one of his favorite spots to think. The cool night felt pleasant, though he sensed the coming of summer in the air.

He could hardly believe he'd been here five weeks. In some ways he felt as if he'd been here longer—this was certainly the longest he'd spent in one place since leaving Idaho—and yet he also felt as if it had only been a matter of days since he'd come to the farm.

A lamp in one hand, Ravena joined him outside, which didn't surprise Tex in the least. She'd likely sensed his ruminating all the way upstairs.

"Do you think Ginny will get back to sleep?" he asked.

"Yes." Ravena shivered and held the ends of her shawl closer together. "She told me about her dream."

Tex nodded. "I think it's more than a dream. She's likely reliving her experience of losing both her parents."

"I agree," she said, moving to stand beside the other porch column. "Thank you for your help, Tex. I could tell she still felt sad when she told me what she'd dreamt, but she wasn't terrified. Not anymore."

"I'm glad." He lifted his knee and placed his elbow there, feeling gratitude that he'd been able to help Ginny. "She thought it was her fault that her father left after her mother died."

Ravena's eyes widened above the light of the lamp. "That breaks my heart to hear."

"I don't think she still feels that way." He described how he'd explained to Ginny what had ailed her father and why he'd left.

"You have a way with the children," she said, her tone full of sincerity.

The compliment pleased him, even as a bit of sadness settled deep inside him at the thought of saying goodbye to these five children who he'd come to care for. And to Ravena too.

"It's funny how I thought the same thing about my

own father leaving. That somehow it was my fault."
He shrugged, trying to recall his boyhood thoughts. "I
guess I believed if I'd liked farming more or hadn't gotten into so much mischief or done the chores without
asking that he wouldn't have left for good."

Ravena sat, setting the lamp between them. "That
doesn't sound funny to me at all. You and Tate were
children, Tex, same as Ginny. You were looking for answers and explanations you could understand, which is
natural. But you weren't any more responsible for your
father leaving than Ginny was for hers."

The realization filled him with as much relief and
hope as he'd seen on Ginny's face in the parlor earlier.
He wanted to shout his happiness to the stars.

But memories of his father spurred other recollections, ones that didn't leave him feeling so happy. "I
may not be responsible for his leaving, but the fact is
he *did* leave and that last time he didn't come back. My
mother was never the same after that." Neither were he
and Tate. That experience had shaped all three of them,
for better or worse.

Pushing the lamp out of the way, Ravena scooted
closer. "I didn't understand back then how hard that
was, Tex. And I wish I had."

"You were just a kid too," he reminded, shooting
her half a smile.

She might not remember giving him a hug the day
he'd confessed to her that he didn't think his pa was
coming back, but Tex remembered. It was the day he'd
first recognized he was in love with Ravena Reid. But
he'd worried then that a poor, fatherless boy might not

be worthy of her. That fear hadn't disappeared over the years.

"Ma used to say I was a lot like him. Charismatic, optimistic, always looking for that next adventure."

Ravena regarded him. "In those qualities, I suppose you were like him, yes."

Fresh guilt and growing fear pushed the next words from his mouth. "It's not just the good qualities, Ravena. He up and left us without saying goodbye." Tex swallowed hard. "Same as I did." He glanced away, afraid to see the truth of it mirrored in her expression.

"You think you take after him in that too?"

"Don't I?" he countered. He hated having to point out the obvious, but he was tired of holding in his anxiety.

He heard her soft sigh. "Tex?" He continued to glare in the direction of the road. "Tex, look at me."

Dread filled him as he pulled his gaze to hers. "What?"

"You aren't your father."

Why did she refuse to see it? He'd up and left her and Tate, just as his father had done with his family. He'd also been ready to leave Ravena again before deciding to stay for the plowing and planting.

"You don't believe me, do you?"

He spread his hands wide in a surrendering gesture. "What can I say? I've always been stubborn."

Ravena frowned, making him wish he'd kept his mouth shut. He didn't want to argue with her tonight. Working together to help Ginny had felt really nice and it was a feeling he wanted back.

"How come you don't ever sit in the rocking chair?" he asked, desperate to change the subject. She'd yet to discover his repair work on the rocker and he suddenly wanted her to know, to understand what he'd done because he cared about her.

Her frown increased. "I know you're changing the subject. And I don't sit there because the rocking chair is broken."

"Is it?" Grinning, he hopped up and made a show of sitting in the rocker. Then he set it rocking back and forth with his bare feet.

"It's not broken anymore?" Rising, Ravena skirted the lamp to step closer. "How?"

Tex stood and motioned to the chair. "Have a seat."

She sat and began rocking. "It works beautifully. Did you pay someone to fix it?"

"Now why would I do that?" he said with a chuckle. "All I needed to do was repair the runner to get it working properly again."

"You fixed it?" Ravena stopped the rocker at once.

He cupped the chair arms with his hands and bent close. Would she recognize that he'd done it for her? "Yes, I fixed it. I'm glad I remembered enough of your grandfather's woodworking lessons."

"He taught you woodworking…" Her tone sounded thoughtful.

Straightening, Tex went to grab the lamp. If they went inside now, maybe he could avoid a return to the earlier topic of his father and their similarities. "Ezra taught me a lot of things. And I greatly wish I'd been here to say goodbye to him."

He waited for Ravena to stand, but she continued to sit. "I'm going to turn in," he said, moving toward the door. "Do you want the lamp left out here?"

Instead of answering his question, she started rocking again. "He respected you, Tex. My grandfather."

"Maybe he shouldn't have," he murmured.

He knew she'd heard him when the rocker stopped moving and Ravena stood. "Why? Because you still think you're like your father?"

He should've kept his thoughts to himself. "I'm beat, Ravena…"

"Tex, just because you left here once doesn't mean you're going to turn out like your father."

Her words, which matched his fears perfectly, stilled his retreat.

"You're back here now, aren't you?" She rested her hand on his sleeve, her touch every bit as imploring as her tone.

He studied her over the lip of the lamp. Her hair gleamed ebony in the light, her dark brown eyes deep and full of feeling. A strong longing to kiss her filled him, but he fought it back with the reminder that he risked breaking her heart if he kissed her before leaving her, yet again.

"I am back, but…" Tex didn't think he needed to finish his sentence out loud. Ravena likely knew what he was going to say. That while he wouldn't leave behind a wife and family, he'd inherited his father's wanderlust.

Ravena shook her head. "No," she said with fervor. "You're different from him, and I have a way you can prove it. To me, to him and to yourself."

It was his turn to frown. "How would I do that?"

"You have to promise to stay."

"Ravena, I've done that—"

"I mean promise to stay and finish the house my grandfather started."

Tex chuckled with disbelief, until he realized she was serious. "What about the rest of the planting?"

"My foot's fully healed, so Jacob and I can finish while you start on the house."

"Why?" He wasn't sure he understood why the house or bringing more orphans to the farm was so important to her.

Her gaze dropped to the floorboards of the porch. "Because I can't bring those four boys here if the larger house isn't completed. There just isn't enough room for all of us to live in the one we have." She lifted her chin, her determined gaze reminding him of her grandfather's. "If I don't finish the house, those boys will be sent farther West on the Orphan Train on the first of July, and they'll likely be separated into different homes and even different towns along the way. It was Grandfather's last wish to give them a home here."

Blowing out a breath, Tex ran his hand through his hair. "So you want me to finish the house in less than a month?" It would mean staying far longer than he'd planned.

"Yes. I can help you, when the planting is finished, but you know woodworking as well as my grandfather did."

"I wouldn't go that far..."

She lowered her hand from his arm, but she continued to study him solemnly. "Please, Tex. I'll even pay you what little I have saved up. I already have all the lumber and nails."

Tex recalled the towering pile of wood he'd seen

when he was working on the rocking chair. "Like I told you before, Ravena, I don't want your money."

He thought she looked relieved. "Then will you do it?"

"Just to prove I'm not like my father?" He'd meant the question to sound more cynical, but it came out sounding curious. Was he really considering her suggestion?

"Not just for that. Though if you do stay longer, then surely that will prove you aren't your father. And..." She looked in the direction of the unfinished walls of the other house. "It would mean a great deal to me and to my grandfather."

The old urge to escape returned full force, tempting Tex to decline her request. The planting would be done in another few days and he could ride away, free of entanglements and regret. But as he peered into Ravena's lovely face, a face he hadn't expected to ever see again, he grappled the wanderlust into submission. She'd given him a gift with her proposal. He could prove to himself, once and for all, that he wasn't his father, and in turn, he could finally put his conscience to rest when it came to Ravena, Ezra and the past.

"All right. I'll stay, until the house is completed."

She blinked. "You will?"

Tex couldn't help laughing. "Yes, Ravena."

Leaning close, she placed a kiss near the corner of his mouth. Tex maintained a mildly surprised expression as she eased back, though he really wanted to kiss her back. Only he wanted to kiss her squarely on the lips, not on the cheek, same as he had in the past. Back then he'd taken their sweet kisses for granted, but now, he felt certain he would treasure them always.

Except he'd already talked himself out of kissing her. Instead of drawing her close and pressing his lips to hers, he relished the lingering feel of her gentle touch to his face and the way she looked at him in this moment. As if he were the greatest, noblest man alive.

"Thank you, Tex," she said. "You won't regret it."

They were the same words he'd said to her when he'd offered to stay the first time. And he felt certain he wouldn't regret his decision just now—as long as Ravena didn't discover the truth about him or the Texas Titan.

Chapter Ten

Rain fell softly against the kitchen window. Ravena sat at the table, writing a letter to Miss Morley. It wasn't her first since Tex's arrival, but after last night and his agreement to finish the house, she couldn't wait to share her confidence with the woman that the four orphan brothers would be coming to live at the farm and not leaving on the Orphan Train.

"Give it back, Luke," Fanny whined as she circled the table after the boy. Luke waved her rag doll in the air.

Ravena blew out a sigh of frustration. The older three had accepted Tex's offer to learn whittling this afternoon, after she and the children had returned from church services. But Luke and Fanny hadn't wanted to join them.

"Luke," Ravena said, setting down her pen. "Please give Fanny back her doll."

The boy frowned, though he did stop running. "She keeps waving it in my face, Miss Ravena."

She supposed she ought to feel a twinge of gratitude that they weren't too shy or afraid to speak their minds—their arguing showed they'd both adjusted to living here. At least enough to act like siblings. "Fanny, why were you waving the doll in Luke's face?"

Swiping her doll from Luke's grasp, she came to stand by Ravena. "I want him to play with me."

"Why don't you two find a game you both like?"

Luke plunked down into a chair, his face despondent. "There isn't one. I want to play outside, but it's still raining."

"How about holding the kittens?" she asked Fanny.

The girl shook her head. "They don't want to sit in my lap anymore."

Ravena tapped her pen, thinking. There must be something they could do indoors, while giving her the space—and peace—to finish her letter. "I know." She shot them each a smile. "Why don't you play train and conductor in the parlor?"

Luke's eyes brightened. "Can we move the furniture?"

"Yes."

Hopping out of his chair, he raced toward the door. "Come on, Fanny. You and your doll can be the passengers 'cause I'm gonna be the conductor."

Fanny gave a happy laugh. "Let's go, Lucinda," she murmured to her rag doll. "We'll be late for our train."

Quiet descended over the kitchen once more, to Ravena's relief, though she could still hear the children talking excitedly in the parlor. She felt a great sense of satisfaction as she completed her letter and set it aside to mail tomorrow. Her grandfather's wish would soon be fulfilled. And with Tex building the house for free, she and the children would be able to keep her meager savings against… She glanced out the window and chuckled. Well, against a rainy day.

Singing one of the hymns they'd sung at church, she rose to her feet to start preparing supper. A short time later, she realized she could no longer hear Luke and Fanny. Had they gone outside? She decided to check and see if they had left the parlor.

She walked down the hall to find the room rearranged. The sofa had been pulled away from the wall and turned around with the armchairs flanking it. As she stepped closer, she spotted Luke and Fanny on the floor on the other side of the sofa.

"What are you two—"

"Look what we found, Miss Ravena," Luke exclaimed. He held bundles of cash in each hand. Ravena could see Fanny was holding something too. One of Tex's saddlebags lay open beside them.

She hurried around the chair and crouched down next to the children. "These aren't your things, children. These are Mr. Beckett's things."

"How come he has so much money?"

Ravena ignored the question. "You need to put everything back."

"Are you mad, Miss Ravena?" Fanny regarded her with large blue eyes.

"It wasn't right to go through his bag, but no, I'm not mad." Hopefully Tex wouldn't be either. "Now hand me those things and we'll get this cleaned up."

Luke nodded and passed her the wads of cash. Thankfully it looked like he and Fanny hadn't completely emptied the saddlebag. "We're sorry, Miss Ravena."

"Thank you for that, Luke." She stuffed the money

back into the bag and reached her hand out for whatever Fanny was gripping. It appeared to be an old piece of paper.

"That one's a treasure map," Luke said in an awed tone.

Was the boy's description true? Ravena took the paper from Fanny and unfolded it, enough to peek at the writing. Sure enough words and symbols met her gaze. Why would Tex have a treasure map? She stuffed it into the bag with the money before she noticed several envelopes scattered about the rug. "Did those come from Mr. Beckett's bag too?"

Luke gathered them up. "They're just empty envelopes, nothin' interesting. Except they have your name on them, Miss Ravena."

"What?" She snapped her chin up as he passed her the envelopes. Sure enough her name and the address of the farm were scrawled on the front of each. Ravena studied the envelopes, wondering why they looked familiar. And why Tex would have them. He hadn't written her once since he'd left.

Sudden understanding drew a soft gasp from her lips. These envelopes were an exact match to the ones she'd received through the years with no note and some money inside. But if Tex had the envelopes, then that meant... She shook her head in disbelief. Tate hadn't been the one to send her the money; it had been Tex all along.

Surprise, gratitude and sadness battled for dominance inside her. Tex hadn't stopped thinking or caring about her after leaving so long ago. And yet, she would have valued a short note from him above any amount of money. Some word that he was still out there and hadn't forgotten her.

"I'm going to ask Mr. Beckett about this," she said, placing all but one envelope back inside Tex's saddle-bag. The remaining one she tucked into her apron pocket. Then she stood and hefted both satchels in her arms. "You two, finish straightening up the parlor. I'll be back."

She stepped out the front door and onto the porch, her mind racing at her discovery. Tex would need to find a new place to stow his saddlebags, especially given how much money he had inside them. Money that she now believed she knew how he'd earned. But she'd need to confirm it with Tex first.

Darting into the rain, she moved with purpose toward the barn.

"That looks great, Ginny," Tex said, nodding at the girl and her small carving of a house. Out of the three children, she'd taken to the whittling lesson the best.

Mark frowned at his piece of wood. "What about mine, Mr. Beckett?"

Tex fought a smile at the irregular-shaped box. It reminded him of his first attempts. "You're getting the hang of it, Mark. Keep carving."

"This is kind of fun," Jacob conceded.

"And relaxing." Tex smiled with contentment and cut another groove into the bird he was making.

He'd felt bad turning down another request from Fanny for him to attend church services. The rain had limited what he could do outdoors while they were gone, so he'd opted for some time in the barn, carving.

But he missed having the children around. When they'd returned, he'd offered to teach anyone who wanted to learn how to whittle. Mark, Ginny and Jacob had all volunteered.

A sound at the barn door made him lift his head. Ravena ducked inside, clutching something in her arms, her long hair damp from the rain. Tex felt his smile deepen. Having her join them would make the whittling lesson even more enjoyable.

"How are things going in here?" she asked as she walked to where they sat at the back of the barn.

Tex gestured to the three children. "They're doing well."

Ravena exclaimed over each of their carvings, then turned her attention to him. "What is that you're making?"

He held up the bird, though he didn't want to tell her yet that it was a raven. Even after leaving Idaho, he'd thought of her every time he'd spotted a raven. The bird's glossy black coat reminded him of Ravena's dark hair and eyes. And the one story he could vividly recall from his mother reading the Bible to him and Tate was the one about the ravens bringing food to the prophet Elijah. To him, Ravena had always embodied a similar spirit of compassion and loyalty.

"That's beautiful, Tex."

Her compliment warmed him more than the barn, until he saw that she was carrying his saddlebags. A prick of alarm shot through him. "You sendin' me on my way?" he half teased.

The three children looked horrified at his question. Mark even cried out, "No, you can't, Miss Ravena."

She shook her head. "I thought it might be best if you stowed these somewhere else besides the parlor." She bent toward him to whisper, "Luke and Fanny found them."

He felt relieved. "If you set them here, I'll put them away when we're done."

"Actually, I wanted to speak with you."

"Oh?" he hedged, watching her closely as she set down his saddlebags. She didn't appear angry or upset. If anything he thought she looked resigned. But was she feeling resigned in a good way or a bad way?

Ravena straightened, her hand moving to her apron pocket. He saw the edge of what appeared to be an envelope sticking out. Maybe she'd received some bad news. "Children, will you excuse me and Mr. Beckett, please?"

Mark and Jacob huffed. Even Ginny looked disappointed.

"We'll only be a few minutes," she said, her face full of understanding at their reluctance. Tex had a sudden desire to go with them. "You can keep carving your things on the porch."

Jacob was the first to comply. "All right. Come on, Ginny and Mark."

Once they'd exited the barn, Ravena turned toward Tex. She rubbed her lips together, a sure sign she was nervous. His trepidation began to multiply.

"Want a seat?" He gestured to the other stool and the overturned milk pails.

"No." She pulled the envelope from her pocket and fingered the front of it. The barn echoed with stillness before Ravena released a sigh. In the quiet, it sounded as loud as a gunshot. "I know about the money, Tex."

He blinked, unsure he'd heard her correctly. "What?"

"I know about the money."

Dread pulsed through him, thundering in his ears and squeezing his lungs. How had she learned about his stolen loot? Did she know he was the Texas Titan too? But if that was the case, why didn't she sound angrier? He feigned intense concentration on the woodcarving in his hand as he casually replied, "You do, huh?"

"Yes, I do." Ravena dropped onto the other stool. "Why didn't you tell me?"

He loosened his grip on the small knife, fearing if he gripped it any tighter it would slip and cut him. He kept his gaze leveled at the little bird. "I wasn't sure…"

"You let me think it was Tate who'd sent it. But it was you," she said, her tone contemplative. "Why didn't you tell me about the money sooner?"

Tex lifted his head, confusion pushing at his fear. "You mean the money I sent here, for you?"

The hint of a smile appeared on her lips—the very ones he'd wished to kiss last night. "Yes. What did you think I was talking about?"

He shrugged, going back to her earlier question. "I guess I wanted to remain anonymous awhile longer." He brushed flecks of wood from his creation. "How did you find out?"

She turned the envelope around, revealing his own handwriting on the front of it. "Luke and Fanny were playing in the parlor and they got into one of your saddlebags."

Had they taken his map? Knowing how much Quincy

wanted it, he was determined to keep it and protect it. Or maybe that was just plain stubbornness.

He ignored that last thought. "Did they pull things out?"

"They did. But I had them put everything back." She motioned to the saddlebags. "I still think it's best if you keep them out here."

"I'll do that."

She nodded, though she remained seated, her hesitation obvious.

"Is there something else you wanted to say?" If so, he wasn't sure he wanted to hear it.

"I think I understand now how you made your money all these years."

Her eyes were on the envelope in her hands, so she didn't see the color he felt draining from his face. Tex swallowed hard, feeling like there was a boulder in his throat and an anvil on his chest.

"And how is that?" He barely managed to push the words out his dry mouth. Maybe she had brought him his saddlebags so he could leave after all, despite what she'd told the children.

Ravena's gaze rose to his. "You've been searching for treasure. The kind the map in your bag leads to."

Tex choked back a startled laugh. This wasn't the answer he'd expected from her, though he felt strong relief that she didn't know the truth. Or at least all of it. In a way he *had* been searching for treasure all these years—but the treasure wasn't hidden, it just belonged to other people.

The easiest option would be for him to tell her that she was right. Treasure hunter was a far more acceptable occupation than thief. But Tex didn't want to lie to Ravena. Not after all she'd done for him and not when they'd become friends again. But what could he say without revealing too much?

"I didn't set out looking for that treasure map," he admitted. "I got it by chance, winning it in that poker game, along with the gold coin."

To his surprise, she climbed to her feet, signaling the conversation was nearing an end. "Is that what the map leads to? More of those coins?"

"Yes, silver ones too."

"Will you go search for them?" A shadow passed over her face as she added, "After you leave here, I mean."

Regarding her, standing there as regal as any queen could have been, Tex had the strangest desire to ask her to come with him when he left. She never would—she wouldn't leave these children. But he was beginning to see that the longer he stayed here, the harder it was going to be to say goodbye to her. He'd been too angry, at Tate and the world, and too afraid to come back to say goodbye to her last time, even if Ravena had deserved a proper farewell. Would he have the courage and the fortitude to say it this time and then ride away afterward?

He cleared his throat and busied himself with the wood. "I'd like to see where it leads to," he answered.

"I hope it leads you to what you're wanting, Tex." Her earlier resignation seeped into her tone, but he knew she was talking about far more than the map or its supposed treasure. She was talking about him, about them. His heart twisted painfully inside his chest. "I'll send the children back in for the rest of their lesson."

She moved toward the open barn doors, then turned back. "Thank you, Tex. For sending that money through the years. It's nice to know that you hadn't…well, hadn't forgotten us."

He forced himself to look from the unfinished carving to her beautiful face. "You're welcome. I hope it helped."

"It did."

Nodding acceptance of her gratitude, he made his mouth turn up in a crooked smile. "I'm glad to hear that." He couldn't maintain his joviality though when he added in a low voice, "And you're right. I didn't forget you."

He hadn't gone more than a few days at a time through the years without thinking of her. Without wondering what she was doing, if she was married, if she'd forgotten him. Perhaps that was the other reason he'd sent the money. Not just as a way to help her and to atone for his abandonment, but also as a way to ensure he entered her thoughts now and then, even if she didn't know for certain if the money came from him.

She shot him a grateful smile before she walked away, taking her warmth and light and goodness with her.

Hanging his head to his chest, Tex gulped in a breath of air. He ought to feel relief that she still didn't know about his outlaw career. But he didn't feel liberated or grateful. Instead he felt like a fraud, an imposter.

"I'm trying to make it right," he whispered, not even sure if he was attempting to say a prayer or not.

He'd helped with the planting and he'd accepted her challenge to finish the house and prove to himself he wasn't like his father. And yet, the more he settled in here, the more Tex knew what he was really proving—that his history as an outlaw and his life at the farm the last five weeks couldn't exist independent of each other forever. Sooner or later they would run together and Tex hated to think what the resulting consequence would be.

Ravena drove all of the children, with the exception of Jacob, to school the next day in the wagon, so she could post her letter to Miss Morley while in town. A slight drizzle began to fall as she headed back to the farm, but she refused to let it dampen her spirits. Tex would start on the house today.

On her return, she and Jacob headed to the fields to work, but by midafternoon, the rain had picked up, making it difficult to keep planting. Raindrops dripped off her hat and soaked her dress.

"We'll have to call it a day," she said to Jacob. The boy nodded, looking grateful. They maneuvered through the rivulets of water and mud back to the house where Tex met them on the porch.

"It's really coming down." He shook water from his jacket and removed his hat, revealing tussled brown hair. His slightly disheveled look and the grin he threw her brought the same blossom of attraction she'd felt yesterday, while talking to him in the barn. Especially when he'd told her that he hadn't forgotten her through the years. "I got in a little more framing before it started to pour." She'd showed Tex, before leaving with the children, her grandfather's plans for the house, and she was pleased to hear that he'd gotten right to work.

After taking off her own hat, Ravena squeezed water

from her long hair and did her best to squash any feelings beyond gratitude for Tex. "Hopefully it clears up by tomorrow."

"It likely will," Tex said with typical optimism as he and Jacob followed her inside.

But contrary to his prediction and Ravena's hopes, the rain didn't let up the following day or the one after that. When she woke to drops against her window for the third day in a row, Ravena decided to send Jacob back to school. There'd been little to keep him and Tex busy inside the house or barn and she had no idea when the rain would finally end.

With all of the children gone, though, and Tex working in the barn to make doors for the new house, a feeling of helplessness pressed in on her. She found herself constantly checking the window, and each time, her disappointment and desperation pricked anew at the steady fall of rain. She couldn't afford a delay, especially since she'd confidently declared in her letter to Miss Morley that everything was going to work out after all for her to bring the other orphans to the farm.

Ravena dished up lunch for her and Tex and set it on the table. Instead of going to the barn to call him inside, though, she slumped into a chair. If she let down the orphan boys, how was she supposed to fulfill her grandfather's wishes and earn his forgiveness?

The sound of the front door being opened caused her to hop up. She didn't need Tex witnessing any more of her weak moments.

"I thought I'd see if lunch was ready," he said as he entered the kitchen.

She nodded without turning around. "It is. I just need to cut some bread."

"Smells good." Tex came to stand near her at the sink to wash his hands. "It's still raining hard out there. Probably was a good thing you sent Jacob back to school."

"Yes." Her voice wobbled slightly, but she hoped Tex wouldn't notice.

She could feel his eyes on her as she placed a slice of bread on each of their plates. Returning to the side-board, she wrapped the rest of the loaf in a towel. "Shall we eat?" Ravena darted a glance at him and found him leaning against the sink, watching her.

"Mind telling me what's got you so glum first?"

"It's nothing," she said, looking away.

His soft chuckle surprised her. "I still know you, Ravena. Even after all these years."

Rather than bringing comfort, his remark prompted anger. "If you knew me, then you'd already know that I'm glum about the rain." She gestured with frustration at the window, then folded her arms. "It's ruining...all of my plans," she ended in a near whisper. Tears swam in her eyes at voicing her fear aloud and she lifted a hand to her mouth to keep from sobbing.

"It won't last forever," he said in a gentle tone. His hands framed her shoulders as he rubbed her arms beneath her sleeves, bringing welcome warmth. "The planting and the house will get done."

"But what if it doesn't..."

As he had after she'd sprained her ankle, Tex pulled her close and wrapped her in an embrace. Unlike the other week, though, Ravena hugged him back. It had been so long since she'd been cradled in his arms like this, and the familiarity of it felt both wonderful and frightening.

Tex wordlessly rubbed her back, his chin resting lightly against her head. His kindness and the absence of his usual teasing touched her deeply and seemed to open up her grief. The grief she'd only allowed herself to feel here and there since her grandfather's passing, in quiet moments when no one else could see.

"I miss him, Tex," she said, the realization spilling out in between shaky breaths and shuttering sobs. "I miss my grandfather so badly. He was supposed to stay. To be around for so much longer."

He stopped his rubbing and tightened his hold around her. "Of course you miss him. And I wish he'd stayed around much longer too."

"Then you understand why I have to fulfill his wish to bring those boys to live here, in our new house." She eased back enough to see his face. "And I can't have a new house if it keeps raining."

He brushed some hair away from her cheek. "You can't control the rain, Ravena. And we'll do our best to finish everything once it stops."

"But what if we don't succeed? What if those boys get sent away on the Orphan Train? I can't fail in this."

His brows rose in obvious confusion. "Why? Your grandfather would understand if something unpreventable stops you."

She glanced away, the desperation threatening to consume her again.

"Why can't you fail at this?" he repeated. His tone was unusually somber.

"Because…" Ravena dragged her gaze back to his. "It's the only way I know that he'll forgive me."

"Forgive you? For what?"

Swallowing hard, she pushed the truth from her lips, each word cutting deeply. "I was going to leave with you that night. I was going to turn my back on the farm and on my grandfather." Her voice hitched higher with emotion. "How could have I even considered that, Tex? After all that Grandfather did for me, for us." She freed one hand to wipe at her eyes. "That's why I have to do this. I have to make amends by fulfilling his last wishes. I have to show him that I'm still committed to what he wanted, to what he lived for, even if he's gone."

Tex frowned, but she wasn't sure which part he found most troubling. Or maybe it was all of it. "Ravena," he said, releasing her to arm's length, "your grandfather loved you. Do you believe that?"

She didn't hesitate to nod.

"That love wasn't contingent on your choices. He loved you unconditionally, just as you did him. Anyone could see that." His expression was more serious than she'd ever seen it before. "Do you feel like he held it over your head that you almost left?"

"No," she admitted.

"I didn't think so. And you know why?" He waited to go on until she shook her head. "I knew Ezra well enough to know, if there was anything to forgive, he did it a long time ago."

Hope rose inside her, pushing at her doubts and fears. "I want to believe that, but…"

His blue gaze softened as he led her to a chair at the

table. She sat as he pulled out another chair to perch on beside her. "I think I know what's tripping you up."

She couldn't help a chuckle. "You do, huh? And what is that?"

"It's something I've been wondering about during your Bible reading."

It was her turn to lift her eyebrows in question. He'd been joining them each Sunday night, but he hadn't spoken of anything they'd read since the night they'd discussed the parable of the prodigal son.

"What have you been thinking?" She was more than a little curious for his answer.

"Well, you've read a lot of stories about forgiveness, right?" He didn't wait for a reply. "Like the one about Jesus telling the disciples that they needed to forgive seventy times seven. Or the publican that asked God to forgive him with more humility than that Pharisee."

She nodded agreement.

"With all this talk about forgiveness, don't you think part of that is forgiving yourself?"

"Yes, of cour—" Ravena stopped talking when he threw a knowing smile. She'd walked right into his argument.

Tex spread his hands in an imploring gesture. "See? It's not your grandfather's forgiveness you need to seek, Ravena." His countenance grew solemn again as he added, "It's your own."

Was that true? She studied her hands where they lay in her lap. Her grandfather had loved her, of that she had no doubt, even after learning that she had planned to elope with Tex.

She knew Tex was right when he said that her grandfather would never have held a grudge, that he'd forgiven her in his heart right away. So why did she still feel guilty? *Does that mean it's myself I need to forgive, Lord?* A feeling of peace, similar to what she'd felt that first night she'd agreed to let Tex stay at the farm, washed through her now.

She might have been ready to leave, but she hadn't. After she knew Tex wouldn't be returning, she'd made a conscious choice to stay, to continue working the farm and helping her grandfather with the orphans. And she'd found much contentment in that. This wasn't just her grandparents' way of life; it was hers too.

"You're right." She lifted her chin.

That boyish grin she adored brightened his face. "Two words I don't often hear."

"I mean it. Thank you, Tex." Her hopelessness had lifted, replaced with peace and gratitude. Not only was Tex helping make this dream of hers and her grandfather's a reality, he'd also helped her understand herself better.

An intensity filled his eyes and made her heart pick up its rhythm. "You're welcome," he murmured.

Ravena forced herself to look away, afraid she'd see the same attraction she felt reflected in his gaze. And if she did, she might give in to her longing to cross the short space between them and kiss him—and not just on the jaw like last time.

"Our lunch will be cold," she said as she climbed to her feet. "I'll warm it up."

Tex would eventually leave again, she reminded herself, so there was no point in renewing their past relationship or pursuing her new, growing feelings for him. And yet, as she moved about the kitchen, she realized that argument was getting harder and harder to remember.

Chapter Eleven

Once the three days of rain finally ended, clear, dry weather followed—the perfect kind of weather for finishing a house. Tex went at the project with all of his energy. To his surprise, he found himself enjoying his time sawing, nailing and building. It felt good to be creating something. And though he planned to stick closely to Ezra's original vision for the house, Tex decided to implement a few of his own ideas into the construction. Like adding bay windows to the front and side of the structure.

After the planting was completed, Ravena made good on her offer to help him with the building whenever she could. Tex liked having her there as he worked, handing him nails or steadying boards, while they conversed. They talked about her grandfather, about the orphans who had come and gone over the years, about memories from their shared youth. The two subjects Tex noticed they both avoided were his eight-year absence and their past relationship.

Ravena wasn't the only one assisting him either.

Whenever the children weren't in school or doing chores, one or more of them would usually scramble up the ladder to see his progress and insist on "helping." They weren't exactly perfect assistants, but he appreciated their eager willingness, and the cheerful company they offered. Jacob, Ginny and Mark in particular had each taken turns working alongside him until late into the evening, after Ravena would bring them a lantern for light.

The days passed far more quickly as he immersed himself in building the house, and Tex found himself wishing they'd slow down. With every nail he pounded, he was fulfilling Ravena and Ezra's dream and bringing an end to his own.

A dream in which he was a needed part of a family. One in which he wasn't alone and running from the law or outmaneuvering angry cattle rustlers and vengeful sheriffs. One in which he could easily imagine he and Ravena together again, embracing the feelings stirring in his heart and reflected back at him in her dark brown eyes.

When there was less than a week left to complete the house, Tex decided to work late that Saturday night, even after Jacob, who'd been helping him, went to bed. A short while later he was surprised to hear footsteps on the staircase. He twisted on the ladder to see who it might be.

"Thought you'd be trying to sleep by now," he said when Ravena appeared, the lantern casting her shadow across the nearly completed walls.

"You too."

Tex pushed up his hat. "I wanted to keep going."

Crossing the room, Ravena peered out the window opening. "Is it possible the stars look even prettier from up here?"

He chuckled. "Maybe they do, or maybe you're just happy the house is almost done."

"Maybe." He sensed more than saw her smile.

"The house looks wonderful, Tex. Grandfather would say you have the woodworker's touch."

The compliment pleased him, not just because it came from Ravena, but also because he liked to think of having Ezra's approval.

"Do you want some help?" she asked as she walked over to the ladder.

Tex handed her the rusted tin of nails. "You can do what you usually do."

"Hand you nails and make conversation?"

Grinning, he accepted the nail she passed him. He loved her teasing. People might think Ravena serious and reserved, but he'd had the pleasure of seeing her playful, lighthearted side too.

"Don't forget looking pretty as a picture in the lantern light," he added before hammering the nail into place.

Her eyebrows shot up as she placed another nail in his palm. "Flattery will not get you another piece of pie."

Tex bowed his head in mock grief. "Can't blame a man for trying, especially when it comes to your pie."

"Ha. So you admit that remark was flattery?"

Draping his arm on the top rung of the ladder, he leaned toward her and lowered his voice. "Two things

I don't joke about—your cooking and how beautiful you are."

Ravena lowered her gaze, but not before Tex caught sight of the gratitude and affection shining there. It took every ounce of willpower for him to turn back to his hammering instead of climbing off the ladder, sweeping her into his arms and kissing her right then and there.

"Jacob's really taken to helping with the building," he said after clearing his throat.

She seemed to collect herself too, making him wonder if she might have accepted his kiss. "I think he's taken to having you around too."

Tex shrugged with nonchalance, but he was happy to hear her say so. Each of the children had wormed their way into his heart and he was grateful. He'd carry the memories he'd made here with them—and with Ravena—wherever he went.

"It's not just him. I think Luke still wants to bring you to school to show the class," Ravena added with a soft laugh. How he loved that sound. "And Mark has stopped saying *ain't* because according to him 'Mr. Beckett doesn't say that.'"

He had noticed the boy slipping the word in less and less. "Is that bad?"

"Bad?" she echoed with a look of surprise. "Not at all. You managed to cure him of the habit in no time."

"They admire you too." Tex positioned the next board into place.

A low sigh escaped her lips. "I hope so. I love them dearly and I'm thrilled to bring another four orphans here. But…"

He hammered the board on one side, then the other. "But?" he prompted when she didn't finish.

"Sometimes I wonder if that's enough." Her expression clouded in the lantern's light. "Now that Grandfather is gone, I worry that they need more than just me to love and care for them."

Guilt rose in him as he climbed down the ladder and positioned it farther down the unfinished wall. He hadn't considered settling down, at least not for the last eight years. But if he were to stay, Ravena wouldn't be on her own and the children would have more than one adult around who cared about them.

"You could marry," he said as much to fill the silence as to see if there was anyone she favored. No suitors had come to the house during his time here, but he didn't know if there were any young men at church vying for her attention.

"That's not funny, Tex." Her tone implied frustration and a twinge of hurt.

He paused with his boot on the lowest rung of the ladder. "It wasn't meant to be." If Ravena wanted to marry, to give her heart to another, he couldn't stop her. And if it would make her and the children happy, well, then he wanted that too. Even if the thought of her falling in love with someone else brought a hard ache to his chest. "You're beautiful and strong, Ravena. Any man would be blessed to call you his wife."

His heartfelt words were met with more uncomfortable quiet. He took the nail she offered him and concentrated on nailing the next board in place. Maybe he'd said too much, but she needed to know he wouldn't hold her to any past promises. And he couldn't be the man to marry her either, though everything in him wished he could.

"I don't plan on marrying." Her answer came out hardly louder than a whisper. "Not anymore."

"Does that mean there are no robust, handsome young men at church?" he asked, trying to avoid the pain her declaration inspired.

Ravena laughed, but it held none of the softness and merriment it had earlier. "Oh there are."

When she didn't continue, he found himself frowning hard at the plank of wood he steadied with his hand. "No one worthy enough to be your suitor?"

"If I only wanted robust and handsome, then yes, they'd be fine." She shook the can of nails, then extracted another for him. "But I want trust and commitment and faith and laughter. I want what my parents and my grandparents had."

Tex kept his mouth shut, uncertain what to say in reply. He could offer her laughter; and he believed that he'd improved in the trust and commitment areas too. But Ravena didn't want someone exhibiting those characteristics for a short time—she wanted them permanently and consistently from the person she married.

"What about you? Do you plan to marry?" Her question took him by surprise, though it shouldn't have. He'd been pushing into her personal matters and opening himself up to her doing the same.

He feigned a casual grin and shook his head. "Naw. I think Tate had it right." He reached out for another nail. "A girl deserves better than being saddled with me."

Instead of agreeing, Ravena squared her shoulders

and fell back a step, holding the nails out of reach. "He wasn't right, Tex. Then or now. Any girl would be proud to have you as a husband. You're smart and capable. And when you set your mind to something, you don't do it by half—you work and work until it's completed. You're optimistic too and kind and have a knack with the children."

Tex lowered his arm and tried not to gape at her. After all the pain he'd brought her, after all the promises he'd broken, how could she defend him? The answer slipped quietly and without fanfare into his mind—she still cared about him.

Stepping down off the ladder, he took a step toward her. Words he'd been thinking for days crowded his head and clamored up his throat. He'd tell her how much he still cared for her and how coming here had been a blessing. He'd tell her how the fact that he was even thinking of anything in his life in terms of blessings was due to her and her beautiful gift of forgiveness and kindness toward him. He'd tell her he'd realized the other day that he was falling in love with her all over again.

But before he could give voice to any of it, she extended a nail to him and asked, "What about the girls you met during your travels? Weren't any of them worthy sweethearts?"

The inquiries slammed into him like a plank to the skull. It jerked him back to reality and away from the futile hopes he'd given too much thought to lately. He couldn't let himself forget that he was an outlaw, temporarily hiding out, not looking for a way to settle down and marry the woman he'd once—and still—loved.

Taking the nail from her, he mumbled "Thanks" and climbed back up the ladder. "I was never in one place long enough," he offered by way of a response, "to come to know anyone that well."

"I imagine there were still a number of broken hearts because of it."

Her tone wasn't condemning, only matter-of-fact. Tex hadn't meant to break any hearts, especially not Ravena's. There'd been a couple girls he'd liked through the years, but his conversations with each and the few innocent kisses they'd shared had left him feeling empty. And always had him thinking of Ravena afterward.

He finished nailing the board, but his heart was no longer in the work tonight. "I think I'll head to bed."

If she was surprised, Ravena didn't say. She simply nodded and set down the can of nails. Picking up the lantern, he followed her from the room, down the stairs and outside to the old house. She reached the porch first and opened the screen door.

"Ravena, wait." He might not be free to share everything he was holding inside, but there was one thing he could tell her—one thing she needed to know. She turned back, her expression unreadable. "There were a few girls I may have liked, but none of them ever took your place." He forged ahead, even as he saw her eyes widen. "I might not have been here in person, but my thoughts…and my heart…never left."

She didn't speak for a long moment, then she stepped toward him. "I suppose the opposite is true for me. I was here…but my heart was with you, even when I didn't know where that was."

He swallowed hard, fighting the longing to either hold her and never let go…or take off for good. "I'm sorry, Ravena. So very sorry." He didn't expound, but he figured she knew exactly what he meant.

"I know. And I'm grateful for that."

She slipped inside, the screen clicking shut behind her. If she'd lingered she might have heard Tex whisper his first real prayer in years. "Help me not break her heart again, Lord," he said, glancing up at the stars. "Help me see things through with the new house. And then, please, watch over her for me."

It dawned on him the next morning that this would likely be his last Sunday with Ravena and the children. The new house needed to be completed before the week was out, so she and Jacob could travel to Boise to bring back the other four orphans before they left on the train. After that, Tex had no reason to stay.

The thought depressed him more than he would have expected. As he shaved and dressed, an idea of how to spend the morning came to mind. It would involve risk, but then again, so had his entire stay on the farm. And if it meant seeing Ravena and the children's faces light up with enthusiasm, then it would be worth it.

He entered the kitchen after everyone else and took his customary seat across the table from Ravena and between Ginny and Fanny. After the blessing on the food, he heaped his plate high with eggs, bacon and pancakes and waited for Fanny to ask him her typical question. But the girl seemed more interested in her breakfast than sticking to her usual Sunday routine.

Jacob and Mark were arguing over who could eat more bacon, and Luke was performing a one-man musical number with his knife and fork, though Ravena kept asking him to desist.

Taking a drink, Tex set down his cup and turned toward the little girl. "Anything you want to ask me this morning, Fanny?"

Her face scrunched in thought. "Did you know I named one of the kitties Mr. Tex?"

He chuckled. "No, I hadn't heard that. But thank you. I'm thrilled to have a four-legged creature named after me." She giggled behind her hand. "Any other questions for me?"

"Um…are you going to marry Miss Ravena?"

Tex wasn't sure who felt more discomfort at that question—him or Ravena. She choked on her breakfast and threw him a pained look, while he shifted uneasily in his seat.

"Fanny, we discussed this the other day," Ravena said with obviously forced patience. "Mr. Beckett is still here because he's helping to finish the new house so we can have four new brothers. That is all."

"Okay," Fanny huffed.

This wasn't going at all how Tex had envisioned. Clearing his throat, he tried again. "The question I'm thinking of," he said, tapping her nose with the handle of his fork, "is one you've asked me every Sunday for weeks."

She frowned in concentration, then her expression brightened. "Will you come to church with us, Mr. Beckett?"

There it was. He feigned a contemplative demeanor,

noting that Jacob and Mark were no longer arguing and Luke had stopped tapping on his plate. Twisting in his seat to face her directly, he grinned. "Yes, Miss Fanny. I would be most honored to accompany you to church."

"Hurray! You're coming." Fanny clapped her hands, her eyes all a sparkle.

Tex looked to Ravena next. Her wide gaze held his, her mouth slightly open in evident shock. Then she smiled, full and sincere, and he felt as if there were no one else in the room but the two of them.

The children, including Ginny, all began talking to him at once, pulling him back to reality and the crowded kitchen. "All right, children." Ravena's voice rose over the happy chaos. "Finish your breakfast and then all of you need to get ready for church."

Now that he'd stated his plan, Tex's gut began churning with apprehension. It had been years since he'd stepped inside a church. Would the preacher call him out? Would someone recognize him as the Texas Titan? He swallowed the bite in his mouth and set down his fork, no longer feeling famished.

He still managed to smile and make conversation, but he was relieved when the meal finally ended and the children hopped up from their chairs. Following them to the sink, he set his dishes on the sideboard. The sooner he got church over and done with, the better.

"Do you have a suit?" Ravena asked him.

Tex glanced down at his regular work shirt and trousers and shook his head. A suit wasn't something he'd considered either. "Guess I might be underdressed."

"Not necessarily." Her dark brown eyes were lit with

warmth. "But I can get you one of Grandfather's suits if you'd like to wear it."

Would he? There didn't seem any good reason to refuse the offer. The rest of them would be dressing in nicer clothes and maybe he'd feel less conspicuous if he did the same. "I'll take it. Thanks."

Ravena's expression brightened, making him grateful he'd accepted. "I'll fetch it from the attic."

"Come on, boys," Ravena called up the stairs to Mark and Luke. "We don't want to be late." Especially today when Tex had agreed to accompany them to church. She couldn't believe it, though she was more than happy at the sudden change to his usual Sunday plans.

Mark and Luke scrambled down the stairs and out the front door. Ravena followed at a more leisurely pace. She'd put on her best dress, a maroon one with a dozen buttons down the bodice, and had taken extra time with her hair, even curling the strands around her face with the curling tongs.

Outside, she found the children already seated in the back of the wagon. Her gaze went to Tex, where he stood chatting with Jacob and Fanny. He looked incredibly handsome in her grandfather's suit, his hair dampened with water and free of his usual hat. There were likely to be a number of girls at church who would be paying far less attention to the pastor and far more to Tex.

"Ready to go?" he asked as he turned in her direction.

Ravena nodded. When she reached the wagon, he offered her his hand to climb up. "You look lovely, Ravena," he murmured, his blue eyes surprisingly void of teasing. "But then, some things never change."

His compliment prompted a shy smile from her. "You look rather dashing yourself."

He chuckled and handed her up onto the seat. In a few moments, he was seated next to her and guiding the horses away from the house. Ravena couldn't help sneaking glances at him as they turned onto the road and headed for town—just to make sure she wasn't dreaming.

Having Tex seated close beside her and the children happily talking in the back felt natural. She could easily imagine this being her life every Sunday.

Except Tex was leaving.

She wanted to ignore that fact, to shove it to the back of her mind, as she'd been able to do for a short time while they'd been talking last night. When he'd told her on the porch that he had left his heart with her, she had let herself believe for a moment that the future held more than another painful goodbye for them. And yet, the fear of trusting him fully had stopped her from kissing him or allowing herself to believe he might still care as much as he once had for her.

"You're quiet," Tex said, nudging her lightly with his shoulder. "Are you wishing I'd stayed behind?"

Gathering her courage, Ravena linked her arm with his. "Not at all. I'm glad you came, Tex. Truly."

The grin he threw her warmed her more thoroughly than the summer sunshine. She resolved to simply enjoy the day. There would be time enough for tears and farewells later in the week. In this moment, though, she would choose to be content with what she had right now.

* * *

Tex's heart resembled a kicking mule as he ducked into the church behind Ravena and the children. Despite the open windows, the main room felt stifling. He stuck a finger between his collar and his throat, desperate for more air. But he lowered his hand and pasted on a false smile when Ravena shot him a questioning look.

He followed them into a middle pew and took a seat. The children separated him from Ravena, and for a brief moment, he wished he were sitting right next to her as he had on the wagon. He would slip his hand into hers and relish the brightness of her smile and the way her dress enhanced the color of her cheeks. Or maybe that was the effect of his compliment earlier.

Tex found himself smiling with sincerity at the thought. She'd practically robbed him of breath when he'd turned around and seen her standing there in her Sunday finery, wisps of dark hair curling around her face.

The church began to fill, pulling Tex's attention to the other members of the congregation—and back to his underlying fears of being recognized as the Texas Titan. He bounced his leg in apprehension, especially when he noticed several familiar faces among the older people entering the church. Too bad he hadn't opted to wear his hat, then he wouldn't feel so visible and unprotected. Of course it wasn't like Quincy would be looking for him here, but he still felt vulnerable.

The children seemed to be whispering something to each other before Ginny, who was seated next to him, motioned for him to lean down. "Miss Ravena wonders if you can stop shaking the bench," she whispered in his ear.

Too late Tex realized his leg had been bouncing faster and faster. He stopped fidgeting and threw Ravena a chagrinned look, then whispered back to Ginny, "I will." He watched with amusement as his message passed from one child to the next until Fanny loudly proclaimed it to Ravena and anyone else listening.

"Thank you," Ravena mouthed, her lips tugging upward.

He tipped his head in acknowledgment, even as he began drumming his fingers on the arm of the pew. If he made it through the entire service without someone shouting out who he was, he'd be as wrung out as a dry rag.

The services began, but Tex could hardly concentrate. He didn't know the words of the opening hymn, though it did sound familiar. Instead of singing along, he took the opportunity to glance about him again. A man a few rows back stared hard at him. When Tex looked away, he found a woman and her daughter watching him carefully too. Panic rose like bile in his throat and he swallowed it back.

By the time the young-looking pastor rose to address the congregation, Tex was ready to bolt for the door. This hadn't been a wise idea after all. Even if no one connected him with his outlaw persona, he was dreading the questions he would likely be asked at the conclusion of the meeting by anyone who recognized him as the rebellious son of the late Mrs. Beckett. He might have voiced a prayer last night, but that didn't mean he was ready to be in church again.

Ginny tugged on his sleeve and he bent a second time to hear what she had to say. "Miss Ravena wants to know, are you all right, Mr. Beckett?"

Tex glanced at Ravena, who looked mildly concerned. Apparently he hadn't hidden his discomfort well. "I'm fine," he murmured back to Ginny who passed the message back up the line of children.

When Ravena heard it from Fanny, she lifted her chin and offered Tex an encouraging smile. The sight of it helped calm his nerves a little. He was here and he would try to make the best of it. Settling back against the hard pew, he stared at a knot in the bench in front of them and tried to focus on the pastor's sermon.

"'For God hath not given us the spirit of fear,'" the man read in a quiet but firm voice, "'but of power, and of love, and of a sound mind.'"

The words jolted through Tex like lightning in a dry storm and he snapped his head up. Did the pastor suspect who Tex was? He expected to find the religious man watching him, but the pastor was still reading from the Bible.

The spirit of fear. If Tex were truly honest with himself—and where better to be than in church—fear had underscored his life for years. He'd left angry, yes, but also afraid. Afraid that Tate was right about him, afraid Ravena would regret having ever loved him, afraid he would turn out exactly like his father. Fear had dogged every heist he'd committed and kept him far from home.

For the first time in eight years, he saw his actions clearly. Not as the adventurous, carefree ones he'd believed them to be but choices born of deep-seated fear—

that Tex Beckett wasn't enough. Not for his father, his brother or the girl he'd loved.

The truth heated his face and he tugged at his tight collar again. Had he chosen a path all those years ago that led him to become someone who *did* seem good enough, glamorous enough, exciting enough? The Texas Titan was famous, larger-than-life, bold. But Tex Beckett? He was a disappointment to his friends and family, to himself and to God.

Wasn't he?

The verse said fear didn't come from God. Then did that mean, his fears weren't from God either? That maybe they weren't rooted in reality like he'd believed for so long?

He darted a look at Ravena, who was earnestly listening. Tex still felt regret and guilt for the way he'd left and for not writing. But regrets hadn't been the whole of their relationship. He could recall the love he'd once given her and received in return. His mother had also loved him unconditionally and her death had affected him deeply. She'd been the only one, besides Ravena, who could see past his mistakes and stubbornness to see *him*.

God hath not given us the spirit of fear, but...of love.

He had known that love in the past. And not just his mother's love or Ravena's love. He suddenly recalled a day, after his father had abandoned them, when he'd been crying by the Reids' stream. His father had promised to take him and Tate fishing before he'd left. Ezra had come along right then with two fishing poles. Tex dried his tears and had a nice afternoon fishing with Ravena's grandfather.

When they'd finished, he asked Ezra if Ravena had told him where Tex was and how he'd wanted to fish. But the older man shook his head.

"Ravena didn't say anything to me, son." He bent down so he was level with Tex and put his hand on his shoulder. "And she isn't the only one to know what you needed today. God knew what you needed, Tex."

"How so?" he'd asked, skeptical.

Ezra smiled. "Because I was headed back out to the fields after lunch when I had a distinct thought to go back and get two fishing poles and get myself quick to the stream. I did and here you were."

Then Ravena's grandfather had told Tex something he thought he'd always remember. "God knows you, Tex. And no matter what happens in your life or where you go, He isn't going to abandon you. He'll be right there always, but you've got to do your part, and let Him in. He won't force you to come."

A feeling of warmth and happiness spread through Tex's chest at the memory. He'd felt loved and good enough that afternoon after realizing God knew exactly what a young boy had been hoping for that day.

The spirit of power, and love, and of a sound mind. He'd once possessed those qualities, even in the midst of the hardest and saddest times of his life. But somewhere along the way, he'd let fear have greater and greater sway inside his mind and heart.

The notes of the closing hymn penetrated his thoughts. Tex glanced around him, embarrassed he hadn't realized the service was over. He listened to the words and to Ravena's beautiful singing voice before bowing his head for the benediction.

Feeling far less dread than he had when he'd entered the building, he exited ahead of Ravena and the children. He shook the pastor's hand, introducing himself as Ravena's newest hired hand. It was the simplest explanation, especially for someone who didn't know their history. The man was polite to him, but the pastor lit up with animation when Ravena expressed what a lovely sermon it had been. Was the preacher one of the possible suitors Ravena had alluded to last night?

Frowning, Tex waited beside her as the man continued talking. When she finally stepped away, Tex found himself placing his hand lightly on the small of her back as he guided her toward the wagon. He was stopped a minute later by the man who'd been staring at him during the service. Tex's heartbeat resumed its wild hammering.

Instead of calling him out as an outlaw, though, the man asked if Tex was Tate Beckett. Tex explained that he wasn't; he was Tate's twin brother. The stranger went on to introduce himself as the one who'd bought the Beckett farm, who Tex had briefly met when he'd gone looking for Tate weeks ago.

When they'd finished chatting about the farm, the woman who'd also been watching Tex in church approached him next, along with her daughter. She told Tex that she'd been a good friend of his mother's. Tex fielded her questions about Tate with vague answers, though he sensed only friendly curiosity in the woman's demeanor. And hearing someone talk fondly about his mother brought happy memories to mind.

A few others spoke to him as well, so by the time

he and Ravena reached the wagon, the children were already waiting.

"Let's go, Mr. Beckett," Mark said, hopping up at the sight of them. "I'm starved." He gripped his tummy in exaggerated fashion.

Tex couldn't blame him; he was starved too after eating so little breakfast.

"You're rather popular." Ravena smiled at him as he settled onto the wagon seat beside her. He nodded acknowledgement, though deep down he'd been surprised at how nice it was to be recognized as himself and not as the Texas Titan. "Did you enjoy the sermon?" she asked.

"Not half as much as the pastor enjoyed talking to you about it."

Her cheeks turned pink, making him grin. "I don't know what you're talking about. He was merely being polite."

"More so to you than to anyone else."

"Are you jealous, Tex?"

"It was nice sermon," he said, facing forward and dodging her question.

Her laughter floated out across the fields of growing crops and distant hills. "I think you answered both questions with that response."

He shrugged and shot her a lazy grin. But she was right. He had felt a mite jealous and he had enjoyed the sermon, at least the part he'd heard. His thoughts circled back to those realizations he'd had during the service.

Was Ezra still right—about God knowing Tex and not abandoning him? He wasn't sure he knew the answer, not yet. But he planned to figure it out. After all, he was nothing but determined when he wanted to be.

And if he came to the same conclusion he had that day by the stream, then he had some big decisions to make.

Glancing at Ravena, who had turned to say something to the children, he couldn't help thinking that coming to church had been more than worth it. And he had Ravena and the children to thank for that. They'd come to trust him during his time here. Now he just needed to figure out if he was brave enough to trust himself, and more important, to trust Someone far greater.

Chapter Twelve

"Miss Ravena, Miss Ravena!"

Small hands pushed at her shoulder, but she didn't want to wake. *Just a few more minutes of sleep.* She'd stayed up far later than usual to help Tex finish plastering the inside walls of the new house and then she'd rested on the floor for a moment...

Ravena sat up in confusion. How had she come to be in her bed inside her room? Luke and Fanny each grabbed one of her hands and began tugging her forward.

"You gotta come see," Luke said.

She allowed them to pull her up and out of bed. She still wore her work dress from yesterday and there were splotches of plaster on her hands. "What is it?" she asked, yawning. "Have you had breakfast?"

"Mr. Beckett made us eggs," Fanny announced proudly.

"But that isn't what you gotta see." Luke released her hand to rush toward the door, motioning for her and Fanny to follow.

Ravena brushed out some of the tangles in her hair with her free hand. "What am I coming to see, Fanny?"

The little girl shook her head and grinned. "It's a surprise. That's what Mr. Beckett said."

I'm sure he did, Ravena thought ruefully as she and Fanny headed down the stairs and out onto the porch. Luke kept his lead ahead of them.

The man of surprises met them as she and Fanny started across the yard. "Morning," Tex called, his expression every bit as excited as the children's. Ravena wondered what time he'd fallen onto the parlor sofa to sleep.

"Good morning. I heard you made breakfast." She'd slept later than she had in years, judging by the sunlight and it felt rather wonderful. "Thank you," she added, sincerely.

His blue eyes seemed even brighter today. "You're welcome. We saved you some, but first I need you to come with me. There's something you need to see before the children go to school."

"All right. Is it something in the new house?"

"It is the—"

Luke's words were cut off when Tex good-naturedly clapped a hand over the boy's mouth. "You'll see." He released Luke with a knowing smile, then turned to Ravena. "Your eyes need to be closed, though."

She lifted an eyebrow at him. "Closed?"

Coming around behind her, he settled one hand over her eyes and cradled her to his side with the other. "Is she peeking, Fanny?"

The girl giggled. "No, Mr. Beckett."

"Good," he said near Ravena's ear. "Now just walk

slowly in the direction of the new house. I promise not to let you trip or run into anything."

His nearness and the low quality of his voice made her pulse speed up, even as she began moving in tandem with his measured footsteps.

"Do you know how I came to be in my room last night?" she asked as they shuffled along. "The last thing I remember was taking a short rest on the floor."

Tex's chuckle stroked her cheek. "After that *short rest*, I couldn't rouse you. So I carried you to your room."

The realization she'd unknowingly been in his arms caused her to blush. But it wasn't out of embarrassment alone. Ravena wished she'd been awake. She very much enjoyed being carried by him. "When did you go to sleep?"

There was a pause as if he were trying to remember. "My pocket watch indicated it was three o'clock."

"Three o'clock?" She stumbled in her surprise, but true to his word, Tex steadied her. "If you were up in time to make breakfast, that means you've only had a few hours of sleep."

"Ravena," he said huskily, causing the skin by her ear to tingle, "I'll be fine. But you have a long journey ahead of you today to bring those four boys here."

"Yes. If the house is done."

Tex stopped her. "Let's go see. We're going up the steps now." She allowed him to guide her onto the porch, away from the sun's early morning rays and into the new house. The children were talking and moving about nearby.

"Can I see it now?" she asked with as much exasperation as excitement.

His warm laughter washed over her. "A mite impatient, aren't we?"

"Tex!"

"All right. All right." She could hear his grin. "On the count of three," he directed the children. A chorus of voices counted, "One...two...three."

"Welcome to your new home, Ravena," he said, an unmistakable note of tenderness in his voice, as he removed his hand from over her eyes.

Ravena blinked, then her gaze went to the white plastered walls of what would be their new, larger parlor and to the children standing there, all eagerly watching her reaction. "It's absolutely beautiful. Just as Grandfather would have wanted."

Mark let out a whoop and the children scattered, some toward the kitchen and others upstairs.

"You finished the rest of the plastering yourself?" She turned to look at Tex.

He shrugged, but she could see his pleasure at her astonishment. "After everyone's help yesterday, there wasn't much left to do." He extended his hand to her. "Want to see the upstairs?"

Nodding, she slipped her hand into his and felt a moment's wish that things could remain just as they were right now. Tex led her up the stairs and into each of the six, large bedrooms that would be for the children. Mark and Luke had already claimed theirs.

"The glass still needs to be picked up and placed in all of the windows," Tex explained as they walked down the hall to the seventh and final bedroom. Her grandfather had ordered and paid for all of the window glass, but it was still sitting at the mercantile in town. "The outside walls need to be whitewashed, and the indoor plumbing put in by someone who knows how. But once the furniture is all moved over from the old house, it'll be livable."

Ravena shook her head. "I can't believe it's practically done."

Pushing open the last door, he released her to let her move past him into what would be her bedroom. This room hadn't been whitewashed before she'd fallen asleep.

"It looks amazing…" Her compliment faded to silence when she caught sight of something sitting on the windowsill that hadn't been there the night before. "What's this?" she asked, crossing the room. Ravena picked up the object and realized it was the bird she'd seen Tex carving several weeks earlier.

She ran her fingertip over the tiny carved feathers of the wings. "Tex, this is incredible."

"It's a raven." He walked over and stopped in front of her.

Lifting her chin, she gazed up at him, her heart resuming its earlier rapidity. He knew the story of how her parents had come to name her "Ravena" because of her raven-black hair. But was there more behind his choosing this creature to carve? "Why a raven? Why not a different bird?"

"Because a different bird doesn't remind me of you." The intensity in his blue eyes made it more and more difficult to draw a full breath.

"I remind you of a bird?" she countered, half teasing. If she kept things light, as Tex usually did, then she wouldn't have to acknowledge the emotion his closeness or his gift inspired. Emotion she wasn't sure she wanted to examine—not when he was leaving for good tomorrow.

His half smile seemed to suggest he knew what she was doing. "I've always thought of you whenever I see a raven." His fingers brushed wisps of her hair from her cheek, warming it as surely as the blush she felt there. "They remind me of your black hair and eyes." He softly ran his thumb over her right eyelid. "They remind me of your compassion and loyalty too. Like in the story with Elijah when the ravens bring him food and help save his life."

Tex cupped her face between his hands then, his fingers tangling in her hair. "How many times have you saved my life, Ravena—or given me something worth living for? First when we were kids and my father left. Then when my mother died. And again when I came back here, shot and bleeding." He cleared his throat as his expression grew more somber, almost pleading. "Why do you keep saving me?" The last question hardly made a sound in the empty room.

Tears filled her throat and pressed hard behind her eyes, but Ravena willed them back. "Because you are worth saving, Tex Beckett."

His gaze widened in surprise before dropping to her lips. Ravena held her breath. He was going to kiss her, for certain this time. Closing her eyes, she only had to wait a fraction of a second before Tex's lips touched hers. The familiarity of his kiss filled her with the happiness of a thousand shared memories. And yet the newness of kissing him now, after all these years, sparked fresh delight and anticipation as if she were a girl of sixteen all over again.

Resting her hand on his shirt, Ravena kissed him back. And in that moment, the heartaches of the past and the uncertainty of their future fell away, forgotten. What mattered was Tex was still here and she was here and kissing him again felt like the most natural, most wonderful thing in the world.

He eased back after a minute or two, his eyes searching hers. "Ask me to stay longer, Ravena."

"What?" she asked with a startled laugh.

"I don't have to leave tomorrow. I can stay and help you, after you bring those boys back. I can even stay until harvest time."

Shaking her head, she tried to make sense of his words. "But you said you couldn't stay. You had to go. You've already proven you're not your father, Tex. You don't have to prove anything else to anyone."

His thumbs caressed her face. "I wouldn't stay to prove something." He pressed his forehead to hers. "I'd stay because I want to."

She didn't quite dare believe his declaration. "But…"

"I'll stay in the old house or in the room off the barn, if that will make it more proper and ward off any gossip."

Sharp hope beat in time with her heart, making her feel lightheaded. Did he really mean what he was saying? "What made you change your mind?" She needed to know, to have everything laid out.

Tex lowered his hands to her shoulders. "You helped

change my mind all these weeks I've been here. And something the pastor said on Sunday helped too."

"Ah. The infamous pastor." She shot him a smile, thinking again how thrilling it had been when she'd realized Tex was a little jealous of the other man's perceived attentions toward her.

He kissed her quickly. "Yes, that pastor." His demeanor grew serious again. "I'm done making choices out of fear. And I'm done running. I want to stay put."

Ravena wet her lips, feeling her own fears creeping in. Could she fully trust him to keep his word this time? And if she could, did she want to remain just friends?

She knew the answer at once. Given more time, she knew she'd want more from their relationship than friendship. But Tex had to want that too. His kisses today were evidence that he might wish for something deeper, and more permanent, between them, but he might change his mind again in another few months.

"What happens with us?" She hated the feeling of vulnerability that came with asking such a question, and yet, she wanted no more surprises. She'd lived with his abrupt disappearance from her life once before; she wouldn't willingly go through that a second time.

Tex regarded her without a trace of amusement or teasing. "I want to be in your life, Ravena. Now and always. If all you're willing to offer is friendship right now, then I'll take that and wait. But you need to know, I'm holding out for more than that." His earnestness was palpable. "I foolishly chose to let you go once. I don't want to do that again."

"You promise?" She could hardly believe he'd voiced the words she'd hoped for so long to hear from him.

"I promise." His firm answer echoed in the room.

She peered deeply into his blue eyes, wanting so badly to trust him again. The sounds of the children playing outside floated up and through the window opening. It was time for them to go to school and for her and Jacob to head to Boise. "All right," she said with a nod. "I accept your offer to stay."

It was Tex's turn to look taken aback. "You do?"

Letting her smile break through, she nodded. "Yes, Tex. I trust you to keep your word this time." She glanced down at the smooth floorboards, feeling suddenly shy. "And if you're willing to wait and stay in the old house once we move into this one, I'd like to see if we could be more than friends too."

He clasped her to him and swung her around, making her laugh. She hadn't felt this lighthearted in ages. "You'd better go," he said when he set her back on her feet. "So you can reach Boise by this evening."

"Will you be all right here?" she asked. He'd already agreed to watch over the other four children and the farm during her two-day absence.

Tex grasped her hand and brought it to his lips. "We'll be fine. Ginny can help me with the cooking, and the boys can help with the chores."

"And Fanny?" she prompted with a smile.

"Fanny can tag along and entertain us with the kittens."

When they reached the stairs, she stopped him, his lovely bird carving still clutched inside her hand. "Thank you, Tex. For finishing the house and for being here so I can go get the others."

His eyes softened right before he pressed another lingering kiss to her lips. "I'm glad it all worked out."

And so was she. As she trailed him down the stairs, she couldn't help offering a quick prayer that things would continue to work out—for the orphans, for the farm and, most of all, for her and Tex.

After seeing Ravena and Jacob off, Tex completed the morning chores, checked on the fields and saddled Brutus to ride into town. He wanted to have as much of the remaining projects on the new house completed as he could before Ravena returned the following evening. Not having a wagon posed a problem, but he would try to find someone willing to cart the window glass back to the farm. He was no longer afraid of someone recognizing him, not after the warm welcome he'd received while attending church.

The bright sunlight, shining down on him as he rode, suited his jovial mood. Today the surrounding hills, farms and fields struck him as beautiful in their familiarity. It was time to hang up his hat, so to speak. Because there was no other place on earth he wanted to be right now than here, with Ravena.

Recalling their kisses earlier, he smiled foolishly at himself. He had to admit he'd wanted to kiss her ever since his first night at the farm when he'd woken up and found her compassionately rebandaging his wound.

And now he was here to stay. Hopefully he could convince her that he'd already fallen in love with her a second time. But for now he'd accept her friendship and the adoration that frequently filled her dark eyes when she gazed at him, until Ravena was ready…to be his wife. He grinned, his chest expanding with the possibility. That's what he wanted, more than anything. To marry her, to be a father to these children, and to stay put.

You can't change that before coming here you were an outlaw. Tex frowned at the intrusive thought. Eventually he'd need to tell Ravena the truth about his past, but he could wait. He'd first let her see that he meant what he'd said about staying indefinitely. His outlawing days were over. No more heists, no more running, no more loneliness.

But his mind refused to let go of the familiar rut of self-denigration. Why did he think he deserved Ravena? *You're still a worthless no-account, who up and left everyone.* The voice in his head sounded exactly like his father's, the words echoing ones Tex himself had often said about the man.

Except he wasn't a worthless no-account. Wasn't he worth saving, as Ravena had declared, worth loving?

And if he was, then the same was true for his father.

The simple but powerful realization struck Tex so hard he stopped Brutus in the middle of the road. Thinking the worst about his father had only made it easier for him to think the worst about himself. They'd both made mistakes—big, painful mistakes. But he wanted to believe those mistakes didn't make them worth less. And chances were, that's what his father had wanted to believe about himself too.

"I'm sorry, Pa," he whispered to the cloudless blue sky. He didn't know if his father was dead or alive, but somehow voicing the words aloud eased the resentment he'd been holding on to for twenty years. "And most important, for me, I forgive you."

He nudged his horse forward again, but he couldn't maintain their earlier languid pace. Kneeing Brutus into a gallop, Tex let out a shout of joy. He felt less burdened than he ever had in his life. And he couldn't wait to tell Ravena about it, after he surprised her with a completely finished house. His life had taken a new direction, had a new purpose now, and he couldn't wait to see how it all unfolded.

Chapter Thirteen

The horses made good time to Boise, which meant it was midafternoon when Ravena and Jacob arrived. Though this wasn't her first trip to the city, Ravena still marveled at the bustle of people and the tall buildings. She considered stopping at a hotel first before going to the orphanage, but she wanted Miss Morley to know they'd arrived.

She drove to the orphanage and parked the wagon out front. "I'll be right back," Ravena told Jacob. "I just want her to know we made it."

Hurrying up the walk, she didn't try to quell the excitement bursting through her. They'd done it—they'd completed enough of the house to bring these boys to the farm, just as her grandfather had wished. She knocked on the door. Small faces pressed up against the windows on either side and made her smile.

The door opened to reveal a young woman near Ravena's own age. "May I help you?"

"Yes, I'm here to see Miss Morley." Best to start there before she went in search of the brothers. Ravena looked past her to see a number of children watching them. Were any of these the boys she'd come to claim?

The other girl offered an apologetic smile. "I'm sorry, but Miss Morley isn't here. She's at the train station."

It took a moment for her words to register. "The train station? Why is she there?"

"The Orphan Train arrived today."

Ravena fell back a step, panic squelching her anticipation. "But it wasn't supposed to come until tomorrow."

"Miss Morley wasn't expecting it either. She only just got the orphans readied who are leaving. Shall I tell her you stopped by, Miss…"

Spinning on her heel, Ravena hurried back down the walk. "I'll find her there," she called back.

"What happened?" Jacob asked as she scrambled onto the wagon seat. "You look awfully white, Miss Ravena."

She slapped the reins and guided the horses up the street. "We may be too late. The Orphan Train arrived a day early."

"That's not good."

"No, it's not good at all."

The train depot seemed to teem with people, causing further alarm inside Ravena. Would she find Miss Morley and the boys before the train departed? Handing the reins to Jacob, she hopped to the ground. "Park the wagon, then come find me. I'll see if I can spot them."

She didn't wait for Jacob's reply. Instead she began pressing her way through the crowd. She had a vague memory of what Miss Morley looked like—tall, gray bun, kind green eyes.

Ravena frantically searched the faces of those around her. "Miss Morley?" she finally called out in desperation. "Miss Morley?"

Up ahead a woman turned and lifted a gloved hand. Relief flooded through Ravena and she rushed forward.

"Miss Reid," the woman said in an equally pleased tone. "I'm so glad you made it. The train came early and we weren't prepared. I would have sent a telegram, but I wasn't sure one would reach you in time."

Ravena clutched the woman's arm. "It's all right. I'm here now." She paused to let her racing heart slow to normal rhythm. "Have they boarded the train yet?"

"No," Miss Morley said with a smile. She stepped back, revealing four solemn-looking boys, each with light brown hair. "Miss Reid, may I introduce Edmund, Felix, Winston and Ralph Wight."

"I'm Ralphey," the youngest boy declared with a scowl.

From their correspondence, Ravena already knew their ages—13, 10, 7 and 5. "Hello, boys. I'm so happy to meet you." She crouched down beside Ralphey. "How would you boys like to come live with me and five other orphans on my farm?"

The eldest glanced at Miss Morley. "Would that mean we wouldn't have to go on the Orphan Train? That we can stay all together?"

"That's right, Edmund." The woman placed her hand on the boy's shoulder. "I wanted to tell you of this alternate plan sooner, but I felt I should wait until Miss Reid's arrival before getting your hopes up."

Ravena stood, already loving the little ragtag group.

"So what do you say? Would you all like to come live with me?"

Edmund eyed his three brothers, and something unspoken passed between the four of them. "Yes, Miss Reid." He turned to face her, his young face finally breaking into a smile. "We'd like that."

Ravena blew out the breath she'd been holding. "Excellent. Now, let's see about your luggage."

"It's over there, near that bench." Miss Morley waved toward one wall of the train station. "One of our older orphans has been minding everyone's suitcases."

With Miss Morley leading the way through the crowd, Ravena fell into line behind Felix. Jacob appeared at her elbow a moment later. "Did you find them?" he asked, his face hopeful.

"Yes." She put her arm around him, feeling giddy. "They're collecting their things now. Come meet them." He followed behind her as she made her way to the designated bench.

Ravena introduced Jacob to the boys. Then as the four brothers set about extracting their suitcases and saying their farewells, she let her gaze wander to the different advertisements and Wanted posters hung on the nearby wall. She casually perused them, until a familiar face met her eyes.

It was Tex, staring back at her from one of the posters.

Certain she was imagining things, she took a step closer. Why would Tex's face be on a Wanted poster? Ravena read the boldface type, and with each word, shock squeezed harder and harder at her lungs and her stomach rolled with nausea.

Wanted: Dead or Alive. The Dangerous Outlaw Known as The Texas Titan. A rather large cash reward was listed, along with a description of the man's crimes— train and bank robberies—and his physical appearance. Not only was it Tex's face, but the mention of blue eyes, brown hair and height measurements fit too.

Ravena lifted her hand to her mouth, certain she was going to be sick. Maybe it was a mistake. Maybe someone else happened to look like Tex. It could even be Tate, she told herself. But she dismissed the thought at once. Tate becoming an outlaw was as likely as chickens learning to fly. Tex, on the other hand—charismatic, adventure-seeking Tex—well, it wasn't out of the realm of possibilities.

"Are you familiar with the Texas Titan, ma'am?"

Lowering her hand, she glanced up to find a heavyset man with a gray beard standing close and watching her shrewdly.

"I…um…" She couldn't seem to speak past the disbelief clogging her throat. Did she know this outlaw? Had she been harboring a Wanted fugitive on her farm? Her head felt heavy and her skin clammy, despite the heat of the summer sun. She feared she might faint.

If the older gentleman noticed, he didn't comment on her visible uneasiness. Instead he went on talking. "He's a wily one. Wanted for train and bank robberies all throughout Texas."

Texas? The dizziness in her head increased. Tex had talked about traveling throughout Texas.

"He robbed a train back in April in Utah Territory too. Took off with six thousand dollars before holing up for a few weeks. Then he headed to Casper, Wyoming."

The amount of money was staggering, making her think of what Tex had in his saddlebags. He'd never said exactly where that money had come from. Perhaps it wasn't from treasure hunting as she'd suspected but from something nefarious.

"That's where he got shot more than two months ago," the man continued. "Some think he died from the wound, but no one found his body."

Ravena swayed before splaying a hand against the wall, below the poster, to keep herself from falling to her knees. The Texas Titan had been shot, just as Tex had been. There were too many similarities to ignore.

"Hey," she heard Jacob say from behind her. "Isn't that Tex—"

His sudden interest snapped Ravena from her fragile, lightheaded state. "Time to go," she said, latching onto Jacob's shoulder and turning him away from the incriminating poster. "Boys, come along."

She felt the stranger's gaze boring into her back as she embraced Miss Morley and herded the brothers after Jacob. Even when they'd reached the wagon and climbed aboard, she couldn't shake the man's words from her mind or those she'd read on the poster. She drove in a daze back toward the center of the city, hardly mindful of what Jacob and the other boys were saying.

A part of her wanted to drive straight back to the farm and demand that Tex tell her the truth about his life the past eight years. Then maybe he would take her into his arms and assure her that the Wanted poster wasn't real; it was all a horrible mistake. Because he wasn't an outlaw, running from the law. He was Tex, the man she'd come to love all over again, the man she'd asked to stay, in hopes of making a life together.

But the other part of her, growing more insistent by the moment, already knew what her mind refused to accept. And for that reason, she would stick to her original plan. She and the children would stay in Boise overnight and return to the farm tomorrow. There was no reason to rush home and hear the horrible confirmation all the sooner.

Her mind made up, exhaustion settled into her bones, making her want to crawl in the back of the wagon and sleep for days. When she awoke, maybe this would all be a horrible nightmare.

Otherwise, Ravena realized as she stopped the wagon in front of the hotel, she was in real danger of having her heart and her trust broken once more. And this time she didn't know if she could weather the damage.

Tex kept wandering into the parlor in the new house and peering through the pristine glass of the front window to look at the road. It was coming on evening, which meant Ravena, Jacob and the other orphans should be arriving any time. The chores had all been completed early, and he and Ginny had done their best to make a nice supper. Fanny had even insisted Tex help tie her hair up in her best ribbon. Mark and Luke had grown restless, as time stretched on and no wagon had appeared, so he'd sent them out to find flowers for the table.

The new house had seen a flurry of activity the last two days. Tex had procured the glass and fitted it into all of the windows. He'd also traded in his gold coin for cash, in order to hire a man to install the indoor pump in the kitchen. Then he and the children had white-washed the outside of the house. There were places where it had gone on too thick or too thin, but he suspected Ravena wouldn't mind. He'd also rallied some of the neighbors to help move the furniture from one house to the other. He'd even gotten a donation of two old bedframes and mattresses that he put in two of the bedrooms for the new boys.

Now everything was ready. He couldn't wait to see Ravena. She'd only been gone two days, but Tex had missed her, terribly. He missed talking with her, making her laugh or simply watching her. He also wanted to tell her the epiphany he'd had about himself and his father the day before.

"Are they here yet?" Fanny asked, coming into the parlor. She slipped her hand into Tex's and looked up at him with hopeful eyes.

He gently squeezed her fingers. "Not yet, but they should be here soon." When she didn't release his hand, Tex found himself wondering how he could have ever contemplated leaving. Everything good in his life was right here. This is where he wanted to be—permanently.

Movement out the window pulled his attention to the yard. "There they are," he declared, his heartbeat kicking up with relief and excitement. What would Ravena think of all they'd done?

He led Fanny to the door, calling to Ginny to come outside too. Mark and Luke reappeared, wilted flowers in hand, and raced to the wagon as Ravena stopped it in front of the new house. He was already watching her, drinking in the sight of her as if she'd been gone two weeks instead of two days, so he didn't miss seeing the furrow in her brow. Something was bothering her. Or perhaps she was simply tired from the long drive.

The four boys in the back of the wagon piled out. Hopping to the ground, Jacob grinned and strode toward Tex. "We barely made it yesterday," he announced. "The train came early, and we had to go to the station to pick them up."

Perhaps that was the reason for Ravena's troubled expression. "It's a blessing you went when you did then."

Ravena circled the wagon, her face brightening when Fanny raced forward to give her a hug. "Meet your new brothers." She introduced the four boys to the other children, then holding Fanny's hand, she approached Tex.

"Hi there." He offered her a smile, which she didn't return. "Long journey?"

She gave a wordless nod.

He kept hoping she'd notice the glass in the windows or the whitewash, but she seemed not only exhausted but distracted too. "We made supper. Ginny and me."

The older girl beamed.

"Smells good," Ravena murmured as she ascended the porch steps of the new house.

"That's not all we did, right?" He winked at Fanny. When Ravena didn't ask what he meant, he decided to just share the news anyway. "The children helped me whitewash the house. I got all the glass put in the windows, and a pump installed."

"We moved all the furniture too," Mark added.

A look of surprise crossed Ravena's face and her lips turned up into a half smile. "Look at that." She stepped back to look at the outer walls and the windows. "It's looks terrific. Thank you, children." Her gaze flicked to his, an unreadable emotion in her dark brown eyes. "And thank you, Tex. You've done far more than I could've hoped."

Why did it sound as if she were saying goodbye? He shrugged it off as part of her weariness and coming so close to losing the chance to take in the four new boys.

"Who's starved?" he called out. Clamors of agreement filled the air as he led the group inside and into the dining room.

Supper was a noisy affair, now that their numbers had increased by four. But Tex welcomed the cacophony. It filled the strained quiet between him and Ravena. He could tell something was on her mind; he just couldn't reason what.

Once everyone had eaten and the dishes were washed, Ravena trooped upstairs with the children to show the newcomers their bedrooms. Tex remained below stairs, unsure if she would welcome his help or not. It was one thing to put five orphans to bed, but it was another to settle down nine. When he heard an excessive amount of laughter coming from what he thought was one of the boys' rooms, he decided to go investigate.

Mark, Luke, Ralphey and Winston were in the middle of a pillow fight. Snagging one of the feathery weapons for himself, Tex got in a few jabs of his own before being overwhelmed by the pack. He was trapped beneath them, laughing, when Ravena appeared at the door. For a moment her expression looked pained as she took in the scene, then she straightened her shoulders and gently told the boys it was time for bed.

After another reminder from Tex, the new boys headed to their room, while Mark and Luke hopped into their beds. Tex took the lamp in hand and bid them good-night. Hearing them call "Good night" back made him smile and filled him with the same contentment he'd felt earlier while holding Fanny's little hand.

The other doors were shut by then, so he guessed the rest of the children were in bed for the night too. He went downstairs, but he couldn't find Ravena in the parlor or the kitchen. Had she gone straight to bed without talking to him? Disappointment wound through him as he blew out the lamp and crossed the yard to the old house.

In the dying light, he caught sight of Ravena rocking back and forth in the old rocker. He grinned, grateful to know she hadn't avoided him after all. "I meant to bring that over to the new house," he said as he neared the porch. "I can do it tonight, if you'd like."

"No, it's all right."

Tex settled on the step, against the porch column. "The new boys seem to fit right in."

"Yes." He heard her soft sigh. "I'm glad."

"Something wrong?"

For a long moment, the only sound was the creak of the rocker moving back and forth, back and forth. "I saw a rather interesting bit of literature at the train station."

"Hmm. What was it?"

The rocker's creaks came faster. "It was a poster."

The underlying sharpness in her tone set off a warning bell inside his head, but he still couldn't reason out what she was referring to. "What sort of poster?"

Silence reverberated through his ears. She'd stopped rocking. "It was a Wanted poster, Tex."

He couldn't breathe for a second as his mind grappled to understand the full weight of her words. A single thought penetrated his paralyzed confusion. *She knows.* Then his chest seemed to cave in on itself and he gulped for breath.

"How long have you been the Texas Titan?"

The question lanced through his heart and he hung his head. "Eight years."

"I see." The rocker resumed its frenetic movement. "And where did the money in your saddlebag really come from?"

It pained him to the core to hear the hurt and anger in her voice. He wanted to crawl in a hole somewhere and hide. But he wouldn't. Now that she knew, he'd face the consequences. He'd told her and himself that he was done running—and he meant it. "It's from my last robbery in Utah Territory."

"I thought you took six thousand dollars from that train," she accused. "There certainly isn't that much in your bag."

Had the Wanted posters detailed his last robbery? "It's only a handful of it, yes. The rest I hid. Like I did with the other money."

"Have you ever killed anyone?" He could hear the fear beneath her fury.

"No, Ravena. I never killed anyone." He eyed her, but the shadows obscured her expression. "I'm not a murderer. You know that."

She stopped rocking again, and when she spoke, the anguish in her words felt like a knife in his side. "I don't know what I know about you anymore. You're an out-law, Tex." Her voice broke. "An outlaw who was hurt and running from the law when you came to my door-step. Did you steal that gold coin and map too? Is that really how you came to have those?"

Twisting to face her, he shook his head, even if he wasn't sure she could see him. "I won those in a poker game, just like I said. It was the only time I ever gam-bled."

"No, it's not."

Frustration bloomed inside him, despite his efforts to keep it at bay. "I'm telling you the truth, Ravena. I only gambled once."

"No, Tex." He thought he saw her lean forward as if too full of hurt to sit up anymore. "Every time you robbed a bank or a train you were gambling. Not with money but with your life."

The truthfulness of her statement rendered him speechless and renewed the guilt he'd been free of the last few weeks.

"Am I right?" she pressed.

He swallowed hard as all the insecurities of the past roared to life inside him once more. "Yes," he whis-pered.

"You could've been killed." There was no mistak-ing the tears in her voice. "What I can't understand is *why*? Why did you do it, Tex? Why did you come back?" The inquiries rose on a wail. "Why have you stayed?"

Everything in him urged him to go to her, to comfort her. But she wouldn't want that. So he forced himself to stay seated. "I made a choice, Ravena. A really bad choice." His mind sorted back through the years to the moment he'd stood, gun in hand, waiting for that first bank clerk to fill his sack with cash. "After my fight with Tate over that keepsake, I convinced myself that I was already a thief, so why not continue down that path?"

The only interruption to his story was the sound of her quiet weeping. "After that, it got easier and easier to justify." He paused, wishing he could stop there, but it was time Ravena knew everything. "I came back here because I was shot and running. But it wasn't just from the law. The cattle rustler I beat in that poker game wanted his treasure map back. So he tipped off the sheriff in Casper. He was waiting for me when I went to the bank the next morning."

He studied his shadowed hands, remembering how they'd been covered with blood after being shot. "I was there to exchange that coin for cash to send you." A soft cry sounded from the direction of the rocker, though he wasn't sure if it was in indignation or understanding. Was she angry to learn that his other contributions had come from stolen funds? "The sheriff found me and managed to get off a good shot as I was riding away. I figured the only safe place to go, where no one would have heard about the Texas Titan, was here."

She remained silent, so he forged ahead to answer her final question.

"As for why I've stayed," he repeated. He rested his head back on the porch column and shut his eyes, feeling suddenly more tired than he could ever remember. "I wasn't planning to. At first I stayed because I truly wanted to help you, whether you believe me or not. Then I stayed to finish the house because I wanted to prove I wasn't my father. And now…"

Should he tell her what he felt in his heart? Would it even matter? His earlier hopes and satisfaction felt like a distant memory, as did the words and kisses they'd shared yesterday morning.

"And now?" she echoed.

Tex steeled himself for her rejection as he opened his eyes. "I want to stay now because…because I've fallen in love with you all over again, Ravena."

For a moment he wondered if she'd heard him when silence met his declaration. Then she spoke, her voice strangled. "What am I supposed to do after hearing that?" He thought he saw her wave her hand in an arc. "With hearing all of this?"

"I can't tell you that. You've got to decide what you want, for yourself." He rose to his feet. "I'm sorry for not telling you the day I came. I was afraid you'd throw me out, but it was wrong of me to keep my past from you." He pulled in a breath, feeling a familiar weight of guilt resting on his chest. However, he felt certain it wouldn't crush him this time and that was something to be grateful for. "I'm done with outlawing, whether you agree to let me stay now or not. I'm done with deceit and hating my father. I'm done blaming him and Tate for my mess and for my choices. Most of all, I'd like to be done loathing myself."

He moved toward the door, and Ravena let him go. He hated leaving her out here, grieving, but they each had to do their own sorting of things. It was time he learned for himself if he was really worth saving and loving. And there was only one way, One person, who could help him figure that out.

Chapter Fourteen

Breakfast was a silent affair, at least between him and Ravena. But Tex didn't think any of the children noticed. Jacob, Ginny, Mark, Luke and Fanny were excited to introduce the new boys at school. And the four brothers seemed equally happy at the prospect of already knowing friends there. There was also considerable talk about the upcoming Fourth of July celebration in town and how there'd be no school that day.

Ravena announced before they'd finished eating that she would drive the children to school in the wagon, so she could introduce the newcomers to the teacher. Tex couldn't help wondering if her motive had as much to do with talking to the schoolteacher as it did with avoiding him.

Once everyone had left, he decided to make himself a lunch, that way he wouldn't need to come back to the house until late afternoon. It would give Ravena the space she clearly desired to think things through. Setting out for the day, he headed to the fields first for a look at the tender crop plants, then he went about fixing a hole he'd discovered in one of the barbed wire fences.

He was more than tired and famished when lunchtime rolled around. Looking around for a spot in the shade, he found himself heading in the direction of the stream. The trees provided a welcome respite from the hot sun as Tex sat to eat. With no one to talk to, his meal was devoured in no time. But he wasn't ready to head back out into the heat just yet.

Picking up a rock, he lobbed it into the stream, thinking again about Ezra finding him here and how they'd fished. *God knows you, Tex. And no matter what happens in your life or where you go, He isn't going to abandon you.*

If that was still true, then he needed to do some praying. "It's just You and me here, Lord." The words fell from his mouth, almost without conscious thought. "So I guess I'd better start talking."

He removed his hat and set it on the ground before bowing his head, his hands clasped loosely around his raised knees. "I've made a lot of foolish choices. Choices that have really hurt the people I love." The pain he'd sensed in Ravena last night washed over him again, bitter and all-consuming. "I've run and hid and done bad things, Lord. But I want to change." His voice cracked with emotion. "I need to change, if for no one else but myself."

His head dropped lower to his chest as Tex kept praying. "I've apologized to Ravena and tried to make amends. I've apologized to my father too, and someday, I hope to do the same with Tate. Which means there's just one more apology to make right now. And that's to You, Lord."

Memories of all his heists paraded through his mind and increased the weightiness inside his chest. "I'm so sorry." His shoulders began to shake as tears slid down his face. "I'm sorry for every wrong thing I did after leaving here and for all the wrong things I did before that. I'm sorry for abandoning Ravena and Tate. I'm sorry for blaming my choices on my brother and my father. On everyone but myself." He pulled in a great, shaky breath. "Please forgive me, Lord."

Tex let the tears run their course, though he kept his eyes shut tight. After a few minutes, he opened them to stare unseeing at the stream. He might not feel drastically different, but he did feel lighter and less burdened.

You need to forgive yourself too. The thought came unbidden and quiet, sounding more like his mother's voice this time, and Tex felt the truthful power in it. Could he forgive himself? Could he let go of his self-loathing over his mistakes?

"I want to, Lord," he whispered. "But I've got to know that I matter enough to forgive myself."

He stayed there, oblivious to time, as he searched his heart and thought back over his misdeeds. This time, though, they didn't bring the same intensity of pain. He still felt sorrow but not the old unshakable ache. And beneath the grief, he felt something he hadn't for years—maybe not since he'd sat here talking to Ezra as a boy. He felt peace. A warm yet solid peace that rose above his regret.

He *was* worth saving. A grin lifted one side of Tex's mouth. He was worth saving and loving, not because

Ravena or his mother believed him to be but because he and God believed it.

Scrubbing his hands over his face, he let out a grateful chuckle. Ezra had been right about God not abandoning him, and now Tex knew it too.

"There's just one thing left to do, Lord." And it would likely prove to be the hardest. "Help me know how to make things right."

He knew from his long-ago days in church and listening to his mother share her faith that it wouldn't be enough to simply give up being an outlaw. To make things fully right, he had to restore what he'd taken. But how?

Ruminating on that, he climbed to his feet. He'd figure out a way to make all that he could right again. In the meantime, he'd wait for Ravena's answer as to whether he could stay or not. Even not knowing her answer though, it wasn't worry or pain that filled him as he headed back out to the fields. It was hope. And that was something he hadn't dared believe he could ever feel again.

Ravena returned from the school to an empty house. With more space now, the rooms seemed to echo with greater silence than they had in her old home. Thankfully there was no sign of Tex. She needed to think, to make a decision, and she couldn't do that with him close by.

Lunchtime came and went without him making an appearance. Had he left, in spite of what he'd promised? She went to the barn and found Brutus still inside his stall. She didn't know if she felt relieved or disappointed by that fact. If Tex had up and left again, then she wouldn't have to decide if she wanted him to stay or not.

She tried to occupy her mind by throwing herself into her regular chores around the house and yard, but she couldn't concentrate. When she'd gone outside for the second time and couldn't remember what she planned to do, she gave in to the physical and emotional exhaustion pressing down on her. She trudged upstairs to lie down on her bed. Perhaps a nap would help.

Sleep wasn't any easier to find than her focus had been. Her thoughts swirled endlessly, always coming back to land on the moment when Tex had confirmed he was the Texas Titan. Touching her cheeks, Ravena realized she'd begun to cry. She covered her face in her pillow and sobbed out all the grief, anger and pain of the last two days.

She wasn't sure she could live with Tex nearby. And yet, she couldn't imagine her life without him now. The tears slowed as she drove a fist into the pillow. Her heart felt as if it were splitting in two all over again—just as it had the night he'd left her behind.

She'd foolishly given him her trust again, only to learn he was an outlaw. How could she have been so deceived? Should she not have trusted him after all?

The answer to her latter question wasn't hard to find. Deep down, beneath the pain and anger, she felt the quiet, insistent truth. She'd trusted Tex a second time because he'd earned that trust throughout his time at the farm. Helping with the planting and the house, interacting with each of the children, listening to their Bible reading and coming to church for what she suspected was the first time in years. All of those things together, however small, had engendered her trust in him bit by bit, until she'd been ready to have him stay for good. To consider sharing a future with him as his wife.

Lifting her face, she stared at the windowsill where she'd placed the raven he'd carved for her. The beautiful gift reminded her of their conversation from the other day. She'd told Tex he was worth saving and she'd meant it. But did the same hold true for him now that she'd discovered he was an outlaw?

Ravena rose from the bed to pick up the intricately carved bird. Her fingers trailed the smooth head and beak. There was no mistaking the care and love that had gone into creating the gift. Sliding to the floor, she rested her head against the windowsill. The sparkling new glass was another evidence of Tex's kindness.

She'd forgiven him once already, for not coming back for her that night. Could she forgive his choices during his eight-year absence? Especially in light of his consistent, heartfelt actions since his return?

"Can I, Lord?" she whispered.

She sat still, searching her heart. Slowly and quietly, the peace she'd felt Tex's first night here began to grow and expand inside her. Forgiveness was the very thing she'd been hoping for from her grandfather and from herself. How then could she expect to gain it if she couldn't give it back?

Tex was the same person he'd been two days ago. And while she didn't condone his past actions, she could see, that outlaw or not, he was still of worth. Just as she was, even after almost leaving her grandfather and her home.

Hopping up, Ravena dabbed at her wet cheeks with her apron. Like the bird she still grasped in her hand, she had a gift for Tex. The gift of her complete forgiveness…and her love. And she couldn't wait another minute to find and tell him.

She found him patching one of the fences. As she drew closer, he must have sensed her presence because he rose to his feet. He didn't say anything as she approached, but Ravena could see there was something different about him. He was still as handsome as ever, his face as dear, and yet, there was an attitude of hope about him that she'd never seen before.

"The fence looks good," she said, stopping several feet away from him. Why did she suddenly feel shy?

He nodded. "I'm almost done."

Grasping the bird tighter within her fingers, she forced her gaze to meet his. "I've been doing some thinking. And some praying."

"Me too."

"You've been praying?" she half teased. She could believe he'd been thinking. Praying? Not so much.

A crooked smile lifted one corner of his mouth. "Yes, ma'am. Took almost my whole lunch doing so."

His affirmative answer and attractive smile set her heart pumping faster. "And what did you conclude?"

"I'd like you to go first."

"All right." She took in a full breath and exhaled slowly. "I wished you'd told me that first day about being an outlaw. And I hope you are sincere about giving it up forever." When he dipped his head in acquiescence, she gathered her courage to continue. "I can't say I understand your choices, Tex, but I do forgive you. Completely. I've realized I can't forgive myself for my mistakes and not forgive you for yours."

He took a hesitant step toward her, then another. "You mean that?"

"Yes." She tilted her chin upward to show her determination. "With all of my heart."

Grinning, he covered the last couple feet between them and gathered her to his chest. Ravena wound her arms around his waist, grateful to hear the sound of his heart thumping beneath his shirt. He might have been lost to her so many times over the years, but here he was, alive and at peace. And right here is where she wanted him to stay.

"Tex?" she murmured. He placed a kiss to her hairline. "I'd like you to stay, just like we decided before I went to Boise."

Instead of whooping with happiness or embracing her tighter as she'd expected, she felt him tense.

Alarm poked at her earlier relief and resolve. "Don't you want to stay?" she asked, easing back to see his face.

He glanced away, but not before she caught sight of the anguish in his blue eyes.

"What is it?"

Stepping back, he threaded his fingers with hers and rubbed his other hand over his jaw. "I can't stay, Ravena. At least not now."

His words made no sense. "I don't understand." She shook her head, her dread growing and knotting in her middle. "You said you'd prayed." Surely they'd come to the same answer.

"I've got to turn myself in."

The shock of his declaration had her dropping her mouth open, but no words came out.

"It's the only way I know to make things right." He hurried on as if he expected her to argue. If she'd been able to speak, she might have. "I sought the Lord's forgiveness and my own. But that's only partway to a change of heart. Setting things right is the other part. And I realized this afternoon that means I need to do the right thing by turning myself in."

"But you could go to prison," she said, finding her voice again. He'd asked to stay and she'd agreed, and now he was going to leave? "Isn't it making things right to stop? To never steal again?" Even as the question left her lips, Ravena knew deep down that it wasn't.

Tex reached out and caressed her cheek. "I'd hoped so, but I know differently now. If I stay, I'll never truly be free of the guilt because I won't have done all in my power to change. Can you see that?"

Lowering her chin, she gave a nod. His explanation, however painful, rang true. In spite of herself, she loved him even more for this proof that he really had changed, that he wasn't going to run from his responsibilities anymore.

"I don't want to leave you, Ravena. Especially not now." He lifted her face and she peered up at him through tear-filled eyes. The way he tenderly regarded her made her want to kiss him firmly but also weep. "I don't know what will happen after I turn myself in, but I promise you, I'll come back. It may be two years or twenty. But if you're still here and free, I'll come back."

"Then I'll be waiting."

He pressed his lips to hers in a firm kiss that filled her with as much resolution as it did sorrow. Unlike last time, he wouldn't be leaving without biding her goodbye or giving her a parting kiss. And yet this time, it would be even harder to let him go. Because today there were no secrets, no guilt, no resentment between them. There was only deep affection and a tenacious hope for the future.

Twisting in his saddle, Tex raised his hand in a final wave of farewell to the ten people standing around the porch of the new house. He wouldn't forget how they all looked in this moment—Ravena hugging the porch column as if for support; Jacob, Mark and Luke appearing sad but stoic; Fanny and Ginny brushing tears from their faces; and the four new boys looking disappointed. Similar feelings of regret and disappointment filled him head to toe.

Somehow he managed to look away, to nudge Brutus forward. Supper had been a glum event after he'd announced to the children that he would be leaving. Ravena had asked him earlier if he'd stay through Sunday and the Fourth of July, but he'd declined. Better to leave now while he was still resolved to do so.

Kissing Ravena's cheek just now, squeezing the shoulders of the boys, and embracing the girls hadn't made his determination to turn himself in any easier. His only solace came in knowing he was doing the right thing. Besides, he hadn't left without a proper goodbye this time, and when he returned one day, he would be a free man.

The ride to town didn't take nearly long enough. Before he knew it, Tex was climbing off his horse in front of the jail. He tied Brutus to the hitching post and hefted his saddlebags. His grief returned as he rubbed the horse's nose for a final time. He'd thought about giving the animal to Ravena, but knowing he'd bought the horse with stolen money, he'd changed his mind. The sheriff could decide what to do with Brutus after he locked Tex up.

"See you later, boy."

Heaving a sigh, he stepped onto the boardwalk and to the jail's main door. His heart kicked double-time within his chest. Inside he found the sheriff himself on duty behind a tidy desk.

"Howdy," the man said, eyeing Tex with curiosity from beneath his hat. White-blond hair poked out from under the brim. He looked to be about Tex's own age. "Can I help you?"

Tex lowered his saddlebags into the one available chair. "Yes, sir. I'm here to turn myself in."

The sheriff's face registered surprise before he chuckled. "That so? What would be your crimes, stranger?"

"Bank robberies, train robberies." Tex shrugged. "I'm an outlaw. Or rather, I was. Pretty famous too, though not so much in these parts."

"An outlaw, huh?" The man's expression changed from incredulity to wariness as he slowly rose to his feet, one hand moving to the gun in his holster. "And which one might you be?"

Tex leveled a serious look at the sheriff. It was the last time he hoped to ever identify himself with the infamous name again. "I'm the Texas Titan."

Chapter Fifteen

"Can we have some pie now, Miss Ravena?" Mark asked, the expectation on his face mirroring that of the other boys.

"Not yet. We ought to let the rest of our lunch settle first." Plus she wanted to draw out the Fourth of July festivities. That way they wouldn't have to return too soon to the house, a house now devoid of Tex.

Mark frowned, then cheered when Jacob announced, "Let's go play some ball."

All seven boys scrambled to their feet and headed off to where a game of baseball had begun amongst some of the other children gathered for the celebration. Ravena smiled after them, but the merriment fell from her lips a moment later.

Try as she might she couldn't enjoy the day. Her thoughts were on Tex, as they'd been since he'd left.

Was he in the town jail? With the holiday, she'd guessed they might not move him to the state penitentiary yet. But the not knowing weighed as heavily on her mind as his welfare did. Was he sweltering in a cell? Was he being fed?

"You're thinking about Mr. Beckett, aren't you?" Ginny's soft voice nudged into her troubled reverie.

Ravena reached out and clasped the girl's hand. "Yes, I am."

"I miss him," Fanny said, laying her head on Ravena's lap. "Will he ever come back?"

"I hope so, Fanny."

Blinking moisture from her eyes, she glanced around at the crowds of people, some seated on blankets as they were, others standing or wandering about. The entire town had turned out for the picnic, and the speeches and music would begin soon.

Her gaze stopped on a gentleman watching the baseball game. She didn't think she'd seen him before at church or in town. And yet he seemed vaguely familiar. As Ravena watched, the man turned to his companion, giving her a clear view of his face.

She sucked in a sharp breath as remembrance flooded through her, along with sudden suspicion. This was the same man who'd questioned her about the Texas Titan at the train depot in Boise. But what in the world was he doing here?

The man stopped talking to his friend and returned his attention to the game, but after a moment, Ravena realized he was watching Jacob. Did he recognize the older boy as having been with her that day?

Alarm pulsed through her, making her shiver even in the hot sun. Something wasn't right. How had the man come to be here, in the very town where she lived? In the very place Tex had been hiding? They hadn't told the children about Tex's past, or his real reason for leaving. If this man spoke to Jacob, the boy wouldn't know to keep quiet about Tex.

Rising to her knees and dislodging Fanny, she began packing the picnic basket as quickly as her shaking hands would allow. "Ginny, would you please go get the boys? It's time to go."

"But what about the music?" Fanny said with a pout. "And the pie?"

"We'll eat the pie at home. Now help me pack, please."

Ginny obediently stood and headed toward the baseball game, while Fanny reluctantly helped gather up their things. Ravena had everything ready when the boys came trooping up, obvious disappointment on most of their expressions.

"Do we have to go?" Edmund asked.

She gave a decisive nod. "Yes. I'll explain later." Though what she'd say, she wasn't sure. She only knew that she needed to leave before the man with the gray beard saw her. Or worse, began asking any of them questions.

To her relief, the children tagged along behind her as she walked to where she'd parked the wagon. She put her things in the back and climbed onto the seat.

As she clucked to the horses, she glanced back at the field to find the stranger from the depot staring right at her. "Let's go," she called to the team, desperate to pick up their pace, especially when the man and his companion began jogging toward them.

* * *

Tex lifted his head from staring at the stone floor of his cell as the jail door opened. A new arrival was a welcome diversion from the warm temperature and the lack of anything to do. Sheriff Clipton's young deputy entered the building, a plate of pie in one hand and a piece of paper in the other.

"That my pie, Jenkins?" the sheriff asked. His hands were linked behind his head and his boots rested on his desk.

The deputy nodded as he set the plate on the desk's edge. "Appears somebody's been looking for you, Beckett."

Confused, Tex stood up from the cot and crossed to the cell bars. "What do you mean?"

"The man claims he's a bounty hunter. He gave me this." The deputy lifted the paper in the air. It was a Wanted poster. Not surprisingly Tex's own face stared back at him. "Asked me if I'd seen you."

The sheriff had started in on the pie. "What'd you say?" It was the same question burning in Tex's mind at that moment. Especially given that he hadn't expected anyone to be looking for him way out here.

Jenkins shrugged. "Said I might have seen the man in question. Something struck me as odd about this fellow. He wouldn't look me in the eye or agree to come back here to talk to you, sheriff, about his search." He studied the poster in his hand, then glanced back up at Tex. "I acted like I was done talking to him, but I kept my eye on him."

"Good thinking, Jenkins," the sheriff said around a mouthful of dessert.

"He wandered around for a bit, but then he seemed real interested in Miss Reid."

Tex felt his heart constrict at the mention of Ravena. He'd thought of little else the past two days. He'd already confessed to Sheriff Clipton and Jenkins that he'd been staying with her and that they were lifelong friends—though he had emphasized that she'd had no idea about his career as an outlaw when she'd taken him in. "How do you know he was interested in her?"

Jenkins frowned. "She and them kids left in a real hurry, but he saw them leave and took off mighty quick after them. I trailed the group long enough to see them follow her to her farm."

Dread had Tex gripping the bars tightly in his hands. Jenkins was right. This man didn't sound like any bounty hunter he'd heard of. "Did he give you his name?"

The deputy shook his head as he set the poster on the sheriff's desk. "Nope, that was another funny thing about him. But he was a real barrel of a man with a gray beard."

Quincy! Tex's stomach bottomed out at the realization. The man had tracked him down after all. "He's not a bounty hunter—he's a wanted cattle rustler with a grudge against me. He's after the map you found in my saddlebag."

Would Ravena and the children be safe? He hoped with him gone from the farm that they would be, but he couldn't be certain. Not without seeing for himself.

The sheriff slid his empty plate forward and twisted in his seat to face Tex. "You sure he's the same man?"

"Positive," Tex ground out, his fear pounding as hard as his heartbeat. "Which means you gotta let me out. Those are dangerous men who followed Miss Reid to her farm."

Clipton raised an eyebrow. "Now hold up there, Beckett. This poster says you're a dangerous man too." He motioned to the paper. "And I still haven't figured out what to do with ya."

"Let me go to see if she's all right, and I promise if I make a run for it, you can shoot me and ask questions later."

Jenkins threw the sheriff a questioning look. "I could go check things out."

"You'll scare 'em off," Tex protested. "That is, if you're not shot first."

The sheriff got to his feet, looking annoyed. "I suppose you've got a point there."

"If you let me go, I can lure them out into the open." Tex kept his expression neutral, contemplative, hoping to hide his desperation to convince the man to go along with his plan. Protecting Ravena and the children was the only thing that mattered to him right now. "Then you'll have five wanted men instead of just one."

Rubbing his smooth chin, Clipton blew out a breath. "All right. We'll go as soon as Jenkins can wrest up a posse. Folks aren't gonna like their festivities interrupted though."

Tex released a breath of momentary relief, knowing he wouldn't rest easy until Quincy was apprehended and behind bars too. "Am I coming?"

"Of course." The sheriff grinned. "Like you suggested, we're gonna use you as bait."

* * *

Worry clogged Ravena's throat. She hadn't out-smarted the gray-bearded stranger after all. Instead he and his three companions had followed her to the farm. Whispering to the children to stay seated, she parked the wagon beside the new house. The men rode into the yard right behind them and stopped their horses.

"Howdy, ma'am," the stranger said, tipping his hat to her as if paying a social call.

She inclined her head in a grim nod. "Can I help you?"

"Well, that all depends." He swung out of his sad-dle and approached her. Lifting his hand to help her from the seat, he said, "We're here to see a man I be-lieve you know."

Ignoring his offered hand, Ravena slipped past Jacob and climbed off the wagon on the opposite side before circling the horses. "I'm sure I don't know what you mean." She feared telling them Tex wasn't here, that it was only her and a passel of children. Especially when she wasn't within easy reach of her grandfather's rifle.

The man folded his arms and threw her a patron-izing look. "You can't pretend we haven't met before. At the train station in Boise. We both had an interest in a certain Wanted poster." He flicked a hand at one of the men who held up a copy of the poster.

"Who's that?" Mark piped up, making Ravena cringe. She tried sending him and the others a warn-ing look to keep silent, but it was futile. They were all staring at the poster.

"This here," the man waved at the familiar face,

"is none other than the notorious outlaw known as the Texas Titan."

Luke frowned. "How come he looks like Mr. Beckett, Miss Ravena?"

"That is rather interesting, isn't it?" She marched forward, feigning confidence she didn't feel. "Now, come along, children. Bid these men good day."

The stranger lumbered in front of her, blocking her way with a hand on the side of the wagon. "Let's not get hasty, *Miss Ravena*," he sneered. "I reckon our old friend is here after all. And we just want to talk to him."

"You're Quincy," she stated with sudden realization. The man whose map Tex had won, the man who'd haunted his dreams when he'd been sick.

Quincy's eyebrows shot up, then dropped low with suspicion. "How come she knows you, boss?" one fellow drawled before chuckling.

"Shut up, Lester," Quincy bit out. He didn't bother masking his annoyance from her this time as he leaned close and demanded, "Where is he?"

Ravena straightened her shoulders and lifted her chin in a show of bravado. "He isn't here."

Quincy eyed her and smiled slyly. "Now why is it that I don't believe you?"

"You're welcome to search the place. But he really isn't here."

His hand latched onto her arm with a steely grip. "Where did he go?"

"Leave her alone," Jacob said, standing, his voice firm. "She's telling the truth. Mr. Beckett isn't here."

"Get those kids into the house," Quincy barked to his men. They swung off their horses and menacingly approached the wagon as they drew their guns. Fanny screamed and shrank back against the seat, but her brother quickly sat to console her.

"It's all right, children." Ravena tried to catch each of their gazes. "Go on into the house now." She licked her dry lips. "We'll be fine."

To her great relief, none of them argued with her. All nine orphans climbed out of the wagon and trudged into the house. Quincy's men trailed them to the door before taking up positions on opposite sides of the porch.

"Where is he?" Quincy squeezed her arm hard.

She wouldn't tell him that Tex was in the jail out of fear that he and his men would ambush the place to get to Tex. "He left."

He studied her long enough that she began to squirm. "By the look of things, I'd say there's a real good chance he's comin' back." She knew he meant Tex would be coming back for her, but she held her tongue.

"Search the place anyway," he ordered. Then wrenching her forward, he dragged her onto the porch and plunked her into the rocker Tex had moved over to the new house before leaving. "Keep an eye on her, Lester."

The other man threw her a grin, making Ravena's skin crawl. "Right, boss."

She watched as the other three men split up. One went into the house, where she hoped Jacob and Edmund were watching over the younger children. Quincy and his other partner moved toward the barn. She sat perfectly still and tried to ignore the barrel of Lester's gun pointed at her. Once they didn't find Tex, they would surely leave.

What felt like hours later, the men congregated back on the porch.

"Find any trace of him or the map?" Quincy asked.

Murmurs of no came from the other three. "I did find a gun, though," the one who'd gone inside the new house said, lifting her grandfather's rifle into the air. Ravena felt like weeping. How was she supposed to protect herself and the children now?

Please, help us, Lord.

Instead of commending the man on his find, Quincy let his fist fly at the porch column. "Blast it. He's split for now. But he'll be back. I can feel it." Turning his shrewd gaze on Ravena, he grabbed her arm once more and steered her toward the door. "You and those young'uns aren't to leave this house, you hear? My men will be posted at the front and back."

She swallowed past the lump of fear in her throat. These men weren't leaving after all. Maybe by sundown when Tex failed to appear, they would go. "We'll stay inside," she managed to say.

"Good." He released her. "We certainly wouldn't want anything unfortunate to happen."

Ravena hurried inside, desperate to see how the children fared. Her gaze went straight to the parlor where all nine orphans sat, some on the floor, others on the sofa and chairs. Fanny was silently crying and Ralphey looked on the verge of dissolving into tears himself.

"Shh. It's okay." She hurried toward them and sank to the rug. Like chicks to a hen, they gathered around her. "I know this is all very, very frightening. But it's going to be all right. I'll explain everything later." Somehow, some way, they'd be safe. Because if there ever was a time she needed to know the truthfulness of her grandfather's words—*the Lord has got this in His hands, Ravena. He's got you*—it was now.

The late afternoon sun cast Tex's shadow on the road as he neared Ravena's farm. It had taken Jenkins hours to gather a posse. The wait had been excruciating for Tex as he sat in his cell, imagining all sorts of horrid scenarios. Quincy could be ruthless when crossed, and if he didn't find Tex at the farm, he was likely to become enraged.

And if anything happened to Ravena or the children, Tex wasn't sure he could forgive himself this time.

Is this my punishment? he wondered as he lowered his head. *For all my wrong choices?*

The question hadn't fully finished forming in his mind before he felt a quiet confidence stirring inside him. He'd done what he could, to start making things right, by turning himself in. What happened now was in the Lord's hands.

The buildings and yard came into view, but he was surprised to see Ravena's wagon and horses sitting out front as if she'd only just arrived home and hadn't yet put them away. Concern fizzled in his gut. Ravena and the children would've returned from the picnic some time ago. Were they all right? Were they inside?

On the porch of the new house, Lester sat in the rocker, his eyes shut and his gun across his lap. Another man stood in front of the old house. It looked like Ravena's rifle sat next to him. Neither Quincy nor the fourth man was visible.

Offering yet another prayer for protection—for the

posse, for Ravena and the children, and for himself—Tex worked his face into a scowl and strode toward the center of the yard. "Quincy," he hollered. "I need a word with you."

Chapter Sixteen

A sudden shout from outside had Ravena lifting her head from where she'd rested it against the sofa. She'd been dozing, along with several of the children. Jacob, she noted, still sat rigid near the window. His vigilance in watching over all of them warmed her heart, though she wished he hadn't had to show his protectiveness under such tense circumstances.

"The man in the rocker just got up," he whispered to her.

Ravena shifted Fanny and Ralphey so she could crawl to Jacob. Sure enough the rocker swung back and forth, empty.

"I think someone else showed up," Jacob said, "but I can't see who." The wagon blocked most of the yard from their view.

Was it another friend of Quincy's? Or perhaps a neighbor who'd seen her leave the picnic in a hurry?

Her curiosity battled with her fear to stay put and finally curiosity won out. "Stay here," she told Jacob.

"I'm going to see what's going on." More information could mean more chances of keeping all of them safe.

He nodded in answer, and Ravena turned to face the children who were still awake. She put a silencing finger to her mouth. When she felt certain they understood, she crept to the front door. Quincy's man had shut it earlier. She twisted the handle and opened the door, but she couldn't see much through the crack.

Drawing in a steadying breath, she widened the opening. The wagon still obstructed her view, but she thought she could see the sleeve of someone standing in the yard. Ravena eased herself out the door, keeping herself slightly bent over to avoid detection, if possible.

"Well, well, well, look who decided to show up," she heard Quincy loudly announce.

She drew to the edge of the porch, then slipped down the steps to the back of the wagon.

"I heard you've been looking for me."

The sound of Tex's voice yanked a gasp from her mouth, which she quickly stifled with her hand. He'd come back! How had he known they were in danger? How had he gotten out of jail? And the most important question of all…what would Quincy do to him? Her heartbeat ratcheting, Ravena inched her way to the edge of the wagon and peered around it. At last she could see the scene unfolding in the yard.

Tex stood there, flanked on either side by Quincy's men who each had a hold of one of his arms. Thankfully they'd holstered their weapons. Quincy stepped off the porch of the old house, along with the last of his comrades. This man hadn't put his gun away. Instead he held it aimed right at Tex.

"I've sure had a time huntin' you down," Quincy said with a smirk. "That sheriff in Casper thought he'd gotten rid of you for good, but I knew better." He came to a stop a few yards away from Tex. "The Texas Titan wouldn't go down that easily."

Tex lifted his shoulders in a casual shrug, though his face was a stony mask. Ravena wished she could know what he was thinking. "What would the fun be in that? Although, you did take your sweet time finding me." He shook his head as if disappointed. "More than two months is rather long, don't you think? I could've been halfway to Europe by now."

Quincy's expression hardened. "Well, you weren't. It may have taken longer than I thought to check for you in every city you bought a train ticket for, but eventually, I reached Boise. After that it was a cinch tracking you here." He waved his hand dismissively at the farm. "I knew keeping tabs on that pretty woman I met at the train depot, who couldn't stop staring at your picture, would likely pay off. And it did. I just didn't know how easy it would be once I got to this sleepy little town and saw your sweetheart again. She is rather charming, Tex. I can see why you chose to hide out here."

Ravena swallowed back a wave of revulsion. She wasn't the only one disgusted by Quincy's praise either. Tex wrestled against the men's hold. "If you so much as look at her..."

"She's not what I came for," Quincy barked, bringing a flood of relief to Ravena and prompting her to take another brave step forward. "Now where's my map?"

"Quincy." Tex tsked. "We discussed this. I won it fair and square in that game."

The other man narrowed his gaze. "Fair and square doesn't hold much water when you're outnumbered."

"You make a valid point." Was Tex giving in? "Tell you what. You come with me. We'll have a drink and I'll hand the map over then."

"Uh-uh. You're gonna hand it over now."

Tex cocked his head in a questioning gesture. "And if I don't?"

"Then I guess you'll need something to change your mind." He turned to the man at his side, the one with the drawn weapon. "Go get the girl from the house." Ravena shrank back.

The man started walking sideways in her direction, keeping his gun trained on Tex, but he stopped when Tex hollered, "I'll give you the map. I've got it right here."

Quincy eyed him with obvious suspicion. "Let him pull it out, Lester."

The man on Tex's left released his arm. Ravena held her breath, certain Tex would pull out his own gun. Instead he withdrew the map from his jacket. What was he doing? She slowly moved forward, away from the shelter of the wagon. None of the men noticed her at all.

"Look at that," Quincy said, opening his arms as if welcoming a long-lost relative.

Tex held it out. "Take it."

Before she saw Quincy nod to the man whose gun was still aimed at Tex, before the ruffian turned slightly to face Tex head-on, Ravena knew what would happen next. Quincy was going to have him shoot Tex and then he'd take the map, while the man she loved lay in the dirt bleeding and dying.

Adrenaline and panic coursed through her veins as she dashed forward. "Look out, Tex," she screamed.

The gunman whirled in surprise and fired off the bullet meant for Tex. The bullet plowed into her shoulder, bringing fire and pain and black dots before her eyes. She crumbled to the ground in agony. Her last thoughts were full of hope that Tex would still get away unharmed.

"Ravena!" Tex shouted in terror, right before chaos erupted throughout the yard. The waiting horses reared as someone fired a second shot, but this one was aimed at Quincy's feet. The rustler leapt backward, just as the sheriff and his posse appeared with their guns drawn.

"Let him go," Sheriff Clipton hollered, motioning at the man still gripping Tex's arm. "You're all under arrest."

The moment the man released him, Tex raced to where Ravena lay unmoving on the ground. Her eyes were closed, her face pale, and blood covered her shoulder. "Ravena?" He took her face gently between his hands. "Can you hear me?" He didn't think Quincy's man had fatally injured her, but she remained so frighteningly still.

He slipped his arms beneath her and carefully lifted her off the ground. Above her limp head, he caught sight of the children rushing out of the house.

"What happened?" Jacob asked, taking a step toward Tex.

He was barely aware of the sheriff rounding up Quincy and his men and taking their weapons. "Miss Ravena was shot, but I think she'll be all right." At least he hoped so. He'd been wondering what was taking the posse so long to make an appearance when Ravena had suddenly rushed toward him. Only after Quincy's man had turned and fired off his shot did Tex realize it had been meant for him.

"Go get the doctor," he directed to Jacob. "Ginny, get some water boiling. Mark and Edmund, find some bandages or towels."

"What about us, Mr. Beckett?" Ralphey asked.

Tex carried Ravena onto the porch. "The rest of you start praying she'll recover quickly." He didn't wait for the boy's response or to see if the other children followed his orders. He kept moving into the house, up the stairs and down the hall to Ravena's room. Coming to a stop beside the bed, he pulled back the blankets with one hand and gently set her down.

After removing his bandanna from his pocket, he dragged the chair from the corner to the bed and sat by her side. "Ravena?" he said softly as he tied the bandanna tightly around her wound. She winced but didn't wake. "Jacob's gone for the doctor."

When he brushed her hair from her forehead, she finally stirred. "Tex?" she whispered.

"I'm right here." He rubbed her cheek with the back of his knuckles.

"Am I dreaming? Did Quincy kill you?"

He chuckled. "No, my love, you're not dreaming. The sheriff arrested Quincy and his men."

With her eyes still shut, she frowned. "But... I didn't see the sheriff."

"He and his posse were hiding nearby. The whole thing was a setup to apprehend Quincy."

Her face relaxed slightly before pinching with obvious pain. "Did I make that harder for them?"

"On the contrary, I think you provided them with the diversion they needed." He swallowed past the sudden lump of emotion in his throat. "And I believe you very well saved my life too."

"About time... I did something...adventurous."

He tried to laugh, but it came out strangled. This "adventure" could have ended in her death, and if that had happened... "How about we table the adventure for a while?"

Her lips creased upward. "Where's the fun in that?" It was so like something he would have said as a headstrong youth.

"This isn't funny, Ravena." Why couldn't she understand the horror that had filled him as he'd watched her crumble to the ground?

"Tex," she murmured, opening her eyes and waving him forward with the index finger of her free hand.

He bent closer, ready to give her anything she desired. "What is it?"

"I am not going to die."

"I know—"

She pressed her finger to his lips. "So please go help the children. They're likely frightened to death."

"What about me?" he said, half teasing.

Another small smile appeared on her lips as she lowered her uninjured arm back to the bed. "Are you that frightened?"

"I was," he answered honestly.

"I'll be fine, promise." She winced in pain again. "Now, go."

He stood, then leaned down to place a kiss on her mouth. "I'll go, but I'm coming back."

"I'm counting on it."

Hours later—after the doctor had extracted the bullet from her arm and bandaged the wound; after Tex had fed the children supper and allowed each of them to peek into the room to see that she was fine— Ravena felt she could finally catalog the events of the day. And all the emotions that came with them. The sadness, the suspicion, the terror. She shivered as the memories marched through her mind.

What had started out as a glum holiday had quickly turned into a terrifying, and then painful, ordeal. Her arm still hurt fiercely, but she was alive. And so was Tex.

As if he'd known she'd been thinking of him, he pushed opened the door and stepped inside. "I've made some tea, per your instructions." He moved toward the bed, a cup in his hand.

"Thank you." She tried sitting up, but the movement aggravated her arm.

"Let me." Tex set the teacup on the nearby table and lifted her higher onto her pillow. Then he took a seat in the chair that was still drawn up to the bed. "Here you go." He lifted the cup to her mouth.

"Smells good," she murmured. She took a swallow and grimaced in disgust. "It tastes horrid."

Tex's deep laugh rolled over her as he lowered the cup. "I told you that, my first night here."

Ravena frowned at him. "Did you follow the instructions exactly?"

"Exactly," he said, his blue eyes alight with amusement. "Want any more?"

Making a face at him, which only increased his chuckling, she nodded and allowed him to help her drink more of the tea. She no longer faulted him or Mark for their protests.

"Are the children in bed?" she asked after he set the empty cup aside.

He nodded. "And all asleep too. They were exhausted."

"It's been a long day. I hope they'll be all right."

Taking her free hand in his, Tex rubbed the back of her palm with his thumb. "I think they will be. We talked through the experience at supper, and again before bed with the younger ones. We can pray for them too."

"*We* can pray?" She arched an eyebrow at him, though inside she was smiling. "Since when did you become a praying man?"

"Since falling in love with this beautiful, faith-filled, forgiving woman. Who, I should add, saw what I stubbornly couldn't see until just recently."

A blush crept into her cheeks that had nothing to do with the warm tea or her pile of blankets. "So what happens now?" The question stole some of the tenderness from the moment, but she needed to know. The thought of telling Tex goodbye all over again so that he could go to jail made her heart hurt, and yet, she understood why he needed to go back.

"Well…" Tex glanced down at her hand, the light in his gaze dimming a little. "The sheriff should be returning for me anytime now."

Ravena shut her eyes as a fresh wave of exhaustion washed over her. "Will he send you to prison?"

"I don't know," Tex admitted. "He hasn't said yet what he plans to do with me."

"I hate the uncertainty."

She felt his lips brush the skin of her hand. "Me too."

Opening her eyes, she leveled him with a firm look. "I meant what I said the other day, Tex. I'll wait for you as long as necessary."

"The pastor won't like that," he said, his tone a mixture of sobriety and teasing.

She ignored the pain in her arm as she leaned closer to him. "He'll get over it."

A slow grin lifted his mouth and he narrowed the distance between them to a few inches. Just as she was anticipating his kiss, she heard someone knock on the front door downstairs.

Tex sat back and she did the same. "That'll be the sheriff, most likely." He squeezed her hand, then released her as he stood. "I'll get the door."

She watched him leave, feeling a part of her go with him. Would it always be this way until they were reunited for good? The murmur of Tex's voice followed by another male's floated up the stairs. After a minute, Tex appeared in the doorway to her bedroom, the sheriff behind him.

"Sheriff Clipton wants to speak with you," Tex offered by way of explanation. "If that's all right."

"Yes." Ravena waved them both inside the room. "Come in."

Removing his hat to reveal light blond hair, the sheriff approached the bed and stood at the foot. "How are you feeling, ma'am?"

Ravena worked up a smile at his thoughtfulness. "I'm going to be all right." And she would. The cloud of despair she'd felt for months was no longer shrouding her. She'd been able to fulfill her grandfather's wishes and her own with the new house and the new group of orphans. There was no doubt in her mind that the Lord was aware of her, protecting her. She threw a tender glance at Tex—the Lord's ways of watching over His children didn't always come in expected ways, and for that she was grateful.

"I'm sorry, Miss Reid, that you ended up taking that bullet." The man's expression conveyed his compassion as much as his words did. "But your bravery gave us the diversion we needed to nab those cattle rustlers. So thank you."

She nodded in response, then looked to Tex still standing near the door. "I suppose it's time for you to go?" She hoped the sheriff would allow them a few moments of privacy to say goodbye.

Sheriff Clipton clapped his hat back on, but he didn't make a move to leave. "I've been thinking on that matter."

"Would you like to discuss it downstairs?" Tex asked.

Instead of agreeing, the sheriff smiled and shook his head. "I have a feeling that what I have to say will affect Miss Reid too."

Tex exchanged a perplexed look with her as he partially closed the door and stepped fully into the room. "What exactly have you been thinking?"

The man waved at the chair. "Mind if I have a seat?"

"Go ahead," Ravena answered, unsure whether she ought to feel trepidation or relief that he wasn't marching Tex away posthaste.

Angling the chair to see them both, the sheriff sat. Tex took a seat on the edge of the bed. "I've been thinking," Sheriff Clipton repeated as he glanced at Tex. "First you turn yourself in, without any compulsion. Second, you help us round up a cattle rustling gang, who according to the authorities I wired in Casper, have been a real plague to the area for a while now."

Ravena glanced at Tex and tried to temper her hopes. Where was the sheriff going with this?

"You've already handed over the money in your saddlebags as well," the man continued. "And you agreed to share the locations of where you've stashed the rest of the money you stole."

Tex dipped his head in a solemn nod, his gaze riveted on the sheriff.

The man rubbed at his chin, appearing thoughtful. "If the law in Boise sends a few men down Texas way to recover that money, do you think you could be of assistance in getting it back to as many of the banks and companies as possible to whom it rightfully belongs?"

Visibly swallowing, Tex cleared his throat. The surprise on his face surely matched that on Ravena's. "I can do that."

Hope was getting harder and harder for her to contain. "Would he still go to prison?" she forced herself to ask.

The sheriff turned toward her. "Well, as I see it, ma'am, if Mr. Beckett is willing to pay back what he can, and he agrees to assist us in the future in rounding up other outlaws or cattle rustlers…" He let the words hang there as he eyed Tex again.

Tex's brow furrowed. "You mean, you wouldn't publicize that you'd apprehended the Texas Titan?"

"I think more good could come from having him show up periodically, don't you?" The first glimpse of a smile appeared on the sheriff's mouth. "And one other thing." He pulled a paper from inside his jacket. Ravena saw that it was Quincy's map. "Deputy Jenkins found this on the ground after the scuffle and gave it to me. Seeing as you won it, instead of stealing it, I'm probably obligated to give it back to you."

"Probably obligated?" Tex echoed with a chuckle.

The sheriff studied the map for a moment. "I think we'll call it found at the scene of the crime. And while our boys are rounding up your stolen goods, they can look for this too." He waved the paper in the air, then pocketed it again. "I know a few charitable organizations that would greatly benefit from some anonymous donations."

Clapping his hands against his legs, Sheriff Clipton rose to his feet. "I hope you're recovered real soon, Miss Reid." He took a step toward the door.

"Th-thank you?" Ravena's mind was reeling from all that the man had said. And yet, she wanted to be certain she wasn't misguided in thinking Tex would no longer be leaving. "Sheriff, are you saying Tex is a free man?" The possibility beat as fast and as hard as her heart in that moment.

A full grin lifted the man's boyish face as he turned toward her. "That's what I'm saying, Miss Reid. Seems only fitting too, given today's the day we celebrate the freedom of our great nation." Before she could react, he faced Tex, his expression suddenly serious. "All that's contingent, though, on your willingness to accept the terms I've outlined, Mr. Beckett."

Tex stood, unmistakable shock and relief in his demeanor. "Yes, sir. Every one of them."

"Then I'll bid, you two, good night." Chuckling to himself, he exited the room, drawing the door partway shut behind him.

Ravena couldn't help a startled laugh of her own. "Do you think he'll change his mind?"

"I hope not." Scrubbing his hands over his face, Tex shook his head. "I really think he meant it." He spun to face Ravena. "Which means I'm a free man." The peace on his handsome face brought happy tears to her eyes.

She reached out her hand toward him, wanting to reassure herself that he wasn't leaving. Not now, not ever. "What's the first thing you'll do as a free man, Tex?"

Pulling the chair near the bed again, he sat and linked his fingers with hers. "I'm going to ask you to marry me."

A half laugh, half sob escaped her lips. "You don't want to wait?"

"No." His blue eyes were remarkably serious. "Do you?"

She shook her head, right before he pressed a fervent kiss to her lips. "The moment I'm able to move about and get to town to find a wedding dress, I'll marry you."

"Now hold up. I haven't asked you proper yet."

Ravena smiled, hardly daring to believe a day that had begun so miserably could end so wonderfully. "Go ahead."

After a long perusal of her face, Tex placed his other hand alongside her cheek. Ravena leaned into his touch. "Ravena Olive Reid, I've loved you for as long as I can remember. I wanted to marry you eight years ago, but I needed time to become the man you saw in me back then." Ravena smiled lovingly at him, joy easing the pain in her arm. "So will you marry me? Proper-like this time. No eloping. I want it in the church, with a pastor, and everything." He leaned forward to press his forehead to hers as he added, "And our good pastor is most definitely not going to like that."

She laughed at his joke, then sobered as she regarded him. She'd thought her love for him would never be as deep as it had been eight years ago, but she'd been mistaken. What she felt for him now eclipsed anything she'd once felt. "I love you, Tex Beckett. And nothing would make me happier than marrying you."

His broad smile increased the tripping of her pulse. "Then we'd better get you well real soon," he murmured right before kissing her again.

Epilogue

One year later

Tex shifted little Olive in his arms and glanced down the pew, past all nine orphans, to where his wife, Ravena, sat, listening earnestly to the pastor's sermon. The good man had married six months earlier—to Tex's delight. He'd felt a prick of sadness at the pastor's hound-dog expression when he'd presided at Tex and Ravena's wedding last year.

As if sensing his staring, Ravena turned her head and smiled at him. He couldn't recall ever seeing her look so radiant. Perhaps it was the glow of new motherhood, but he suspected it was more than that. There was peace in her, just as there was inside himself, and it was a glorious thing to behold.

He leaned toward Ginny seated next to him and whispered, "Tell Mama Ravena that she's beautiful." The girl smiled, then passed the message on to Ralphey, and so on down the line, until Fanny shared it with Ravena.

Her gaze jumped to his and she tried to frown, though he could see she was really fighting a smile. Bending toward Fanny's ear, she whispered something. The message ran the line of children until Ginny murmured in his ear, "Don't talk in church. And Daddy Tex looks handsome."

He coughed to hide his laughter as he glanced at Ravena. "I love you," she mouthed before focusing on the pastor again.

Pressing a kiss to his daughter's dark hairline, he did his best to concentrate on the man's words as well. But something deep inside him kept nudging at him that there was a change in the air. He'd quickly come to appreciate and respect the inklings about the land and the weather that came to him as a farmer now. Looking at his family, he hoped whatever the change, it was good. All of the children were thriving and so was the farm. His side business of making furniture had taken off in the past year too.

At last the meeting was over and he led his family outside. He handed Olive off to Ravena and helped everyone into the wagon.

"Everything all right?" she asked as he drove away from the church.

"Sure, why?"

She smiled and nodded at the horses. "You seem in a hurry to get home."

Realizing she was right, he slowed the team. But the feeling of change grew stronger within him the closer they came to the farm. When he drove into the yard and saw another wagon parked out front of the big house, he wasn't surprised. He could see a man and woman standing on the porch, though he couldn't quite make out their faces.

"Who do you think that is?" Ravena shaded her eyes.

Tex shrugged, "Not sure."

He drove toward the barn and parked the wagon. After helping Ravena and the baby down, he strode toward the front of the house to see who the visitors might be. He made it to the center of the yard as the man rounded the other wagon, giving Tex a clear view of his face.

"Tate?" Tex halted to a stop, more than a little shocked at the sight of his twin brother. It had been more than nine years since he'd last seen him.

Tate stopped as well. "Hello, Tex."

They stood there watching each other. Tex tried to decipher what Tate was thinking, but he couldn't read his brother's expression. Was he still angry at Tex? Or happy to see him?

"We've been looking for you," he said; at the same moment, Tate declared, "We only just found you." Tex had been trying to locate his brother since last year, but with no results.

Both of them chuckled, easing the tension in the air. "We didn't know if you were home." Tate waved toward the porch, where a pretty blonde woman stood smiling.

"We were at church," Tex said by way of an answer.

The woman's bright laugh rang out. "I told Tate that's where I thought you were."

This time it wasn't hard for Tex to read his brother's expression—it was one of pure astonishment. "*You* were at church?"

"He's been there every week for the past year." Ravena came to stand beside Tex, her hand resting on his arm. "It's good to see you, Tate."

"You too, Ravena." Tate darted a glance at the baby in her arms, and a surprisingly soft smile lifted his mouth. "Looks like I've missed some things," he said, looking at Tex again.

There was no anger in those blue eyes identical to Tex's. No resentment or bitterness. Only cautious hope. And hope was something Tex had a solid understanding of now.

"I reckon we both have a bit of catching up to do." Tex reached into his pocket, extracted their mother's earrings and held them out for Tate to see. "Starting with these. I never did sell them, Tate."

His brother studied the earrings, while everyone seemed to hold a collective breath. Then Tate pulled him in for a tight embrace, heartily clapping him on the back. "It's real good to see you, Tex."

"You too, Tate," Tex whispered over the lump in his throat as he hugged his brother. He and Tate had both come home at last and there was no other place on earth Tex would ever prefer to be than right here.

* * * * *

*If you missed Tate's romance, be sure to go back
and get swept away with*

THE OUTLAW'S SECRET

*Find this and other great reads
at www.LoveInspired.com.*

Dear Reader,

Some stories are just plain fun to write and others are a labor of love. Tex and Ravena's story is the latter. I have a soft spot for these two and the trials, choices and changes they experience. It was a journey and a pleasure for me to redeem this outlaw and reunite him with the woman he never stopped loving.

Like Tex and Ravena, I hope readers will know that each one of us is worth saving and loving. No matter our choices, none of us are too far gone to change. We aren't what we do or don't do—we are each of unchangeable worth in God's eyes.

While I don't name the town where Tex grew up and Ravena lives, in my mind, it is Horseshoe Bend, Idaho, a town in a picturesque valley, located about thirty miles north of Boise.

The first train depot in Boise was located away from the city. For the time frame of my story, I have Ravena going to the train station in town, even though it wasn't built until the following year, in 1893.

The orphanage in Boise is my creation; however, the Orphan Train really did exist. That program was in operation from 1854 to 1929 and helped place orphaned and homeless children from cities back East in homes in other states. About 250,000 children were relocated, including some in Idaho. However, for the sake of my story, I had orphans *leaving* Idaho on an Orphan Train to be placed in homes farther west.

I love hearing from readers. You can contact me through my website at www.stacyhenrie.com.

All the best,
Stacy

Get 2 Free Books,
Plus 2 Free Gifts—
just for trying the
Reader Service!

Love Inspired HISTORICAL

*When the wrong mail-order bride arrives with another
woman's baby, Trace Warren's marriage of convenience
brings back the memory of the wife and baby he lost.
Can Katherine help him love again?*

Read on for a sneak preview of
WEDDED FOR THE BABY *by* Dorothy Clark,
part of her STAND-IN BRIDES *miniseries.*

"I'm sorry I've gotten you into this uncomfortable position, Katherine. I never meant for you to be embarrassed or—"

The baby let out a squall. Katherine rose, then lifted Howard into her arms. "You owe me no apology, Trace. I chose to stay to help you keep your home and shop for Howard's sake. I'm not sorry." She looked over at him and met his gaze. Tears glistened in her beautiful eyes. "I may be hurt by my choice, but I'll never be sorry." Her whisper was fierce. She bent her head and kissed Howard's cheek. The baby nuzzled at her neck, searching for something to eat. It was the perfect picture of what he had longed for, prayed for and lost.

His chest tightened; his stomach knotted. He looked down at his plate, picked up his fork and forced himself to take a bite of salmon loaf.

"Trace…"

He braced himself and looked up.

"Please hold Howard while I warm his bottle." She handed the baby to him.

He looked at Katherine standing by the stove, holding a towel while she waited for the bottle to warm. Her lips curved in the suggestion of a smile. His heart lurched. She was so beautiful, so kind and softhearted, so brave to take on the care of an infant of a woman she didn't even know. Katherine Fleming was an amazing young woman.

He jerked his gaze away and stared down at his plate. He had to think of an acceptable excuse to leave as soon as the baby's bottle was ready. It was far too dangerous for him to be here alone with Katherine every day.

She set the baby's bottle on the table. "I'm sorry. I just realized I forgot to pour our coffee. I'll get it now. Would you please start feeding Howard before he begins to cry?" Her skirts flared out as she turned back toward the stove.

He swallowed his protest, clenched his jaw and shifted the infant to the crook of his arm. The baby's lips closed on the offered bottle; his tiny fingers brushed his hand and clung, their touch as light as a feather. Pain ripped through him. The pain of a broken heart vibrating to life again. It was his greatest fear coming true.

Don't miss
WEDDED FOR THE BABY by Dorothy Clark,
available August 2017 wherever
Love Inspired® Historical books and ebooks are sold.

www.LoveInspired.com

Reward the book lover in you!

Earn points from all your Harlequin book purchases from wherever you shop.

Turn your points into *FREE BOOKS* of your choice

OR

EXCLUSIVE GIFTS from your favorite authors or series.

Join for FREE today at
www.HarlequinMyRewards.com.

Harlequin My Rewards is a free program (no fees) without any commitments or obligations.

MYR17

Inspirational Romance to
Warm Your Heart and Soul

Join our social communities to connect with other readers who share your love!

Sign up for the Love Inspired newsletter at **www.LoveInspired.com** to be the first to find out about upcoming titles, special promotions and exclusive content.

CONNECT WITH US AT:

Harlequin.com/Community

 Facebook.com/LoveInspiredBooks

 Twitter.com/LoveInspiredBks

LISOCIAL2017

Looking for inspiration in tales
of hope, faith and heartfelt romance?

Check out **Love Inspired**®,
Love Inspired® Suspense and
Love Inspired® Historical books!

New books available every month!

CONNECT WITH US AT:

www.LoveInspired.com

Harlequin.com/Community

 Facebook.com/LoveInspiredBooks

 Twitter.com/LoveInspiredBooks

www.ReaderService.com

Love Inspired®